THAT'S ALL, FOLKS!

a novel

GREG SNOW

Random House   New York

Originally published in Great Britain as *Surface Tension* by André Deutsch
Ltd. in 1991.

Library of Congress Cataloging-in-Publication Data

Snow, Greg
That's all, folks!: a novel/Greg Snow.—1st ed.
p.   cm.
ISBN 0-679-40273-X
I. Title.
PS3569.N615T47   1992
813′.54—dc20   91-52687

Manufactured in the United States of America
2 4 6 8 9 7 5 3
First U.S. Edition

Book text set in Bookman

Book design by Lilly Langotsky

For Mark Kidd

THAT'S ALL, FOLKS!

The night my monstrous illness premiered there were six for dinner at my place. By my own epic standards of proportion it was a pretty small canvas, but dining at home has enjoyed a temporary vogue among my set, stimulated initially by our style baron, Marcus Trilling. Last winter he broke both legs skiing and thus could not keep up his usual punishing restaurant itinerary. That was six months before, and his legs had healed, but the habit continued to amuse.

Naturally I had it catered, by three moronic noovo debs, set up in business by their fathers. They'd called their company Sloane Rangers, a piece of wit so subtle (in their eyes) that they'd explained it to me three times when I'd made the booking. Two of them, as fate would have it, had been chalet girls on Marcus's star-crossed skiing trip. For some reason they blamed themselves for his accident, so he took advantage and "forgave" them in exchange for home phone numbers. I had to admire the way he demanded, then wrote them down in full view of the girl he'd brought with him. What was her name? Anjelica, I think. It's hard to keep track of Marcus—something I commented on at the time.

"Oh, they're just like paper underwear to me, women," he said, "disposable," and laughed his emetic laugh. As usual I joined in, wonder-

3

ing how this talent-free fuck had gone so far, so fast. The piece, Anjelica, was sharper.

"And you're like paper underwear to me, too, Marcus," she said sweetly. "So cheap I couldn't care less if I shat on you."

At this everybody wanted to laugh but didn't. Except, that is, my girlfriend Lucy, who likes to think she's better than my friends. I shut her up with a playfully firm kick under the table.

Laughing longest and loudest at Marcus's crack about the paper underwear was Rory McKaine, dreary dealer in financial futures and boyfriend (fashionably long-standing) of my art director, Christian Kidd. Rory always laughs hardest at masculine bad behavior. Despite the virility of that name, this one is a faggot. The worst kind: a drunken, sporting, fat-assed, backslapping, *heterosexual* faggot. The sort who still thinks nobody knows, even when he's on all fours getting gang-banged by an entire saunaful of *other* faggots. He calls Christian "lassy," which is strange, since he's the real dog, and treats people to detailed descriptions of his talent on the rugby field. Christian once confided to me that Rory had never once kissed him on the mouth. I told him to be thankful: McKaine's mouth looks like Chinatown. But it was one more piece of evidence to add to my case against him. He is a boil in the scented armpit of our set.

Then there was Lucy. My Lucy. "Long-suffering Lucy," as her friends generally call her. It's rather a fitting description; she does look like someone born to suffer, with the sort of face sixteenth-century religious painters would have paid good dosh to use as a model in one of those "martyrdom of so-and-so" paintings, popular on drawing-room walls of the time. Of course, her friends do not call her long-suffering for that reason: it's because she suffers *me*. In my opinion it should be because she suffers *them*. Lucy's friends are of the organic variety. They have grown slowly, together, nurtured in the seedbeds of school and university (or "college" as they insist) and now thrive like dull salad vegetables in the cloches of the civil service or voluntary organizations. They are organic, too, in their likes and dislikes: of food, clothing, music. One of them refuses to speak to me because I work in advertising; another (get this) because I once admitted a liking for veal.

4

I am most grateful not to have to speak to them, and as for long-suffering Lucy . . . when the sinewy golden arc of my body is poised over hers and she is moaning foul-mouthed imprecations to the goddess Vulva she doesn't look as if she's doing much suffering to me.

The dinner party ended acrimoniously, though not without a certain Augustan balance, when all three couples argued. McKaine, as so often, was the catalyst, performing one of his favorite tricks: flirting with somebody else's woman. He does have an appeal to the hormonal sections of some females and it's part of his sad act to exercise it publicly. Anjelica didn't need much persuading to play the game but Christian, unusually, was not to be humiliated. Anjelica was left in no doubt about what Rory does on Hampstead Heath when he isn't playing rugby there.

After the boys had gone, separately, Marcus and Anjelica traded insults. When Marcus announced he was ready to leave I called two taxis.

"Why did you call two?" he asked.

"Because . . . I thought . . ."

"You *twat*. Women don't dump *me* like that. Really, Nicholas, I do wish you'd stop applying your rules to other people. Anyway, cancel the cabs. We feel like walking."

. . . . .

Later, Lucy and I had one of our regulars, about what she sees as the ghastliness of my friends, and I knew there would be no golden arc–making that night. So when she had locked herself in the bedroom I decided to clean up the mess. Marcus had dismissed my caterers before they'd washed the dishes; and since I am still at the stage, career-wise, of spending all spare cash entertaining people who make more money than me, there is none left over for a little woman who does. I tell people otherwise, of course, but the irritating truth is that I am sometimes compelled to wield the Hoover. I draw the line at the laundry, which has to wait until Lucy takes it away. Even then I have the tedious task of packing the newly laundered items into bags marked JEEVES OF MAYFAIR. I pinched hundreds of them when we had the adver-

5

tising account at work. Oh, there are no flies on Nicholas Guy Dennet Taig.

It really wasn't too terrible, just the usual postprandial muck: crockery; glasses; ten or so empty bottles of wine—Marcus's the cheapest, I noted; a razor blade and mirror, remarkably still bearing traces of toot (remarkable because Marcus usually has his vacuum snout and flypaper tongue over any leavings); a couple of ashtrays, heaped high enough to commit suttee upon; but no bloodstains, which there were the last time Christian and Rory argued there. Trying hard to rise above the meniality of the task I gathered the plates and took them to the kitchen. My kitchen is rather smart. With its studded black rubber floor and stainless-steel industrial fittings it is, I have to admit, a little too high-tech, too 1984, to be truly à la mode now, near the close of the decade. But I can't afford a new one and it still draws gasps of admiration from first-time viewers. So it fulfills its function. Naturally I don't use it, except to prepare coffee. Lucy sometimes insists on *cooking* in it, but I can't help my woman's lower-middle-class genes.

I scraped the leftovers into the waste disposal, knocked the handle of the surgical tap with my left elbow, and switched on. There was a crunch, followed by a constipated whine. Shit, I thought, something's jammed: more hand dirtying. Having switched it off I peered down the hole and couldn't help laughing at the cause of the problem. It was, or had once been, Marcus's coke spoon. A very expensive coke spoon: platinum with a tiny diamond set in its handle. That'll teach him, I thought, for being such a gold-plated little turd. It looked as though retrieving the remains would be easy. I reached into the hole and groped. For a reason I still don't understand the machine turned itself on. It was then that my life changed completely. That may seem an obvious statement: mutilation tends to be life altering; but mutilation is precisely what did *not* happen. The first odd sensation was no sensation at all. No pain. Christ, I thought, this must be bad. I'd read that the victims of truly horrible physical trauma are spared pain by some mysterious internal chemistry. Until much later, anyway. The machine ground on. My arm began to rotate in its socket. I wanted to cry out but couldn't: I was hypnotized with horror. And still, no pain.

6

From somewhere I found the wit to stamp on the emergency cutoff. The machine stopped with a grunt. Boy, was I ever going to sue the bastards who installed it. I thought of calling Lucy, but no; I wouldn't have wanted to look at *her* in that state. I wasn't risking my one good arm in a rescue attempt, so I simply pulled. Peering through squeezed eyelids I waited for the emergence of a handburger. Instead it came out uninjured. The relief I felt stopped me noticing that my fingers remained in the machine and I began to back away from the sink. Then my brain registered the impossible: my fingers were four feet long. I shrieked and pulled harder. With a twang my fingers shot from the hole. At the same time my arm, now twisted and bunched along its entire length like the rubber band on a toy plane, unraveled with a whirr of stored energy that flipped me over in the air before tossing me to the floor.

I lay rigid and panting. The smell of my black rubber floor reminded me of the mask I'd had slipped over my face when my tonsils were removed, twenty years before. At least then I'd gone to sleep; now I was all too awake. I wanted to puke, I wanted to pee. I wanted to wake up.

"Nick? Whatever's wrong?"

"Marcus's coke spoon. It's stuck in the waste disposal."

I realized that that was hardly an explanation, but nothing else seemed to have any basis in reality. If I had lost my marbles I wasn't losing my woman, too.

"Well? Why are you on the floor?" She's no fool, Lucy.

"I don't know. I tried to get it out and . . . I must've got a shock or something."

"Oh, Nick. Poor baby," she said as she swooped down, suffering and saintly. Her nipples brushed my cheeks and I felt much better. There was no doubting the reality of those.

· · · · ·

"I've always hated your silly industrial kitchen anyway," she said, as I sat on my imitation (good imitation) Le Corbusier chaise longue, sipping sweet tea. Lucy is the type born to make sweet tea. My drawing room, with its clean lines, its polished floorboards, its chrome, steel, and leather, was no place to feel weak. I needed fake countrification.

An overstuffed sofa, scatter cushions, a gas-log fire, and a dog. An Old English sheepdog. No, wrong commercial: a red setter.

"All that industrial stuff," she continued, "it's not so idiot-proof as the domestic kind. They expect professionals to be sensible."

"Thanks a lot. That makes me either unprofessional or an idiot. Or both."

"Yes," she said. "Now come to bed. I'll get cracking on this mess in the morning."

· · · · ·

The morning after was Saturday. I awoke to an empty bed, with a worse than predicted hangover, and hurgled through to the drawing room where I lay naked on the chaise longue, watching Lucy's quiet efficiency. My vulnerable state led me to wonder (briefly) why she stayed. The phrase most commonly employed by Lucy's friends, when there was still some entente between us, and by her mother, whenever she gets me on the telephone, is *"You don't deserve her, you know."* So why then do I have her? It cannot simply be that I am gorgeous, though I am: tall, patrician Byronic, dark. A man but not, thank God, a "hunk." But Lucy is a very passable piece of skirt. If we weren't *à deux* she could certainly find another man, perhaps one as attractive as me. What I am, for her, is exciting. Lucy's life is all strapped up: by decency, by commitments, by thoughts, consideration, care. She works for a charity. Charity is her middle name. Literally. But I know another Lucy, one who likes her occasional line of coke, whose silence sanctions my opinions—opinions that would lose her her membership to the Worthy Society; who comes with me to the sundry bacchanalia to which I am constantly invited. She complains, she nags, she disapproves; but she still does these things. So you see, "You don't deserve her" is not quite accurate. Lucy knows what I know. *She doesn't deserve me.* And that is why she stays.

When she had finished clearing up she came in from the kitchen with the corpse of the coke spoon. She was laughing.

"Don't laugh," I said, "it cost Marcus a fortune. I'll probably get the bill." I would, too, if I knew Marcus.

"That's just why I'm laughing," she replied, "it didn't. If this is a

genuine diamond"—she held out some broken glass on her palm—
"then your waste disposal is from Venus."

I jumped. Until then the mysterious workings of memory had
blocked out the previous night. Perhaps the waste disposal *was* from
Venus.

"Really," she went on, "Marcus is the biggest fraud. Platinum and
diamond! It's silver and glass. Why does he have this need to impress
all the time? He's stinking rich, he's a 'TV personality'—hasn't he got
enough already?" She dropped it in an ashtray and gave her "thank
goodness I don't have an ego" look. It annoyed me.

"He's got a really small cock," I said in Marcus's defense.

"Oh, I know that. But that can't be all there is to it, so to speak."

"How do you know that?"

"Anjelica told me so last night. I liked her but I don't suppose we'll
see her again, do you?"

"No. Not if she tells perfect strangers about her bed partner's lack of
tackle."

"Don't be pompous, Nick. Marcus reaps pretty much as he sows.
You can't expect to keep your physical shortcomings quiet if you're
famous. And if you're as big a shit as Marcus, well. Why do you insist
on defending him all—"

"OK, Luce. This is what we went to bed on. I've had a shock. Be nice
to me."

"All right," she said, sitting down next to me on the chaise, "I'll be
nice."

She had on a bra and knickers. Housework in the raw is a little too
Bohemian for Lucy. Still, the effect was pretty erotic. She has my favorite type of body: a proper waist and 1958 tits. Howard Hughes
would have enjoyed the intellectual exercise. I looked down. My cock
was on its hind legs. I tensed my arse. "Take it," said my hips. Lucy
bent her head forward.

"But not that nice," she said, flicking my knob with her thumbnail.
Laughing, she jumped up and scampered from the room.

"Bitch," I called, half joking. Suddenly feeling my nakedness I went
to dress.

9

In the bedroom Lucy was ahead of me. She had on her frigidity gear. Green corduroy jeans and a brown jumper like a large wet dog. Considering that we were suffering *(again)* the hottest June "since records began" I knew she must mean what her clothes were saying.

"Is this an official atmosphere or just a temporary interruption of services?" I asked, sitting down on the bed.

"It's neither," she replied, to my astonishment adding a jacket to her outfit. "I'm sorry that your prick doesn't always cause the preferred Pavlovian reaction."

"So it is an official atmosphere. Just wanted to know. Thanks."

"Nick, look. I'm sorry," she said, sitting next to me. "It's not you, it's last night. It's lots of things. Last night I found you on the kitchen floor. I thought you were injured. This morning you seem to have forgotten it, and you want a bonk. I can't change hats that quickly. All right?"

"All right."

"Are we going to this party tonight?"

"I suppose so."

"Good. Pick me up at half-seven." She stood up, gave an adult smile, and strode from the room without looking back. At the front door she called out, "I've switched the waste disposal completely off. Don't touch it till you've called a little man. See you at seven-thirty," and was gone.

With sex no longer an option I decided to take a shower. Generally I disapprove of showers. English showers, anyway, with their pressureless dribble and their poor nylon curtains which wrap you up like dolmades. My shower is not like that. It has a room of its own—at least, a space—off the bedroom. And, by the simple expedient of an electric pump, it goes like a Harlem hydrant. I despair of my benighted countrymen sometimes.

I had a most enjoyable Showering Event. Starting with Aramis Invigorating Body Grains I followed through with Giorgio Armani Scalp Life and climaxed with Oscar de la Renta in my groin. For daytime use I seriously feel that the body should be a bouquet, not a single rose. I have heard that some "trendsetters" consider it wrong to use perfumes. I have also noted that these insignificant stylists seem always to come from the unemployed classes who thus cannot afford such things. A prescription based on envy spends little time in *my* manifesto.

After I'd toweled off (noting that my pecs could use a little more work at the gym if I didn't want to lose the central fjord that looks so exhilarating when I sweat) I thought about breakfast. What I was trying not to think about, though it kept goosing my subconscious, was the previous night's brush with insanity, or perhaps the supernatural. In either case, I did not want to think about it.

My kitchen cupboards offered scant diversion. The choice was between Whole Grain Salt'n'Sugar-Free Wheatettes, left by my mother as part of her lifelong campaign for the health of my bowels, or crackers and black olives. I settled for the Wheatettes, which in the absence of milk I had to lubricate with neat cream. I was pleased at this nullification of their bowel-bracing ability. It amused me to think of my mother's scandalized expression, could she have seen me breaking the law. Sitting down at the kitchen table I tried to concentrate on my Wheatettes but the business with the waste disposal insinuated itself. I was, after all, eating with a spoon. Each time I brought it to my mouth I couldn't help notice the perfection of my hand and arm, a condition that should not really have pertained. When I say "perfect" I do not simply mean "whole." My arms, like the rest of my body, really are perfect. Pleasingly balanced, neither too muscular nor feminine, sun-kissed golden with a good but not vulgar amount of hair. I ponder my outrageous physical good fortune sometimes, feeling almost sorry for the twisted leprechauns, lolloping jellyfish, splay-footed bog creatures, and rheumatoid zombies comprising the mass of humanity. It does seem a shame. Still, tough shit.

My arm continued its action. There was no sign of what had happened the previous night. Yet it had either happened or it hadn't. If it had not, then I'd gone mad. Perhaps only temporarily; but that was hardly reassuring. And if I hadn't gone mad the implications were as bad, or worse.

11

I realized that I'd stopped eating and was now staring, fascinated, at the dormant waste disposal. I turned away, trembling, but turned back again almost immediately. The machine had me by the balls. I shivered: *that* was a horrible image. Tiptoeing to the sink I looked into the waste disposal. The oversized black plug had been removed by Lucy, affording me a clear view of the tubular innards and the heavy, stupid blade. What on earth had happened yesterday? I paced the room, not really thinking, just trying to keep back the inevitable con- clusion. But there was only one way to find the truth. I knew that I had to put my hand down that hole again.

I marched up to the sink like a man. I wasn't having the frighteners put on me by a waste disposal: it was ludicrous. Gripping the edge of the sink I hollered, "All right, you little turd! We'll see who's boss around *here!*" and went for it. Nothing happened. A gibber of brief relief escaped my lips before I remembered that Lucy had switched the thing off at the mains. Angry now, I pulled my hand from the hole and went beneath the sink to find the switch. I pressed it. The motor hummed. When I stood up I was scared again. In one clear moment I saw the absurdity of the situation, yelled a Samurai yell of courage, and plunged my arm into the humming orifice.

Pain, of the comically overdone variety beloved of footballers, knocked me flat. It ravened me, like a hungry, living thing; and the words I screamed as I lost consciousness were "Mad *and* crippled! Mad *and* crippled!," or something similarly histrionic.

ooooooooooo T W O ooooooooooo

I had never before been inside a National Health Service hospital. Any sick person I had ever visited—and they were few—had taken the trouble to get private insurance. The best thing about private hospitals is that they realize how very depressing sickness can be, for the visitors. There are comfortable chairs in every room, and a large television. Thus one is even spared the anguish of looking at, let alone speaking to, the patient. With a box of chocolates and the lights dimmed the experience can be no more distressing than a visit to the cinema, albeit a somewhat dull one. I remember that not one of my family noticed my grandfather die, so engrossed were we in *The Ascent of Man*. When the credits had rolled my sister Katia had said, "I think Grandpa may have gone."

My mother, who had never approved of her father's bowel cancer, on the grounds that it was self-inflicted, looked and agreed. A doctor had been called. He agreed too, and broke the news to us. We'd comforted him in his distress and left the hospital with Grandpa's things in a briefcase, for minimum embarrassment. It had almost been a pleasure, like leaving a bad hotel.

But now, through circumstances beyond my control, I came awake in the casualty department of a public hospital. A young doctor stood over me. He had bulbous, superficial eyes that roamed around, looking as though they might drop out at any moment.

13

"I've got private medical coverage," I said.

"Yes, Mr. Taig, and a pint less blood than you had this morning. You could have gone private, of course, but that would've taken longer to arrange. Still, it might have been nice to bleed to death in comfort."

His tone of voice, like his eyes, was barely under control. "I might add," he chuckled, "that your insurance was about the only cover you *did* have, when the ambulance got to you."

"Ah," I said. He wanted me to feel awkward. Since my body looks like the Apollo Belvedere's on a healthy diet, I was hardly going to be fazed by a couple of ambulancemen admiring it.

"Who dialed 911?" I asked.

"A neighbor. An American chap, I believe."

So it was Tom, the mad Californian acupuncturist. That would explain my nudity: Tom is too blasted on dope most of the time to notice whether people are alive, let alone dressed. I was amazed he'd had the savvy to remember where my spare door key was hidden.

"Are you a psychiatrist?" I asked.

"A psychiatrist?" he said, his delinquent eyes rouletting around their sockets. "Why on earth should I be? You've injured your hand. You're not *mad*, er, mentally ill. Unless you put your hand in that waste disposal with the deliberate intention of injuring yourself?"

I groaned.

"Mr. Taig, what happened, exactly?"

I lied with characteristic aplomb, about the machine jamming and then starting without warning. He believed me, and said that the damage to my finger was slight: lots of blood but little thunder. A couple of nails ripped off, a good chewing, everything usable again in a fortnight. I felt a bit cheated at not being ill enough to command sympathy.

"We're keeping you in overnight. For observation," he said, with an emphatic bulge of those organs which fitted him so well to such a task.

I was handed over to a black porter with a pink hearing aid, who wheeled me to a ward. It had some corny name like *Crimea*. Sitting up in my flaking metal bed I stared around. A nurse with a stirring body but an antierotic uniform rushed up to me.

14

"Mr. Taig, will you lie down?" she asked, as if for the tenth time. "You're probably still in shock."

She was right. I was in shock, at the condition of the ward. *Crimea* was a good name. Florence Nightingale could have walked in and felt right at home. From the cracked maroon linoleum through the blistering green walls to the buzzing fluorescent tubes the place was a nightmare of bad design and worse management. The social distribution of the inmates was roughly that of a large public lavatory. Sixty percent blue-collar, thirty-nine percent white-collar, and one percent forced in by the call of nature who would much rather have been using the executive washroom, thank you. That one percent was me and an actorly man across the way who pretended all afternoon to be doing the *Times* crossword.

The blue-collar contingent, all of whom looked like nightclub bouncers and had names without vowels, kept up a shouted crossfire conversation. Snooker, coons, Thatcher, and women were the preferred topics at the symposium, especially women. One of them held up a magazine centerspread of a woman with her center spread, for general approval. When a nurse hollered at him to put it away he replied that he didn't have "it" out but the man in the next bed claimed that they were just brushing up for anatomy finals, which made me laugh. I didn't expect such a person to know what finals were.

The library trolley made a pass after lunch, a meal I would not have been able to identify without the menu, which assured me it was lamb cutlet, sautéed potatoes, and cabbage. On the trolley's literary wasteland I discovered *Sense and Sensibility* and began to read. At teatime I thought, as I ate an electric-pink cake, of my circumstances and the advantage to be gained from them. It was my intention to lie low overnight, discharge myself in the morning, go back to my flat, and dress. Then I would arrive at the lunch party I'd been invited to, waving my bandaged hand. Lucy would not be there so I decided to tell everybody that the injury was the result of saving an old lady from a mugger. I looked forward to the congratulation but more to the prospect of getting Victoria Smale into the sack on the sympathy ticket. I smiled. Things were working out well, as ever.

15

At seven a bell rang. A group of women with skin like peach pits shuffled in, dragging their distorted spawn behind them. I settled back, preparing to enjoy this sociological sideshow, and was just thanking God for sparing *me* visitors when Marcus entered the ward. Marcus Trilling, like many television folk, is virtually Lilliputian. He is also overweight, in a cubic way, with a malevolent cherub face, and dresses in a Fauntleroy motley of flounces and satin bows. The result is not unlike a fancy box containing something useless and self-indulgent, which is about right.

"Nicholas!" he called from the end of the room, pulling a lace handkerchief from the pocket of his lavender satin jacket and waving it. This had the required effect of drawing the attention of the one or two people still left who had failed to notice him. As he processed up the ward, nodding to left and right as though about to dispense alms, I watched mouth after mouth literally fall open. At my bedside he paused and cocked an ear, waiting for conversation to erupt in his wake. Only when it had did he greet me.

"Nicholas, Nicholas, Nicholas."

"You already said that, Marcus. Why are you here?"

"Now that's hardly the attitude, when a friend calls."

I looked at him dubiously. He wouldn't be seen dead in a public hospital, unless it was part of some jokey report for his TV show.

"All right," he said, "Tom told me you were here. I paid a call this P.M. to collect my"—here he leaned down conspiratorially and hissed—"coke spoon."

"It's because of your coke spoon," I said very loud, relishing its effect, "that I'm here at all. It got jammed in my waste disposal and I had my hand eaten trying to get it out."

Marcus gasped and threw up his baby hands.

"Nicholas. I hardly know what to say! That's simply too appalling. Awful, dreadful. It was a platinum-and-diamond coke spoon. It cost a fortune. An hour's pay at least."

"Thanks for the concern, Marcus. And it was nothing of the sort, it was silver and glass, as you probably know."

"I've been robbed!" he squealed, dabbing at his brow with the table-cloth of a handkerchief.

"Well, Lucy fished out what was left. I probably still have it if you need it as evidence."

Marcus pounced.

"*Lucy* fished it out? I thought you said . . ."

"Look, Marcus, could we just forget it? It's been a day."

"No, Nicholas," he pouted, "we cannot. I don't believe you lost that coke—that item of jewelry—in your waste disposal at all. In fact it is my surmise that you have pawned it."

"Pawned it? Marcus, send me the bill."

"I *shall*," he said with a smile of forensic triumph.

"Now please, could we change the subject? Why are you really here?"

"Well, I was trying to ring you all morning. I just had to tell you about that bit of totty I brought last night—Angelina."

"I thought it was Anjelica."

"Was it? No matter. What matters *is*, she can suppress her gag re-flex."

I resisted the temptation to point out that anybody capable of bear-ing Marcus for more than five minutes must possess that ability.

"Well?" he chivvied, "what about that?"

"What about it?"

"It *means*"—he went into his conspiracy position again—"that she can perform *Deep Throat*."

It occurred to me that this wasn't very special. Considering the famed inadequacy of his tackle a sparrow with laryngitis could do the same.

"What, all the way down?" I asked. He nodded. "You mean, she can take it right down the back of her throat, down her windpipe, without choking?"

He nodded more.

"*All* of it? Every last inch?" His head bobbed enthusiastically. Squeaks of self-satisfaction emerged from his compressed lips. My

17

irony, like most things, went over his head. "So how does it feel then, when you're four fathoms down?"

"Indescribable, Nicholas. Ecstasy. Like . . ." he reached into the air and plucked, as usual, a cliché ". . . like tight velvet. Can't Lucy do it, then?"

"No, Marcus, she can't," I lied. "And what's more, it wouldn't matter if she could. My cock's not long enough to get down that far," I said, in a final effort to prick his conscience.

"Oh, that's a dreadful shame, Nicholas. I suppose I'm just lucky. Still, fret not. Your, er, little secret is safe with me."

I suffered another half hour of him displaying the many facets in his Koh-i-Noor ego. My injuries, my plight, in fact my self, none of these were inquired after. As always with Marcus, I asked myself why I tolerated him, while already knowing the answer. Finally an Asian nurse came and told him it was time for visitors to leave.

"Leave?" he said. "*Leave?* My good woman, do you realize to whom you speak? I am Marcus Trilling, presenter of *Simply Trilling.* I don't suppose you've been in our country long, but nonetheless . . ."

"Oh, I know who you are all right," she interrupted, "even if I have only been in 'your' country for thirty years. I watched that load of rubbish you did last week about Asians in Britain."

"What about it? The ratings were stupendous, actually."

"Maybe. I just don't think curry's that funny."

"Well, then you're in a minority," said Marcus blithely.

The nurse looked at him as though he were a transparent bedpan, then clicked out of the ward.

"That told her," he said. "They're cheeky, the Pakis. As if I could leave right now! There are people wanting my autograph."

I looked around the ward.

"No, there aren't."

"And whose fault is that? If she hadn't sidetracked me I could have signed a few. I could see them waiting."

"Perhaps you *should* go, Marcus. You don't want trouble, it might get in the papers."

The thought of bad publicity made him stand up instantly.

"Yes, perhaps you're right. I don't want *another* libel suit so soon after the last one. But before I go—you haven't forgotten it's my annual bash next Saturday?"

"As if I could forget to go to the party of the year."

"No, quite. Anyway, there's a most marvelous girl I want you to meet. I think you were made for each other. It's really time you dropped that dead weight of yours."

"Lucy's not dead weight, Marcus. I love her, sort of."

"Whatever, you *shall* meet Miranda. And now I must fly."

He fopped his way to the end of the ward. In the rubber doorway he met the Asian nurse.

"So!" he burst out. *"This* is what I pay my taxes for!"

"Very original," she called after him. "Why don't you write to your M.P. while you're at it?"

She moved around the beds, dispensing care and drugs, making notes. It was an easy ward; she had plenty of herself left for banter. But my temperature was recorded with taut professionalism. When she'd done she moved to go, but turned instead.

"Nice friends you have, Mr. Taig," she said.

· · · · ·

I looked casually at my watch. 7:45. Had I really been there for seven hours? I thought about discharging myself. The damage was done, nothing more could drop off. I jumped. The previous night's events still had no rationale. The injury to my hand was proof that the arm twisting and the finger stretching could not have happened. But I *had* seen them. What kind of madness causes spontaneous hallucination? None that I knew. Yet there is a condition that sometimes occurs as a result of taking LSD, called flashback. I had taken acid a few times when I was much younger but I'd never believed in flashback. I did now. A rational explanation. I looked at my watch again. 7:50. Not bad, I thought, five minutes thinking to put my world back on its axis. I thanked God for a sharp mind and a good memory. 7:50? Damn, damn, damn! I was meant to be collecting Lucy at 7:30.

· · · · ·

19

"Lucy?" I banged the telephone on the wall. The connection was dreadful: two tin cans *without* a piece of string would have been better.

"Nick?" shouted Lucy as she fried eggs in a hurricane somewhere the other side of the galaxy. "Why aren't you here?" Despite the so-called connection the anger in her voice came through perfectly.

"I'm in hospital," I shouted back.

"What? This is a dreadful line. I thought you said you were in hospital."

The ensuing conversation began sympathetically but degenerated into an argument when Lucy discovered how I came to be there. Had she not warned me to leave the waste disposal? It was odd to argue when we had been shouting from the very beginning. Since there was nowhere left for the tone of voice to go it all had to be in the language. So we settled for plenty of that. Then, just as my phone credit ran out, Lucy deployed her favorite stratagem: the unexpected apology.

Pip-pip-pip went the phone, hungry for cash.

"Look, Nick, I'm sorry. Shall I come and get you?"

Whenever she does this it is always too late to stop the juggernaut of my temper, so I roll right on, leaving her on the moral high ground and me wondering how much the reconciliation is going to cost.

Pip—"Fuck"—pip—"off." Pip.

I replaced the handset and backed out of the hairdryer-style booth. On my way to the ward the nurse whom Marcus had offended told me I should be getting ready for bed. *Bed?* At 8:15? It was worse than prep school. At least Tom had given the ambulancemen my soap bag. Miserably I collected it and shuffled off to the bathroom.

The administrators of the hospital had obviously taken the government's admonishments to economize seriously, for the bathroom was doubling as a petri dish. Exotic fungi thrived on the damp porcelain surfaces. I looked warily at the dendritic sinks. It had not been my day for sinks. The first had had teeth; these had pyorrhea.

20

Placing my soap bag (chic, calfskin, Paul Smith) in a clearing I addressed the problem of how to wash with one hand. When we were children my sister and I had often played at being cripples but had always rejected unidexterity for its fundamental lack of romance. A pity, I thought; the practice would have been handy. Inserting the plug and running the water were simple. The soap, however, eluded me. I dropped it in the water and chased it around but it had a slithery life of its own. It was far more at home in the swampy bathroom than me and dodged my cursing sorties for a minute or more. I did make momentary contact but it leaped from my grasp and skittered across the floor. I went to fetch it and marched back with it pressed against my chest. Now I've got you, I thought, but failed to see the trap it had laid, in the form of a treacherous slime trail. As I reached the washbasins my torso stopped but my legs did not. I grabbed with my good hand as I fell but it was too late. Down I went, giving my chin a tremendous crack on the high, square sink. For the second time in twenty-four hours I found myself lying on a floor. This one smelled of some martial antiseptic for the killing of plebeian foot rot. Although angry at fresh misfortune I was pleased that at least it hadn't hurt. Levering myself to my feet I went to the mirror for a damage report. Then I realized why it hadn't hurt.

I stared insanely at a complete stranger. He looked as shocked as me, which was some comfort. His—*my*—chin had caved in, leaving a perfect impression of the sink edge. Worse, my nose, as if to compensate for the depression, had grown a frankfurterlike extension which (in case it hadn't already caught my attention) waved up and down. I shut my eyes, willing the hallucination to stop. When I opened them again nothing had changed. I stood there, far too scared to panic. I might never have moved until the gentlemen with the straitjacket had come for me—but the sound of approaching footsteps unlocked my fear. I bolted for a lavatory cubicle and slammed the door. Too late I realized that my soap bag remained outside.

Two working-class voices stood at the sinks. As expected, it did not take long for their criminal gaze to fall upon my bag.

"Ooooh!" said one, mock effeminately, "nice 'andbag."

"Oosisat, then?" asked the other in a voice full of cheap living.

"Dunno. Lemme look."

I heard a zip crackle open. So, this was rape.

" 'Airbrush, toofbrush . . ."

"Toilet brush?"

"No ha ha . . . Buncha keys . . . 'airjel . . . wossis?"

"Look like nail clippers."

"Fuckin' funny-shape nails, then."

They obviously referred to my nostril-hair remover. I could hardly expect them to know, people to whom lavatory paper is a dangerously feminizing innovation. I could imagine the pubic thickets dangling from their nostrils.

"What the fuck's this? Coal? Wossiwant coal for?"

"Lemmisee. No, it ain't coal, iss *kohl*. Like eyebrow pencil. My missus gets it."

"Eyebrow pencil? This ain't a bloke, it's a *tart.*"

I stiffened. My nose waved with indignation.

"I reckon iss that geezer in the bed next to you, Alfie boy."

"Nah! Leave off."

"Stands to reason, dunnit? Oo issy?"

"Dunno," continued Alfie "boy," whom I knew to be at least fifty-five. "Some posh cunt. 'Urt 'is finger."

"Aaah, poor little bubba. Queer, gotta be. That 'is boyfriend then, come in just now?"

"I reckon. That cunt off the telly, werenit? Reckons 'e's funny. D'ya get a look at the clothes? What a state! Like an accident in a fuckin' parachute factory!"

"Yeah," laughed the other one lewdly, "and I bet the uvver one pulls 'is ripcord for 'im!"

That was it. It wasn't so much the affront to my sexuality I resented as the suggestion that I would have a boyfriend so unattractive as Marcus. Ripping open the cubicle door I jumped out and confronted the louts. One of them was spraying shaving foam onto his chin; when he saw me he gasped and filled his mouth with the stuff. Alfie boy, still rootling in my soap bag, tried to cry out but it caught in his throat. He dropped the bag and fled. I advanced on the other, who seemed not to have noticed the shaving foam dripping from his mouth. In a kind of trance he held out the aerosol like a gun and backed from the room. I felt pleased, that I had asserted my masculinity, that the authority of

my presence could frighten two such animals of the forest into running scared. In my temper I had quite forgotten my condition. Then I
caught sight of the monster in the mirror. My chin remained sunken,
my frankfurter proboscis still vibrated obscenely. Now it was my turn
to panic. Without stopping to collect my scattered belongings I rushed
from the bathroom, down corridor after decaying corridor, and fled, as
they say, into the night.

ᴏᴏᴏᴏᴏᴏᴏᴏᴏᴏᴏ T H R E E ᴏᴏᴏᴏᴏᴏᴏᴏᴏᴏᴏ

Getting a taxi at eight o'clock on a Saturday evening, in a busy London street, while wearing government-issue hospital pajamas should have proved troublesome. God knows it's generally impossible to make the bastards stop, even when one is dressed, white, down on one knee, and brandishing a fifty-pound note. But for some reason I managed to hail one immediately. The cabbie, half asleep, didn't notice my deformities when I gave him my address.

It wasn't until we were on our way that I remembered I had no money. My first thought was to ask the cabbie to stop at a cash machine—but I had no card. All right, he could wait outside my flat while I went inside. The next problem was how to speak to him without revealing my face. I took off the pajama jacket and tied it beneath my eyes like Jesse James. Thus prepared I tapped on the glass partition. The cabbie glanced at me in his mirror. A moment later he slammed on the brakes, almost propelling me into the front. When I breathed again it was down the barrel of an air pistol.

"Right, you *bastard*! Just try it!"

"No, no—you don't understand! I'm not trying to rob you. It's just—I've had a terrible accident and I don't want you to see my face."

"Oh yeah? Think I'll fall for that? You ain't the first *bastard* tried to roll me!"

24

"Honestly. Look." I lifted the pajama yashmak to reveal my chin.

"So what do you want?" he asked, putting the gun away with a short-changed expression.

"Nothing. I just want to go home."

"Thought that's what we *was* doing?"

"Yes, but I don't have any money."

"Here we go again. Shall I get me gun out?"

"No! Look—couldn't you take my name and address or something? Do I look like a criminal?"

"You look like a nutter to me, John."

"Please?"

Cruelly, I thought, he reached into his jacket, where the gun was— and handed me a pen.

"I want every little bit of your address. If you don't know the postcode, *out.*"

I wrote it down, inventing a postcode, and we set off again. Slumping in the seat I closed my eyes, listened to the traffic, and imagined I was someone else . . .

· · · · ·

"Well I seen it all now. That's a good one, that is. How you doing that, then?"

"Pardon?" I asked, sitting up. The cabbie was laughing.

"That—what you're doing with your hooter."

"Doing what? Oh Christ—"

My nose was rampant. It shot from my face like sausage meat, out the window, over the roof, into the front with the driver. Vainly I hauled, but it was renegade. Completely beyond my control it wrapped around the steering wheel and drove us into the oncoming lane of Buckingham Palace Road. The cabbie was laughing too much to no- tice, but I wasn't. Desperately I yanked at the greasy tube, pleaded with it to behave, and it relented. When it had contracted to a more manageable fourteen inches or so I rearranged the pajama jacket over it, like a nun who'd exposed her knees.

} 25

"Why didn't you say you was in the business?" said the cabbie, still laughing, suddenly my friend.

"What business?"

"Come on, you can't kid me. *Show* business."

"I am not in show business."

"Well, how come you can do a trick like that? It's the funniest thing since that geezer who could fart 'Rule Britannia.' "

"It isn't a trick, it's a—" I stopped myself. "All right, I admit it—it's a trick. But I'm really not in show business. I just do it for my friends."

"You should do it professional. Ever heard of a bloke called Herman Coprolite?"

"Yes, I've heard of him."

Herman Coprolite is London's top publicist. He rose in the late seventies after realizing that money was to be made from the fatuously famous. Most of the famous have done something remarkable, but Coprolite's clients have only ever done some*one* remarkable. People like "actress" Allegra Assai, bearer of the love child of a certain cabinet minister; or Kevin Domby, the man who used to wash the prince of Wales's underwear.

"Yeah? He's a regular of mine. I'll give him your name."

"No! I—I don't think my act's good enough yet. Thanks, all the same."

"All right, if you say so. Here, don't s'pose there's any chance of another turn?"

"Sorry, I'm really rather tired."

"No. Shouldn't've asked. 'Nother time?"

"Another time."

· · · · ·

When we arrived at my block of flats the cabbie waved away my offer to go inside for the fare.

"Have it on me. For the show."

"Well, thank you."

"Cheers," he said. "Good elf."

"Good health" seemed the most inappropriate salutation possible at that particular moment.

The block in which I live, filled as it is with successful young people intent on Pleasure, was deserted at eight-thirty on a Saturday evening. Even Calvin, our hunchbacked Irish porter, is granted Saturday to himself. Thus I managed to make it up to my flat without provoking further hysteria. I took my keys from their hiding place, still amazed at the uncharacteristic presence of mind shown by dopehead Tom, and let myself in.

The front door hissed shut behind me. I leaned against it, breathing in great relieved chestsful of security, knowing the feeling could not last. It didn't. Ten seconds later I was once more a shivering column of panic. A drink, a drink was what I needed. Juddering my nerve-wracked way to the drinks cabinet (table, actually, though I do have my eye on a little Chippendale cabinet. I like to mix antiques and the *moderne*, it shows such self-assurance) I found it almost bare. That meat 'n' onion faggot Rory McKaine had drunk me out of Glenmorangie the previous evening. I wouldn't have minded, but he drank it with *lemonade*. The only remaining alcohol was the stuff I keep by for my mother. Despite her health obsession, she has an itsy-witzy problem with the booze. She denies it but since her favored fluid is sweet sherry it's easy to tell. She smells like an approaching trifle. Even in my overwrought condition I recoiled at the prospect of neat sweet sherry. However, it was a straight choice between drunkenness and complete nervous collapse, so I poured almost half the bottle into a large tumbler and drank. At least, I attempted to drink but my new nose dipped into the glass like the beak on a "drinking bird" toy, preventing my lips from reaching the calming liquor. In an ecstasy of frustration I went to the kitchen to find some straws.

"Drink half a pint of sherry through a straw"—it was like one of McKaine's rugby club rites. I managed it in about thirty seconds. Real fear was a new experience for me; it coursed around my bloodstream like the Japanese bullet train, stopping unpredictably to disgorge chattering hordes of buzzing Nips. My heart, head, ears, lungs; each in turn was shredded by the flailing hands of Terror. Then the sherry found its mark and a brittle calm began to return. There was no deny-ing it this time, no blaming it on LSD, no reductio ad absurdum to

27

be worked. Something seriously awful was happening to me. But what?

I fingered the canyon in my chin. It needed a shave. I laughed, yes, bitterly, at the idea of trying to shave such a surface. Subjected only to the sense of touch it had a certain rugged charm. It was rather too large to pass as a dimple but its appeal, I began to think, was of the same type. A flaw, certainly, but the horizonless perfection of my features could use a little perspective. Yes, there was advantage to be culled from this. Perhaps the trawl net of my charm would have to be cast in new waters but I had no doubt that the fish in a different sea would still find me hot bait. Closing my eyes I reached out for the glass and brought it to my lips. My nose smacked on the bottom, knocking it from my hand. As I clutched my nose, which now hurt like a two-day hard-on, I realized that a frank assessment of my new physiognomy was needed before I started calculating its aphrodisiac potential.

I delayed the inevitable, choosing which of my many mirrors to use. The bathroom one, with its theatrical surround of naked bulbs? No, too brutal, too real: only used to check for skulking hairs or treacherous zits, on the very rare occasions when such things afflict me. My antique gilt hallway mirror? No, not real *enough*. The one in the bedroom seemed the best compromise. My bedroom is itself a compromise. When the decoration of my flat was nearly complete Lucy had asked whether I intended to have the bedroom done in a similar style to the rest. I'd said that I did. "If you think I'm going to make love in a room like a cross between an operating theater and a saddlemaker's workshop, you're wrong," she'd said. "I imagine you'd prefer Laura Ashley?" I'd replied, in an effort to show her the error of her ways. Foolish me. "Yes, actually," she'd said. "At least I'd feel like I was making love, not visiting the gynecologist. I mean it, Nick. If you insist on decorating even the bedroom to score points with your shallow friends I won't sleep here. Ever."

28

I never bend to Sabine tactics but I'd seen that she did mean it. Now my bedroom is a field of asphodel, a carnival of High Street feminity. There is even, shame, a doo-vay. But at that moment, as I switched on the orchid-shaped pink Tiffany lamps and moved fearfully toward the curlicued cheval glass, I was glad of the room's effect.

It was the first time I had looked at myself since the hospital. As the monstrous alien and I held each other's frightened gaze one of us realized it was going to take more than a pint of sherry to cheer him up. I posed for a while, searching vainly for a flattering angle. I turned my back and spun around, trying to catch myself off-guard, to see how I would look to somebody seeing me for the first time, but I had to admit defeat. Whichever way I looked at them my chin was a crater and my nose a jumbo hot dog.

"It's no good, Nick," I said aloud, "the only person who'd fuck that is Jiminy Cricket."

Experimentally I twanged the end of my nose. Flaccid vibrations ran along it. With the flat of my hand I pressed inward. It slipped to one side. I got a firm grip and pressed again. To my surprise it went in. More extraordinary still, my chin came out. I pushed harder and my face regained its normal proportions. Now I was in a fix: if I let go, would my nose and chin stay in place? I could hardly spend the rest of my life with one hand pressed against my face. Cautiously I released the pressure, expecting the worst, but everything stayed put. The relief was a physical force, it made me jump up and down with delight at my deliverance. The telephone rang and I ran to answer it, Lazarus himself.

"Hello?" I said, laughing. It was Lucy.

"I thought you were in hospital."

"I was."

"Nick, what exactly is going on? Have you got someone else there? If it's that little slut Victoria Smale I swear I'll . . ."

"There's nobody here but me. Can you come over? I've got something extraordinary to tell you."

"I'll bet."

"Look, just come."

"All right. I'll be there in twenty minutes. That should give you time to change the sheets."

"Lucy, I . . ." But she was gone. It didn't matter. She'd soon know the whole story, and it gave me time to shower and dress.

· · · · ·

"So then I just pressed my hand on the end of my nose and everything sort of popped back in place."

Lucy eyed me with horror and contempt, mixed in imperial measure. She sat on the very edge of a chair with her shoulders pinched and her knees almost up her nostrils. She stirred her cup of coffee and stared into it, like an Aztec priestess examining entrails.

"They do say, Nick," she said at last, in the voice she reserves for men who wolf whistle at her, "that only the most unbelievable excuses can be true. But there's a difference between unbelievable and plain barmy. You were never even *at* the hospital, were you? All that business about a terrible connection. What did you get her to do? Stand next to the phone and *hiss*, the little snake?"

"Luce . . ."

"Don't call me Luce. You are. I am not."

"Lucy. I know it sounds crazy but it's true," I whined. "You've got to believe me."

"Why? Prove it."

"Marcus, " I said. "Marcus came to see me. Call him."

"Bad choice of accomplice, Nick. I can't think of anyone less likely to visit somebody in hospital."

"But he *did* . . ."

"Can *you?* He wouldn't visit his own mother."

"No," I sighed. She was right: Marcus wouldn't visit his own mother. Marcus wouldn't visit *himself*. And it was too late to explain that he'd only come for his jewelry.

Lucy stood and sucked her teeth. She didn't exactly count down from ten but she might as well have done.

"OK," I said, waving my bandaged hand at her, "you want proof? Here's the bloody proof. The literally bloody proof."

She snorted and rolled her eyes at an invisible companion. "Go on, then. Show me."

"All right, I will. I hope you feel awful if this leads to gangrene."

I tore at the bandages. They dropped to the floor and I stood brandishing my chewed hand at her. Except it wasn't chewed at all. It was
fine. No more ruined than the average nail biter's. Less in fact: I don't
bite my nails.

"That *was* stupid," she said. "Not like you at all. You should've called
my bluff."

"Lucy, I swear, I swear . . ."

"Oh stop swearing, and pleading. It doesn't suit you. It's time I went.
Really went. I'm tired of all your nonsense. You think I care about
those silly little girls you screw, the ones you find it so easy to impress? Of course I don't. What I mind is being treated like a fool. I'm
going now. I'll send Anne or someone round to collect my things. *Do* try
to be in one piece when she calls."

She was dressed for the party we never went to, in cream crepe de
chine. Somehow it added to the awfulness. I was still staring, shocked,
at my uninjured hand, but Lucy was moving away. She paused halfway across the room and dug her hands into the pockets of her jacket.

"It's funny, you know," she said in that exclusively female tone of
sour wisdom, "but those silly lies you told me, about your hand and
your nose and your chin, they were just the sort of things that happen
in cartoons. And that's all you are, really. The two-dimensional man. A
bad cartoon. A *fucking* bad cartoon."

She tried to slam my door as she left. You can't actually slam it, it's
hydraulically damped, but I knew what she meant. I listened to the
fading drone of her clapped-out car along the quiet street, then went to
seek comfort in the act of coffee making. I have a beautiful machine, a
vintage Gaggia. With its high-chromed pipework and compression
tanks it is like a classic sports car, rippling its lusty guts. I find its low-
throated processes exhilarating, identify with its trouser-busting sexual energy. I am master of all this Latin horsepower, I control it. And
my reward is . . . well, coffee. But coffee I would be proud to serve to
an Italian.

31

I sat down to think about what Lucy had said. I could not be turning
into a cartoon. It was fantastic, impossible. Who could help me? Doc-

tors? *"Doctor, doctor. I'm turning into a cartoon . . ."* It was the first line of a bad joke. Walt Disney Studios?

> *Dear Sirs,*
> *I have recently become the world's first human cartoon. In these times of escalating film costs, I wonder: could you use my services as a substitute for expensive special effects?*
>   *Yours,*
>   *Nicholas (call me Mickey) Taig.*

I imagined the reply I would pen to the fruitcake who wrote *me* such a letter. There had to be a rational explanation for what was happening. There had to be.

The day took its toll without warning. No sooner had I lifted my cup than I was almost asleep. Just as I reached that melting point on the edge of oblivion my telephone rang again.

"Nick Taig? Hi!" asked an unknown voice.

"Yes. Who is this?"

"Your pal, your savior! *Jesus!*"

"What?" I asked, wondering whether the Evangelical Christians had taken to telephone canvassing.

"It's no good, Nick. Your talent is just too damn big! The world is waiting!"

"Look, if you don't tell me who you are I'm putting this phone down."

"OK, OK! This is Herman Coprolite. Know me?"

Herman Coprolite. I made myself a silent promise to find that taxi driver and kill him.

"Yes, Mr. Coprolite. What can I do for you?"

"You mean what can we do for each *other.* I heard about your act. When can we meet up?"

"We can't meet 'up' at all. I told your friend I'm not ready to go public."

"Staggering Christ, you perfectionists! When *will* you be ready?"

"I don't know."

"How about a little private show, just for me? Whaddya got to lose?"

"I don't do private shows. Now please, go away."

32

"Don't do private shows? How come you did one for Eddy?"

"If he's your taxi-driving friend, that was different."

"Oh right, you did it for your cab fare. Come *on*, Nick! I'm offering you a cab ride to the *moon*. Dough! Fame! The whole global number!"

"Mr. Coprolite . . ."

"Herman . . ."

"Mr. Coprolite. I'm not wasting my time talking to you on the phone."

"Now that's what I like to hear!" he said, inexplicably. I cut the connection halfway through his next sentence, left the phone off the hook, and went back to my tepid coffee.

· · · · ·

Among the items on my personal shopping list of absolute necessities to be acquired before death, Fame is first. It jockeys around up there for position, alongside Fortune, but most of the time it leads by a head. Other people may wish for Beauty or Charm or Intellect but I already have a superabundance of those. I just need Fortune and Fame for the five-card trick. Naturally I deny it, especially in the company of the fame-famished. I do not intend to appear on the hit lists of those already on mine. It isn't the notoriety of Fame that I crave; I am already noted for myself. It is the lubricant effect. When I am out with those of my friends who have already become famous there is never any *problem*. Troglodytic nightclub bouncers discover the power of human speech and welcome you across their thresholds; otherwise blind bartenders regain their sight for just long enough to serve *you;* gorgeous ice maidens find that they're wearing nonstick knickers; and best of all, people insist on giving you things. For instance, I have a friend (Edward Geary, the newscaster) who *never buys clothes.* He simply tours those streets of London where mere window shopping requires a bank loan, and when something takes his fancy (some half-million-pound suit, say) he mentions that he will be wearing it on television and the grateful tradesmen almost pay him to take it away. Such is the power of Fame. It removes the burrs from the clothing of life as nothing else, not even Fortune, can. And now that it seemed to be searching for me I was desperate to hide from it.

33

· · · · ·

I was brought from my reverie by the doorbell. I had had an awful job finding the right one; most of them are so blue-collar. "Ding-dong!" they go, like Big Ben castrated. A better class of bell is the no-nonsense "Brrring!" but there's not much style about them. Mine, for which I was brutally robbed by some Jewboy in Bermondsey Antique Market, is a Victorian servant's bell, the type used to summon those below stairs. It was installed by a tattoo-infested electrician named Gary (or "Gow," as he preferred) who made connecting it to the entryphone sound as complex as a heart transplant and charged me accordingly. Still, I am pleased with its distinctive tinkle.

I picked up the entryphone, hoping to hear Lucy. Instead, Herman Coprolite sang me the first verse of "Ev'rything's Coming Up Roses." Whether he sang the second and third is a mystery: I was halfway down the stairs by then.

There are two entrances to my block of flats, but only one has bells and name plates. The other is hardly ever used. Praying that Coprolite didn't have the wit to see my stratagem I stepped into the street. It worked: he stood at the other door, pressing my bell with the persistence of a starving encyclopedia salesman. I'd seen his photograph many times in the papers, his hairy hands like bird-eating spiders clutching the waist of some production-line bimbo. I'd never imagined he'd be trying to get them around *me*.

I thought about risking a confrontation, but saw it would do no good. He was so obviously the type to whom abuse, even of the physical sort, is nothing but coyness. As he continued to harangue my bell I slipped away.

In my rush from the flat I'd forgotten my wallet and car keys. Once again I found myself without money, or the means to obtain it. I wasn't giving my name to any more taxi drivers, so I started walking. The area where I live, Pimlico, is smart and expensive. I can afford it because my father owns my flat and lets it to me for a reasonable rent. Reasonably reasonable, anyway. He could *give* it to me, as he did with my sister Katia's—but she got into Oxford. I didn't, and he won't forgive me. He says he's charging rent to recoup the years of school fees he wasted, with only a redbrick degree to show for it. The problem with Pimlico, at that moment, was that I didn't have any friends within walking distance. The only one was Rupert Ridout, a little prig I was at school with, where we called him Snoopy Roopy. He hasn't changed: now he's a lawyer of the legal-aid-only variety, which is fairly rare for someone who went to our school. If you have just been seen, by a crowd of witnesses, mugging and raping a seventy-five-year-old woman (prior to slitting her throat), Roopy's your man. Provided, of course, you are black. His worthiness is wearying, his every look a lecture, and I hadn't spoken to him for three years.

· · · · ·

"Rupert? It's Nick Taig. Can I come up?"

"Ye-es," he said, his sinus-centered, judicious voice sounding more irritating than ever via the tin loudspeaker.

He was waiting for me at his front door, wearing a fuzzy maroon dressing gown and holding a mug of cocoa. His wiry orange hair had sprinted away from his forehead since I had last seen him. He made no effort to greet me.

"Hello, Roopy!" I said in my school voice, imagining it would summon instant camaraderie.

"Ye-es?"

"Can I come in?"

"We-el. I was just going to bed. What is it?"

"Oh, nothing. I was just in the area, you know . . . and I thought 'I haven't seen old Roopy for a while' . . . so here I am."

"I see. So . . ."

"Come on, Rupert. Surely you can make a coffee for an old chum?"

He gave this statement his best lawyer's look—not surprising, since I'd spent half our schooldays at Winchester beating him up. He turned and went back inside, leaving the door open. I interpreted it as an invitation.

35

His flat, which I'd never seen before, was very much that of a lonely person. It was arranged selfishly, the television, hi-fi, and bookcase in a tight semicircle around a single chair. Far outside, in one corner, stood a sofa heaped with clean books and dirty laundry. Most telling, piles of legal papers lay around the floor.

He continued to stand, sipping at his cocoa. I cleared the sofa and pushed it nearer to his enclosure.

"It must be the lawyer in you, Rupert," I said, in an effort to lighten the mood.

"What?"

"Standing up like that."

"Oh. No."

"Where's Nelson?" I asked, hoping that a domestic inquiry might ease the atmosphere. Nelson is Rupert's beloved. Another hopeless case, rescued from the gutter; a stinking, incontinent cripple. Black, of course; a labrador.

"Around, somewhere. What was it you said you'd like? A cup of coffee?"

"Please."

"Very well. I shan't be a minute."

He went off to his kitchen, leaving me wondering whether I should have stayed with Herman Coprolite. When he returned it was as though he'd taken some mood-altering drug. He was smiling at me like his long-lost brother, and had prepared a plate of biscuits. Nelson staggered after him, dribbling dog pee on the rug.

"Hallo there, boy!" I said, patting the reeking compost heap on its head. He snapped, almost catching my hand in his petrified teeth.

"Actually, Nick, I'm glad you've come," said Rupert, proffering ginger snaps.

"You are?"

"Yes. Well, you're a man of the world, and I've got a worldly problem."

I checked the impulse to tell him that I had an *other*worldly problem.

"Sounds like I'm your man."

"It's a problem with women. No, not women—just one woman."

"One's enough, in my experience."

"Hmm. Look, would you mind if we rearranged the furniture?"

"*What?*"

"It's just . . . I thought . . . if I could lie on the couch, and you sort of sat behind me, I could talk better."

I could smell him sweating. Redheads are so distinct, don't you think?

"OK. If that's what you'd like."

When the furniture was arranged to his satisfaction, Rupert lay on the couch. Nelson lay down, too, in his personal piss pool.

"Are you ready now?" I asked.

"I think I might be."

"So fire away."

"Right. Well, I was picketing the South African embassy last week—I do that on alternate Saturdays—and I got beaten up by a pig." He paused, expecting me to sympathize. I did not. "All right, not exactly *beaten* up, tripped up—but it was down some stone steps. I got some nasty cuts and bruises and a bit of concussion. I was lying there and this girl—sorry, woman—came and picked me up."

"Oh," I said, hoping that my curiosity had not been whetted, merely to hear Rupert mourn his virginity. Nelson eyed me. With a huge effort he staggered to his feet and dribbled his way toward my chair.

"Yes," continued Rupert, "I mean *literally* picked up—bodily. She was absolutely gorgeous. I know that's sexist, but she was."

"It isn't sexist at all."

"All right, I shan't argue. Anyway, her name was Jenny. I was still a bit dazed and she put me in her car and drove me to her flat."

"Good," I said, uninterestedly. Of more interest to me was Nelson, who had taken a grip of my right foot.

"She gave me food. She was very nice. Kind, politically aware. We had some drink and then . . . God, this is difficult."

"Carry on," I said. Nelson was pulling at my foot with a strength I didn't think the rabid invalid possessed. Fear settled on my shoulders once more. I knew something bizarre was about to happen.

"Then we went to bed, made love. It was great, for both of us. It was my first time, by the way."

I was no longer paying even vestigial attention. My leg had started to stretch. Rupert droned on.

37

"It was fantastic. I knew, right then, that I was going to fall in love with her. There was some magic, it's hard to explain . . ."

Nelson was halfway across the room, my foot still in his mouth. I whimpered and shook my leg, which turned like a skipping rope. Nelson enjoyed that a lot and pulled some more.

"But afterward, Nick, oh this is the terrible thing, afterward she told me who she *is.* . . . She's the daughter of the South African ambassador! And I love her, God help me!"

Rupert was crying now, like an American, but I was disconnected from his confession. Nelson was almost in the kitchen with my leg.

"NELSON!" I yelled. The mangy incontinence pad let go in alarm. My foot shot back at high velocity, the force propelling me and the chair two feet. Rupert turned around, tears plopping from his nose.

"Nick, please, don't move away! I'm not a leper, just a hypocrite!" he wailed. I giggled with relief. "Now you're laughing at me. I knew I shouldn't have told you."

"Rupert, I'm not laughing at you. It was just Nelson, he had hold of my foot. I think it's great if you're in love. What's the problem?"

"The problem? Have you been listening? Here I am, the radical young lawyer and I'm in love with the daughter of the South African ambassador! It's a bit worse than buying Cape oranges, you know."

"Oh, don't worry," I said. "You can't *catch* apartheid, you know. Besides, it doesn't sound as though she holds the same views as her father. And you can at least claim to be fucking the regime."

"I suppose you think that's funny? You just can't take this seriously at all, can you? It's what I expected. You and your crowd. Anything's good material for a wisecrack, anybody else's misfortune, so long as it's not your own. All I can say is thank God. Thank God there are still some people around who care for the weak, the underprivileged, the emotionally maimed . . ."

38 {

I really had had enough for one day. I neither needed nor deserved a lecture. "For your information, Rupert, I *am* suffering personal misfortune at this very moment, and it's a lot worse than having put my cock in a politically unsound hole. I don't suppose it occurred to you that *I* might need help? No, of course not. I couldn't possibly need help, I'm not black, am I? You couldn't patronize me."

Rupert stood up, put his hands in his armpits and stamped, twice. Doubtless he'd learned the gesture on one of his Bantu dancing evenings. On my way out I took revenge on Nelson's tail.

· · · · ·

When I got back to my block Coprolite's white Bentley was gone. Inside the lobby, on the mat, lay a golden envelope. My name had been printed in a showbizzy typeface, as though in lights. Inside was one of those Nip devices: a mosquito orchestra played "There's No Business Like Show Business" while I read the letter.

> *Hiya Nick!*
> *So sorry I didn't catch you! What the heck? Why not phone me at home?—I won't be sleeping! 222 1234 is the number to AT&T me on. Could be AT&T for Two!!*
> *This Could be the Start of Somethin' BIG!*
>   *Your old pal,*
>   *Herman. xxxx.*

I took the letter up to my flat. The tireless little orchestra would not stop playing, and before I could go to bed I had to flush it down the lavatory. Something told me I would not deal with Coprolite so easily.

ooooooooooooo F O U R ooooooooooooo

The subway has always upset me.
It's such a humanity amplifier, with its abattoir lights and the fact that
I invariably stand with my nose pressed into someone's kebab-scented
hair. But my journey to work that Monday morning dished up a
double helping of fear and loathing. So many opportunities, in the
crush and the syrupy heat, for my new talents to give a show. Stiletto
heels, until then mere objects of mild fetishism on my part, now looked
anxious to skewer my feet; the horse-bollocks grab-handles seemed
created only to hit me and cause another nose-extension episode.

As it happened there was that rarest of things, an empty seat. It said
THIS SEAT IS RESERVED FOR THE USE OF ELDERLY OR DISABLED PEOPLE etcetera. There
was, in fact, an ancient cripple lurching toward it and I had to strike
out athletically to get there first. I plopped down with such an intense
sigh of relief that my neighbor, a middle-aged woman in a scarlet
blouse and black vinyl skirt, said loudly, "You poor old soul! We'll have
to send you to a rest home!" Some other passengers laughed and
waited for me to explain myself. I have never known what to do with
working-class pleasantries except ignore them, but the expectant
looks on the faces of my audience led me to give a thin smile, which
seemed to satisfy. I dared not open my newspaper or make any movement at all and sat, set solid, until Oxford Circus. There I rose, clutching myself like fine tableware, and shuffled to the doors. As I went, red

blouse stage-whispered, "See that? See where he sat? Shame. Only a boy, really. Shame."

She was right. It was a bloody shame.

My brief walk to work multiplied the possibility of mishap in an alarming fashion. To dodge the unpredictable swirl of bodies I danced a lone minuet. So much so that a young American tourist, convinced she had found some genuine British eccentricity at last, curtsied outside the John Lewis department store and said, "Sir!" coquettishly, like Olivia de Havilland with a rucksack. I gave her my genuine British eccentric's barmy stare and danced on.

Still minuetting I arrived at the premises of Zane, Zane, Darkly, the world's largest advertising agency and my employers. The building, an empty bit of sixties modernism by some Dutch madman, is hard to describe. Five stories high, featureless, with twenty aluminum-framed windows across the width of each floor. The prefabricated concrete sections doubtless looked all right when new but now have ugly yellow streaks across them, like a giants' urinal. I'm told the streaks cannot be removed, they come from within like cancer. Inside is a standard corporate lobby of the white marble variety, meant to make clients feel more important than they are, with three large Jackson Pollocks and a bewildered security man. The truth about our office building is that it is no longer modish enough, which reflects the position of ZZD itself. It's not a hot shop any more. The accounts we get are mainly for other huge corporations who want nothing more from their advertising than to demonstrate how much it cost. So both the building and the business within it are terminally ill. I am creatively frustrated at ZZD, and intend to move, *when* I get an offer that deserves my gifts.

I wished I hadn't taken the lift. It's the sort that shoots up at Mach 1, leaving the air behind and you with an ache in the groin. As it hurtled skyward I literally contracted, by at least a foot. The only other astronaut was Dolly the tea lady, a once-handsome woman who is now simply rugged. She looked startled. I was running short on appropriate reactions that morning and could not think of another. Then Dolly let out a shriek of laughter, poked me in the ribs, and growled.

41

"Gawd. I'm a bit the worse for wear s'mornin! I could've swore you shrunk just now. No, well, I was out on the tiles yesterday, weren't I? Me granddaughter's christening. Teach me to drink champagne, won't it?" I agreed that it would and she stabbed my ribs once more. "Tata, Mr. Taig," she called as I minced from the lift, "I'll try and sober up by dinnertime!"

· · · · ·

As I looked across the subdivided football field of our office the Monday hubbub in the partitioned rat runs told me that my story would have to wait until lunchtime. Our semiopen-plan offices offer the worst of all worlds. One is lulled into a false sense of security. I've lost count of the times I've been bitching about someone, only to have them pop up from behind a partition like Mr. Punch. That day I had an especial need for privacy. I wanted to tell Christian what had been happening. Sunday I had spent locked indoors, without the will or the courage to go to the lunch party. Now my need for sympathy had me overbrimming with self-pity.

Christian didn't notice my entrance. He sat in one of our hideous chairs which look like scrapped bicycles, drawing with his Magic Markers. For once he looked absorbed, his tongue poking right out and almost up his nose. Like many commercial artists, Christian would like to paint only for himself but can't afford it. Unlike many commercial artists, he has talent.

I delicately inserted myself into one of the dangerous chairs and lit a Park Drive. I tell people it's my vulgar little joke, a bit of token kitsch. The truth is that ZZD has the account and Akron Darkly says, "What you flog, you hog." I have tried putting another brand into the packet but there is always some lurking toady ready to go running upstairs. So I lit my Park Drive and blew the smoke in Christian's direction. He ignored it. I coughed, tapped my fingers on the desk. Nothing.

"What the fucking hell is so important that you can't manage a 'Good morning' for your copywriter and the man who bought your dinner on Friday night?" I inquired.

"Sssh!" was my reward.

"And, may I add, allowed your barbell-brained boyfriend to drink me out of Glenmorangie?"

"Did he?"

"Yes."

"Sssh!" said Christian again. A few seconds later he spun around, flourishing the finished work. "There! See, that's nicer than a boring old good morning, innit?"

Christian's drawing whisked my guts. It was of my head, sitting on Donald Duck's body. The thought of the future it might portend made me jump up, knocking over the chair.

"Nicky?" said Christian. "Are you all right? You look like you've seen a ghost."

"I have. Why did you draw that?"

"Why not? To give you a laugh. It's Monday morning. What's wrong?"

"I don't know. Something terrible, I think."

"You *think*?"

At that moment, Tony Belden slid around the edge of a partition. He is an account executive. Like most of his breed he thinks he's creative. I get lots of free advice from Tony. His physical appearance makes liking him, even if I wanted to, impossible. It's not that he's ugly; in fact he's irkingly handsome. He gives off no foul odors, dresses well, doesn't come from Birmingham. The problem is this: he has absolutely no facial expression whatever. His skin looks squeaky, like a thrice-lifted Florida dowager's. Although he's thirty-something there is not the shadow of age on his face; no crow's-feet, nor even baby sparrow's-feet. When he laughs his face does not. Instead, his lips part fraction-ally and he goes "H-, h-, h-." The robotic effect is actually frightening. There is an unofficial office competition; the prize, a magnum of Krug. To win it you have to discover where to put the battery in Tony Belden, or Anthony Android as he is generally known.

"Morning, chaps," he said through the vinyl lips.

"Hello, Tony," I replied.

} 43

"Ertcha," said Christian, whose phonemes fly back to Bermondsey in the presence of Belden. There was a silence. There always is when he's around. The only words anyone wants to say are "Fuck off."

"I really can't stand around chatting," continued Belden, "so about this Elephants' Graveyard account. Presentation Wednesday. Final."

Christian and I groaned. Elephants' Graveyard is a chain of stores selling complete crap. Plastic gilt carriage clocks; musical lavatory-roll holders; *The Monarch of the Glen* in Technicolor—that sort of thing. Imagine something tasteless and Elephants' Graveyard will have it in spades. Or rather, for them. I personally have not met (and can hardly believe exists) a single person with any of these items. So somewhere out there are entire houses crammed full of Day-Glo "tapestries," in-jection-molded polystyrene dueling pistols, and poodle-shaped tam-pon dispensers. Now that the chain has become part of a huge retail conglomerate (another of ZZD's dull, golden accounts) we have to do their commercials. My lack of interest in it equaled my dislike for Belden and it had been shuffled around my desk for more than a month. Now he was demanding the goods. I stroked my chin saga-ciously.

"Mmm. Elephants' Graveyard. We aren't quite happy about it yet."

Christian sniggered. Belden slipped his shiny fingers into the thin portfolio he was carrying and withdrew some notes.

"Is there a problem? You've had the brief for six weeks, I see."

"Nah, Tone son, nah problem," said Christian. "S'just the shops sell dog-do and we can't work out how to break it to the punters."

Belden swiveled his head at Christian. "And what, exactly, do you imagine we pay you for?"

Christian pinked. "We? *You* don't pay me, android, ZZD do that," he said, tactfully. The lights behind Belden's eyes flickered; human emo-tion was almost simulated.

"Well, *Mr. Christian*"—Belden thinks that's very witty—"the com-pany just might not want to continue paying your inflated salary un-less you pull your greasy little finger out. Is that clear?"

"Inflated? They pay us birdshit!"

"And that is probably because your *work* is birdshit."

"Listen, Belden, in a minute I'm gonna . . ."

"Tony, Tony," I interrupted clubbily, placing a hand on his shoulder, "you'll have your work. Tomorrow, I promise."

"I better had," he replied, this time without opening his mouth at all.
As he seethed back around the partition Christian started after him,
whirring and clicking like a tin robot.

"Transformers!" he sang. "Robots in disguise!"

"Christian!" I hissed. "Sit down."

"What's the matter? Lost your nerve?"

"I've definitely lost something. Maybe my mind."

"Blimey. Wanna tell Aunty Christy?"

"No, not now. Will you come to the park at lunchtime?"

"I can't afford to be seen sitting on a park bench with a notorious
heterosexual! I've got a reputation to keep down."

"Please, Christian."

"All right. But I dunno why you can't tell me now. You know I'll only
broadcast it five minutes after you spill the beans, anyway."

"I don't think you'll tell anyone this. They wouldn't believe you."

He drew breath, in preparation for some more wheedling, but something in my expression must have told him that I was not being melo-
dramatic and he said, "So, what about Elephants' fucking Graveyard,
Mr. Taig?" and took the cap off a Magic Marker.

· · · · ·

In fact, he had enough gossip of his own to divert me from my problems. Muscles McKaine, his bullock of a boyfriend, had been arrested
on Sunday, cottaging. "Cottaging," in case you're unsure, is not an
activity sponsored by the National Trust but a slang term for having
sex in public lavatories. Some men do it for pragmatic reasons: they
are married, ugly, or possibly both. Some simply enjoy it. But
McKaine, the snob, cottages because he approves it socially. His self-
oppression is so deep that he feels public lavatories to be the only fit
places for sick perverts like himself to indulge their vice. The latest
arrest (it is a regular event) had extra degradation value, for one of the
policemen on the bust played rugby with him. Christian told the tale
with his usual insouciance, which only added to my detestation for
McKaine. $\}$ 45

"Why do you stay with that bonehead?" I asked.

"Oh, I dunno. I think it's me Blanche Dubois complex."

"But I thought she relied on the kindness of strangers? Rory's neither of those."

"No, but old Blanche still wanted Stanley to sit on her face, didn't she? I can't help myself, Nicky. I know it's not the way a modern queen oughta be but I'm just a sucker for mindless laborers. It's me background, me genes. All them villains I grew up with, I loved 'em all."

"But Rory's not a bit of East End rough trade, Christian. He's a futures dealer. He went to Gordonstoun, for God's sake."

"No, but that's all them City types are, half of 'em. Just mindless laborers. Paddies in Porsches I call 'em."

I laughed. "So what's happened about the arrest? Has he been charged? South Ken Magistrates' Court must have a chair with his name on by now."

"That's the trouble, that's what all the palaver's been about. The copper who knew him let him go."

"So, good?"

"Not good. He let him go, but told him he'd have to leave the rugby club."

"Oh. That must have been a real kick in the athletic supporter for old Muscles."

"No joke. 'Course, muggins paid for it. I'm black and blue."

"Christian, you must dump the moron."

"Nah," he said, winking. "Loved it, didn't I?"

· · · · ·

We went to work on Elephants' Graveyard. Christian, despite his earlier bravado, showed uncharacteristic application and rolled only one salami-sized joint the whole morning. The problem was quickly solved once I could be bothered to blow a few brain cells on it. I came up with a clutch of inappropriate ideas, to let Belden have the pleasure of rejecting them, and one real peach, perfectly attuned to the client profile (flat nose, thick lips, sloping forehead, frizzy hair, that kind of client profile). A train of elephants, laden with panniers of fabulous goods, and driven on by imperial-looking mahouts, makes its way across deserts, over mountains, through forests until finally, wearily, they come to a resting place. It is a sort of magical grotto, like Aladdin's

cave, heaped high with glittering gewgaws. A merchant tells the mahouts that they cannot rest, that the goods must be packed and dis-
patched. Tired, but happy in their work, they put the goods into crates
marked ENGLAND—WITH CARE and a fruity Raj-type voiceover says something like "Elephants' Graveyard—from the ends of the Earth to your
front room." The expression "front room" pleased me especially. I
laughed at the stupid easiness of it all. Really, I didn't know why I
could not just stay at home and let ZZD send me my salary, simply for
existing.

Toward lunchtime Marcus phoned.

"Nicholas? What's all this I hear?"

"I don't know. What have you heard?"

"Oh don't be shy, Nicholas. Your *talent.* I've been hearing all about
it."

"What talent? I haven't got a talent."

"Now that's just what *I* said, when he told me."

"Who?"

"Herman Coprolite, of course. I didn't know you were friends."

"Marcus, we aren't friends. This is all a misunderstanding."

"Well, that's not what Herman says. He says you've been seen doing
the most extraordinary things in the back of a taxi. *And* he wants me
to feature you on *Simply Trilling.* Naturally I've agreed—apart from
anything you could do it for nothing, in lieu of that spoon you de-
stroyed. Now, I want you here at the studio tomorrow morning, at—let
me see—eleven."

I know Marcus when he's on the trail of a feature. Protesting would
do me no good, and appealing to friendship was out of the question. I
put my hand over the mouthpiece and turned to Christian.

"Christian, get me off this phone."

"Why?"

"Just do it!"

He lifted his own receiver.

"Calling all employees! The biannual Zane, Zane, Darkly nuclear-
attack rehearsal is about to begin. Please stop what you are doing and
proceed to the shelter."

47

Marcus was still talking, so Christian pulled the cord from the socket.

"There you go," he said.

"That was very credible, wasn't it?"

"Don't be ungrateful. Why did you want to get rid of him anyway?"

"It's all part of the same thing. I'll tell you at lunchtime."

"It is lunchtime. Come on, I fancy a McDonald's and some juicy gossip."

· · · · ·

Regent's Park was fat with people when we arrived. Office escapees mainly, parts of their winter-white bodies rather touchingly exposed to the sun. I kept my jacket on, content to let my golden hands and face tell these starchy clowns about the difference in our life-styles. Christian gamboled in the throng, pointing to the occasional clearing and asking, "There?," only to find it occupied by a new light worshipper when next he turned his back.

"It's no good, Christian," I said after five minutes' exploration, "there's nowhere private enough."

He gave a cheated pout and stuck his hands in his pockets.

"I know!" he said, "the zoo!"

"The zoo? That would be worse than this."

"Not where we're going it won't. Not today."

"Well?" I asked. "Where?"

"Aha. That's *my* secret."

I looked at my watch. "We don't have time to go to the zoo, it's too far. Belden's really on our case and I've lost enough this weekend, without adding my job to the list."

"Christ, you've really got the shakes today. Fuck Belden! I swear if he says a dicky bird I'll find that fucking battery and pull it out. We're going to the zoo."

I dithered but Christian grabbed my tie and began pulling in the direction of London Zoo. Not wishing to see the effect it might have on my new condition, I followed. Besides which the tie cost forty pounds.

· · · · ·

Our lunchtime was almost used when we arrived, but Christian was right; he did know a deserted part of the zoo. The temperature that day was about eighty-four. The humidity, ninety. The location was the elephant house and the result not hard to imagine. To ensure our complete privacy we sat on the uppermost of the semicircular concrete tiers, where the air had concentrated in a stinking soup that would have made a witches' brew look like watercress consommé. There were no other people. Even the elephants looked grossed-out.

"See?" said Christian, evidently proud of his achievement, "told you. And we can say it's research for the commercial."

I gagged. It was like being sick backward or, perhaps, drowning. I knew that the oxygen was there: the problem was in the packaging. Christian unwrapped his cheeseburger and began to eat robustly. It was the coup de grace.

"Christ almighty! How can you eat? Just breathing this stuff is a meal in itself."

Beneath us a party of hairy-backed Australian hardnuts had wandered in and were now busy pretending to vomit into each other's T-shirts.

"Oh, shush," he said between mouthfuls. "I'm bloody starving. Aren't you gonna tell me the dirt, then?"

"When you've finished eating," I replied.

He ate for a couple of minutes more, ostentatiously smacking his lips, while I sat with my handkerchief pressed to my face like a Victorian gentlewoman on slum duty.

"Fee-nished!" he sang. *"Now* will you tell me?"

I lifted my handkerchief over my lips. "Something beyond belief has happened to me," I said baldly.

"You won't shock me, Nicky," replied Christian, delving into his McDonald's bag and removing a Triple-Thick Strawberry Shake.

"I'm turning into a cartoon."

"Aren't we all, dear? I feel like Olive Oyl at the hands of Popeye lately."

"No, Christian. I'm serious. I really am turning into a cartoon. Physically."

He sucked hard on his shake. Then, screwing up his left eye, he made an artists' square with his thumbs and forefingers, and set me in it. Still keeping his look of concentration he reached out and rapped me on the side of the head with his knuckles, before taking another ruminative slurp.

"You are serious, ain't ya?"

"Deadly." Wheezing through the cotton I told him everything. The more I said the madder I sounded, even to myself. It was standard loony babble—perhaps a touch more colorful than imagining myself to be Napoleon, but no more sane. Christian may have been calculating how best to keep me quiet until he could call an ambulance. But I did him a disservice. His only reaction was to start laughing, with real delight. The strawberry shake frothed and dribbled from the corner of his mouth.

"That's fucking brilliant!" he giggled, wiping his mouth on his sleeve. *"Brilliant!* What tricks can you do? Can you tie your legs up in knots? Or can you do that one where your bonce goes one way and your bum goes the other?"

"Probably. I haven't tried."

"Well show me, show me. Do something cartoony!"

"I can't just do it, Christian. It's unpredictable. I'm a sick man, not a sideshow."

"Don't be a bleeding spoilsport. Give us a laugh!"

For the first time in three days I felt free. To have been believed was almost a cure. Recklessly I stood up.

"All right!" I shouted, "you asked for it!" and took a running jump from our lofty perch. There was a moment of ghastly wisdom when I thought my illness wouldn't do its stuff. Turning my first aerial somersault I caught Christian's horrified expression as he thought exactly the same thing. But then I was off, splatting fatly down the tiers of the elephant house, like a drunken octopus with a weight problem. Christian's hollers of encouragement did me no good at all, but they certainly drew attention to my performance. A superexcited Nip, thrilled to have found a use for the motor drive on his Nikon, tracked my progress down the last few levels and out the door, where I came to a halt, limbs knotted fiendishly like a schoolboy's elastic-band collection. His heavily pregnant wife squealed in terror as I rolled at her feet: for a moment I thought she might add her own little mess to the one that now lay before her. But I could not have cared. I just laughed, laughed, laughed, as Christian caught up, singing the Looney Tunes and Merrie Melodies theme.

ooooooooooo F I V E ooooooooooo

The two Nips were mere early arrivals at my performance; soon it was cheap seats only at the entrance to the elephant house. Christian continued to find it all wildly funny, shaking with laughter each time he failed to undo my knotted limbs, but the massed whispers of the startled gawpers began to take on dark undertones in my mind. Just as I felt certain that they were about to demand a lynching I saw somebody making their way through. A zookeeper breaststroked from the crowd.

"What the bloody hell are *they* doing?" he asked Christian while pointing at me.

"They? There's only one."

"Well? What is it?"

"It's a human being. *Please.*"

"Anyway, I don't care what it is," said the keeper, loosening his tie, "I ain't having him do it here."

Christian stopped giggling. "This bloke, this person, happens to be a mate of mine, and he's got a rare illness, cartoonitis. He slipped and fell up there and now I'm trying to untangle his poor, deformed little arms and legs. This load of bloodsuckers ain't helping and neither are you. I hope someone shows you a bit more consideration when you're sick."

The zookeeper looked chastened. "All right, mate, I'm sorry. S'just I thought it was two . . . well, never mind what I thought. Just didn't look natural, did it?"

"Didn't it?" asked Christian in his gay-rights voice.

"Not to me, it didn't," said the keeper, turning to the crowd. "Come on now, move along, make room! Man's not well here. Move along!"

· · · · ·

While the crowd was being moved "along" (why do they say that?) Christian managed to decipher my body. The left leg had been the problem, trapped as it was in the right-hand pocket of my jacket. I noted with dismay that my trousers, new the previous week from Emilio Bastanquez, were ruined. A pity, I reflected, that my clothes did not seem subject to the same bizarre laws that now governed my person; but my mourning was cut short by the approaching hee-haw of an ambulance.

"What shall we do?" I asked wetly.

"Leg it!" cried Christian, and did. I followed. At least, I tried to. I left the ground, in the first stride of a run, but stopped there. I looked down to see my legs whistling around, making a dust cloud and a noise like a threepenny xylophone. My body bobbed serenely on the air, seemingly unconnected with the tinkling turbine beneath it. The zookeeper arrived, keen for a fresh chance to exercise his office, and stood gaping.

"Christian!" I bawled at his disappearing form. He stopped, saw, started to laugh once more, and began running back to me. He needn't have troubled. Like a flywheel, the energy in my legs was released in one burst and I shot the three hundred yards from the elephant house to the restaurant in about half a second. I slowed then, to a more manageable fifty-five or so, and somehow managed to point myself in the direction of the exit. Whistling along like Roadrunner I zapped through the turnstile, leaving an unfortunate six-year-old with no trousers and a lifelong spin-drier phobia.

It was a further four hundred yards before the energy began to drain and I could execute an emergency landing. Christian arrived, breathless, a minute later. } 53

"Meep, meep!" he chirruped, flopping down next to me on the grass.

Throughout the entire episode he had not relinquished his milk shake and began now to suck at the dregs.

"Do you think you could stop that awful noise?" I asked. "It feels like my leitmotiv."

"Touchy, touchy," he said, adding a particularly fartlike slurp.

"What am I to *do?*" I whined. Christian poked the straw into the corner of the soggy carton and hoovered out the last bit of shake.

"The way I see it, you've got two choices."

"Suicide or what?" I drizzled.

"Nope. Get cured or get rich. I reckon old Herman Whatsisname is right—you could make a bundle out of this if you want. Start with the chat shows. You could work out a proper turn—you know, Uri Geller bends spoons, you bend your legs. Then you write your life story. Instant best-seller. Then they sell the film rights. Imagine it, directed by Spielberg, special effects by old George Lucas's lot, you'll be the cutest freak since E. fucking T.!"

"No thanks, Christian. I think I'll choose the first option. If there's a choice involved. I might be stuck this way forever. It seems to be getting worse."

"So why not collar a bit of moola while you're about it? You could need it."

"Look, I just could not debase myself in that fashion, Christian, OK?"

"A jest cawd nart debaize mayself in thet fesshun, Chreestyarn. Air care?" he mocked. "You're so effing hoity-toity sometimes, Nicky. If you knew what it felt like to be hard-up you wouldn't be so sniffy about making an honest bob or two. Million."

"I am hard-up. But I still don't want to be a touring freak."

"You, hard-up? Your old man's loaded!"

"But he doesn't give it to me. Everything's going to my immaculate sister."

"Well, even if your old man's a mean old bastard you still don't know what it's like to be poor."

"Spare me the 'we had it hard' routine, will you? You'll be telling me how you had to wear your brother's hand-me-downs next."

"Sister's, actually, dear."

I laughed. "Thanks, Christian."

"What for?"

"For believing me. It meant a lot."

"Didn't give me a lot of choice, did you? Bouncing down them steps like a rubber tit. You looked like Squiddly-Diddly when you got to the bottom. Remember Squiddly-Diddly? I really used to laugh when . . ."

"No, you believed me before I jumped off those stairs. Thanks."

He rested his head on his shoulder. "I reckon this illness is affecting your brain, you know."

"Why?"

"Never thought I'd hear you say 'thank you.' Not your style, is it?"

Ridiculously, I felt tears stinging. I was not going to add that special embarrassment to my collection.

"It's almost three. Perhaps we should go back to work. Assuming we still have jobs to go to."

"OK," he said, standing up and brushing grass from his hilariously unfashionable flared trousers.

We set out across the park.

"I hope you realize I've ruined my clothes for your entertainment," I said. Christian laughed.

· · · · ·

Belden had not noticed our absence: he had been away all afternoon on a shoot for a lager commercial. Christian refused to believe the story, suggesting instead that he was in fact having some malfunctioning components replaced by his creator, a man Christian imagines to be like Frankenfurter without the same sense of design. If anyone lacked a sense of design that afternoon it was me. At five-thirty he suggested we went for a drink, but I didn't like the thought of entertaining any more people that day, and refused. He didn't press me.

We left via the lift, and this time I didn't shrink. I stretched upward instead. When we stepped out Dolly the tea lady was nattering to Stan the security guard. She, like half the office, wondered what had happened to my clothes, but Christian gave her some kind of coded working-class look and she shut up with a clatter of dentures.

Outside the building I bade a bleak farewell to Christian, who had grown more maternal all afternoon and now cooed bedtime noises at me. He made me promise to call him if I needed to and "not to do anything *silly.*" I said all right. Then he made me do scouts' honor. In the street.

He beeped his horn four times as he drove away on his ludicrous moped, the kind with three wheels and a shopping basket the size of a tea chest. I wondered how it is that some people can have so little regard for the way they present themselves to the rest of the world. Don't they know the game, the war? Why won't they fight, these style pacifists? Away he went, on a vehicle designed for suburban house-wives, wearing clothes that even charity shops had remaindered, waving to me as though none of it mattered. I shook my head with amazement and a kind of respect.

· · · · ·

I had considered braving it out below ground but decided instead to walk home. The occasional rude stare at my clothes was a better prospect than the commuter *jihad* of the tube, and the walk was only half an hour. By the time I reached Green Park I was having regrets. It wasn't, however, the expected rude stares which were the problem—it was the envy. My envy. To envy power, fame, immense riches, these are the green-eyed moments that punctuate the complacency of the best-blessed lives, but to envy people their normality, their bog-standard humanity, was more than I could bear. I envied people I used to think I would rather be *dead* than be: sales rep types with pub-poodle hairdos and Ford Escort suits; mock yuppies with aluminum briefcases, red spectacles, and the effrontery to believe that they're just like me; fried-faced teenagers; women (all women); even, finally, blacks. I wanted to rush up to all of them, offer my life, my *self,* on the condition that the Condition went too. Yes, Envy and me were big buddies by Green Park.

He must have found me dull company, for he whistled up his old pal, Fear. Fear really got his money's worth. "So what about this illness then, Nick?" he hacksawed. "Why has it picked on you? What caused it? Pretty terrible, eh? Pretty fucking *frightening.*" I did not know what could have caused it. Any physiological explanation I could offer was just laughable. Had I been contaminated by any poisons lately? I *had* been swimming off Turkey on my spring vacation and I know the dagoes are none too fastidious about where they pump their sewage, but if this was holiday tummy, doner kebab was *cuisine minceur.* Did my mother stray into any radioactive areas when she was carrying me? Of course she fucking didn't, she never left Virginia Water the whole nine months. She even refused to watch television, lest the rays damage little fetus features. "Uh-oh," cut in Fear, "looking worse, Nick. How about a cure, what about getting cured?"

I wondered.

"Forget it. For-fucking-get it. Noooo chance." He was right, I knew. I was doomed to live as a monster. A harmless one, perhaps, but that made it worse. Where is the point in being a monster if you can't have fun scaring the shit out of people?

· · · · ·

When I entered the lobby of my block of flats I was beamed brightly at by Calvin the distorted porter. He smiles at everybody, young Calvin. Strangers think he does it on account of his effervescent Gaelic soul but he is in fact a miserable sonofabitch. He smiles only to display his four front teeth, which are gold. With his green livery and gold teeth he looks like a particularly unappetizing petit four. Nonetheless, he was well within the catchment area of my Envy that night. "Hello, Calvin," I wanted to say, "feel like swapping lives?"; but I didn't, I took a sharp left inside the lobby to avoid him. "Fock yow," I heard cheery young Calvin say as I mounted the stairs. I thought perhaps I should turn back, take him into my confidence. After all, he'd had to learn to cope with physical disadvantage, what was his method, his chirpy little scheme, his recipe for success? Ulcerous, weeping hatred for the entire human race, that was his method. I climbed sighingly on, my despair deepening with each step. At my door I stopped and rested my head against the wood, collecting the energy to face the poignancy of the Past within.

}
57

Another of Herman Coprolite's golden envelopes lay on my mat. I felt like going back to Calvin and shouting at him for letting an unauthorized person into the building, but I didn't have the spite. The envelope contained no electronic gimmicks, just a card. I opened it. A photograph of Coprolite's porky features popped out on a spring. He'd cut a slit in the mouth and poked through a fifty-pound note, folded to resemble a tongue. There was a message written on it.

> Nick baby,
> Ouch! You're hurting me! Why no contact? I'm a nice guy—ask
> Marcus Trilling.
> Sorry I can't see you tonite. But tomorrow I'll catch you in action
> at the studio. Can't wait!
>   Herman xxxx.

I put the money in my wallet, then went to phone Marcus, to tell him I had no intention of going to the studio, but I never finished dialing. There was no point. I already knew how to solve my problems. Suicide.

There are those who would say it was a bit early in the game to kill myself; that suicide is the last refuge of the hopeless. Yes, but it's the *first* refuge of the hope*ful*. Or it should be. If a life is mapped out in vibrant colors, where the contours defy geography, describing only peaks; if the life, in other words, is mine, what point is there in letting it plunge into darkened valleys or barren plains? None. My own death was a far happier prospect.

I'd tried it once before, in a limp adolescent way, after forgetting to take a penis to my first fuck. In books, in films, in women's magazines, the girl is supposed to say something like "It really doesn't matter. Let's just lie here awhile. I'm happy, *(your name here)*, just being in your arms." In real life she pointed at my baked worm and hooted, "What do you call that? I've seen bigger pricks on drawing pins." I slunk away with revenge in my heart but suicide on my mind. The attempt at autostrangulation resulted only in concussion, damage to school property, and shame, a lot of shame. This time there would be no mistakes.

58 {

It took about two hours of sitting, staring, and smoking before the centrifugal force of circumstance drew me to its hub. Even then my drawing room almost talked me out of killing myself. I watched its smart shadows change in the falling dusk, loved its sensitive aggregate of possessions and wondered, could I leave it behind? Roaming my demesne for a last time I caressed the clever, sexy curves of the mock Le Corbusier chaise longue, sniffed the honest weight of my curtains, let my fingers linger on the newly finished *craquelure* walls. I admired the broad-shouldered self-confidence of my flatter, squarer television; lifted into my arms the whisper-thin elegance of my video recorder, and, finally, paused at the futuristic promise of my compact-disc player. "Good-bye," I said, and kissed it. A tear splashed down on the black casing.

So, I had had to repair to the harsher world of my industrial kitchen and there I now sat, planning suicide. It was something I had always imagined to be simple, even haphazard; but I found myself with a growing list of rejected possibilities:

1) Pills and Booze? No, only sherry and aspirin in the flat.
2) Slash Wrists?—*No* (might hurt).
3) Car Exhaust? Perhaps a little obvious? (Car parked in street).
4) Hanging? *Again?* Get creative.
5) Electrocution? Get serious.
6) Falling? Now you're talking. This one's got legs.

I felt frightened by the last suggestion. "One instinctively knows when something is right," I thought to myself and laughed. It was the strapline from a booze commercial. So, death by falling it was. I felt giddy. "You'd better do it properly, then," I said aloud, gripping the edge of the table. I went back into the drawing room and shuffled, a ledge walker already, to the window. The pavement looked a long way down but very close at the same time. It was no good, I had to make a telephone call.

"Hello? Samaritans?"

"Mmm, how can I help?" replied the suicide counselor in a strawberry-jelly voice.

"I'm writing a book," I lied.

"Mmm, mmm. All got a bit on top of you, has it?"

"No. It's just . . ."

"Take your time, take your time," he said. I had only paused for breath.

"It's just . . ."

"Mmm?"

"If I could *finish!* It's just that, well, someone's going to kill himself, in my book, by throwing himself from a building. And I wondered how far one would have to fall, to make a proper job of it. I thought I'd ask the experts."

There was a silence. It seemed offended. Then there came the sound of muffled laughter.

"Hang on," said the counselor. "Ooops, no pun intended. Carol! Carol, bloke on the phone here writing a book. Wants to know how far you'd have to jump to do yourself in properly."

Before my counselor came back on the line there was some spirited technical debate.

"About six floors, we reckon."

"Thank you. Sorry to have distracted you from more important things."

"Oh, no problem. Made a change. What's the book called, by the way?"

"My autobiography," I said.

"Really? That's very . . . *Christ!* Look, don't—"

I cut him off. Six floors! It seemed unnecessarily far. It was only death that I wanted, not full "the body cannot as yet be identified" honors, but the Samaritans had concurred: six floors. My flat is on the fourth. I could hardly ask an upstairs neighbor to borrow their window, which meant I would have to go from the roof.

. . . . .

I considered the question of the suicide note for a further twenty minutes but was forced to abandon it because I could not calculate the correct distribution of guilt. I thought that perhaps the timeless simplicity of "Dear ———/ I'm sorry/ Don't blame yourselves/ I love you/ Good-bye" might have maximum impact, but it was too open. Anyone reading it could take my advice literally. On the other hand, a blame-specific note would be too unfair: anybody not named could feel exonerated, and I did not want *that*. But on the third hand, a note that blamed my illness would only lead to my being branded a sad loony, and then *nobody* would feel bad. An accident seemed the most multi-layered means of departure. The problem was how to make my fall from the roof look accidental.

Twenty more minutes later I had compiled yet another list, and was beginning to wonder whether anybody had ever died from exhaustion caused by the planning of their suicide. There were very few reasons for me to be on the roof, all of them equally implausible. There was no television aerial to need adjustment; no sun to bathe in; no view worth appreciating—in short, no excuse at all. I wondered whether my dearth of imagination was a common problem among those of similar inclination, or whether I was the first to suffer from suicides' block. I decided to employ my favorite method of stoking up creativity: the *Telegraph* crossword.

The very first clue provided the answer to my problem. It was an anagram. As I wrote the letters out in a circle at the foot of the page I noticed a small box with the information that there was to be a total lunar eclipse that night. It was perfect: I could be up on the roof to watch the eclipse. A little overenthusiastic peering and a fall from the roof looked distinctly credible. I drew a triple circle in red around the story, then went to collect my binoculars and Walkman.

I smiled to myself as I climbed the service stairs. It was so typically *me* to end it this way; so quintessentially Nick Taig, creative unto death. The door to the roof, as if in premature mourning, was painted black and the cinders on the asphalt crunched beneath my feet like the bones of all the dead before me. I went to the low guard wall and laid down my props. The binoculars on the *Telegraph* said everything with classic understatement. How glad I was, not to have left behind some florid novella of self-pity.

I retired to a distance of fifty feet and donned my Walkman. It had been hard, choosing the music for my closing credits, but "March to the Scaffold" from *Symphonie Fantastique* had won against tough competition from Sarah Vaughan singing "Life Is Just a Bowl of Cherries"—rejected for being that touch too ironic. I didn't want to arrive at the Pearly Gates and be accused by Saint Peter of musical sarcasm. I switched the machine on and began walking to the accompaniment of the opening timpani. At the entrance of the cellos I mounted the guard wall, turned up the volume, and waited for the brass. I felt I had waited all my life for that fanfare and when it came I stepped into the darkness with the sure knowledge that I was making the very best of entrances. As ever.

○○○○○○○○○○○ S I X ○○○○○○○○○○○

DEATH CERTIFICATE

Name	TAIG, Nicholas Guy Dennet
Sex	M
D.O.B.	11/26/58
Address	27 Brecon Mansions, Cambridge St., London SW1
Cause of Death	Severe brain damage from multiple cranial fracture. DOA.

That was how I had wanted it to look: spare, uncluttered; a designer death certificate. My leap from the roof could never have been put down as the "cry for help" of the average hysteric. It was, even the least charitable would have to allow, rather more serious in intent and execution than five aspirin and a Pepsi. However it may as well have been five aspirin and a Pepsi, for all the effect it had had. On me, at least.

For a few seconds I had hung in the air, three feet from the building. Gravity's hot lips sucked at my bowels but I remained motionless. If I'd taken the trouble to apply my life's new rules to my intentions I should have predicted failure: Tom never dies when Jerry tricks him from the top of a building, does he? When I did realize what was going on I decided to walk back onto the roof, but the laws of physics revolted at this affront to their pomposity and shot me at the ground. My Walkman was left behind, Berlioz buzzing eerily in the jetstream.

When I awoke it was to complete paralysis. Inches from my eyes a thigh-thick psychedelic python spat fire, foul water tricked about my ankles, cordite was in my nostrils, and looking up I saw what I had feared: low in the sky an orange lozenge, the sun of Hades itself.

Pimlico certainly looked different from three feet beneath the pavement. I had tailored myself a bespoke sarcophagus, from Westminster Council property, which explained the paralysis. It did not, however, relieve it and I could now smell the unnatural smell of natural gas which, added to the sparks beginning to crackle from the broken telephone cable (not a python), led me to feel somewhat alarmed. I tried to move. It was useless. Short of levitation there seemed no escape. The sparks and the growing smell of gas looked about ready to do the job on my behalf when it occurred to me, for the first time since my illness had begun, that perhaps I might turn it to my advantage. I simply *decided* to sit up, and did. In fact I rolled up, like the lid on a sardine tin, and spilt out onto the street, where I rocked back and forth for a while with my foot in my mouth, unsure how to reverse the maneuver. The problem solved itself when my foot slipped from my shoe. I sprang open like a broken clock and lay there on the pavement, one empty shoe crammed into my mouth. My head hung back into the hole and the humiliation was complete when I realized that the smell was not that of gas at all, but human sewage. A pioneering and evidently snake-hipped turd had made a break for it through the narrow crack in the pipe and swam insolently an inch from my face. Only the prospect of being discovered with a shoe in my mouth and my head in a cesspool gave me the will to stand up; otherwise I know I would have lain there till I drowned.

When I had put my shoe on I stood back for a good look at the damage to the road. To the unimaginative it would seem like a bizarre subsidence; evidence, for those who wanted it, of the government's neglect of the "infrastructure." But to many it would look the exact shape of a perfectly proportioned young adult male. In other words, me. It seemed prudent to run away but I found myself vibrating with fear, unable to move my legs. And at that point, inevitably, a police car drew up.

64

The Westminster Police drive BMWs. It's rather clever of them, because a BMW is as popular and affordable a means of transport in these parts as Nikes are in Brixton. Thus if the police go to arrest a drunken stockbroker as he tries to park on the right side of the pavement and the law, the chances are he'll mistake them for another drunken stockbroker in *his* BMW, and continue blithely to incriminate himself. The flashy understatement of a BMW is not, of course, my style. Instead I drive a 1946 Citroën Avant. It comes from the end of the age when car designers were influenced by the horse and carriage and has a high, straight passenger compartment that seems unconnected with the engine section. I bought it from a restorer at Waterloo who specializes in those and nothing else. His workshop is a fabulous sight, with ten or fifteen of them parked outside, like a postwar French cabinet meeting.

Two policemen alighted from the car, closing the doors in perfect unison and then smirking at each other when their little bit of theater had worked. One was a smudged Xerox of Burt Reynolds, the other so slim and fey he might have been his wife. Overplaying the joke they walked toward me in step, stopped, and folded their arms quizzically. My knees knocked as I feigned ignorance of their presence. Together they scratched their ears. Blood roared in the Jacuzzi of my head. Burt coughed.

"This your hole, sir?" he asked. Fey Ray sniggered.

"Oh! Officer! I didn't see you there!" I said like a hyena.

"No? Fancy that."

"Yes."

"Well?" he continued, "is this your hole?"

"Of course not, officer. I heard some commotion and came down to investigate. I live in these flats, you see. Amazing, isn't it?"

"Not really," said Ray in a voice as slight as his body, "loads of people live in flats."

Now it was Burt's turn to chuckle. I saw why vaudeville had died.

"So you didn't see what caused it, then?" asked Burt.

"I'm afraid not. As I said, I heard a noise and thought I'd do the right . . ."

I was interrupted by the bang of a door. Turning, I saw Mrs. Estroy-Jones, an old army widow who lives two floors below me. Lucy calls her "delightfully dotty"; Christian never comes to see me without taking her chocolates; even Calvin the porter polishes her doorknob. But for some reason she holds me responsible for the premature death of her cat, and goes out of her way to make my life difficult. Like many army people, the E-Js collected tasteless ephemera from around the world during their working lives and she was wearing a bit of it now, a clogged and fetid kimono.

"This," hissed the fossilized Mama-san, "is the hooligan I referred to on the telephone."

Burt made comic show of a suppressed grin. It looked evil.

"Oh oh oh oh oh oh *oh.* I do believe you have been telling us porkies, young sir," he said.

"I don't know what you're talking about, Mrs. Estroy-Jones," I said, trying to sound aloof and hurt at the same time. It had no effect. She sliced her hand through the air.

"Corporal," she said to Burt, "I distinctly saw a large object fall from the roof. It looked like a person but obviously was not. The next thing I saw was Mr. Taig standing by this hole. It seems an open and shut case to me."

"Then you know this gentleman, madam?" asked Ray with the insight of a blocked proctoscope.

"It is my great misfortune to do so, yes," foamed the geriatric geisha. "He is a vandal and vicious hobbledehoy. He murdered my cat!"

That was the old harpy's big mistake. The policemen had already put her down for crazy and the discovery of a motive for her telephone call made the crucial connection in their unpromotable minds. I saw the blame in Burt's eyes shift from me to her, as he gestured with his head that he wanted a private word, in the car.

· · · · ·

"It's really terribly sad, officer. She's off her rocker. I never touched her cat."

66 {

"Do this a lot, does she?"

"I wouldn't say a lot," I said with unimpeachable fairness, "but she does make my life difficult, yes. She's never phoned your good selves before, though."

I smiled. Burt smiled too.

"Still don't clear up the little problem of one large hole in the road, though, do it?"

"No," I said with regret, "but I was only doing my best to be a useful citizen. It's a sad day when—"

"All right, knock it off, I'm not going to nick you. I just want to know if you saw anything at all."

"No, I'm afraid not. As I was saying before Mrs. Estroy-Jones appeared, I heard a noise and came down to investigate."

"Loud noise? Bomb noise? What type of noise?"

"At the risk of sounding facetious, the sort of noise a road might make when it's subsiding," I said, facetiously. Burt leaned on the steering wheel.

"OK. If I could just have your name and address, sir?"

"Most certainly. Nicholas Taig. T-A-I-G, 27 Brecon Mansions, Cambridge Street, SW1."

"Thanks, Mr. Taig. We might be in touch."

"Thank *you*, officer. Er, what about Mrs. Estroy-Jones!"

"Leave her to me," said Burt.

Outside, Mrs. E-J raved on. She was telling Fey Ray how I had administered the poisoned Kit-E-Cat when Burt cut in with stunning ferocity.

"Now listen, you old bat! Wasting police time is a serious offense, and a woman your age should know better. If we get any more of this we'll call the social services and have them shut you away. Understand? Now go home and count yourself lucky. I've got a real job to do here."

For some reason Mrs. E-J first undid, then refastened the buttons on her kimono before shouting, "A curse on your house, Nicholas Taig!" and disappearing back inside Brecon Mansions. I shrugged at Burt, who gave another of his sinister suppressed laughs, this time placing his hand over his mouth.

67

"Be a bit noisy down here tonight, sir," he said. "I'll have to get the emergency services on the blower to clear this lot up, soon as the boys from forensic have had a shufti. Bloody incredible. Wonder what happened?"

"I'd love to know, I really would," I said.

Ray, I'd noticed, had been walking around the perimeter of the hole for some time and now paused at exactly the point I'd hoped he would not.

"I've got it!" he said. "You know in cartoons, like when old Tom's chasing Jerry, only Jerry dodges out the way and Tom falls off of somewhere, and when he hits the deck he leaves a hole shaped like a cat? Well that's what it looks like. Only man-shaped instead."

He looked smug. My skin crêped. Burt walked around to where Ray was standing and looked at the hole.

"See?" said Ray. "See it?"

Burt rocked his head.

"No, I'll tell you what. I reckon what happened is that a bloody great prehistoric *monster* with one leg missing came hopping this way about half an hour ago, that's what I reckon. You *wanker,* Sedgely. You'll have to excuse him, sir, he's a bit new. Aren't you, Sedgely?"

Sedgely gave Burt a new-boy smile, craven and violent at once. I said goodnight.

· · · · ·

I took the last of the sherry to bed with me and lay there drinking it from the bottle like a serious wino, not caring when it ran down my face onto the sheets. Laura Ashley's exploding meadow across the soft furnishings reminded me of Lucy. I wanted her. In one of those clichéd moments that can only happen in real life I found a lone hair on the pillow. I wrapped it around my little finger and fell asleep cuddling the bottle.

· · · · ·

The *Daily Telegraph* lay threatlessly on my doormat when I managed to make my way from bed next morning to collect it. In the kitchen, having selected from my cupboards' *embarras des richesses* (coffee or coffee) and chosen coffee, I sat down to cheer myself with the stories of human frailty which the *Telegraph* makes its speciality. People tell me that *The Independent* is equally amusing but I could never trust a newspaper so smarmily evenhanded in its opinions.

Page three seemed promising. A large photograph of an extravagantly deformed person, his limbs knotted into a boy scout's masterpiece, made me laugh out loud. Until, that is, I recognized the poor freak:

MYSTERY CONTORTIONIST AT LONDON ZOO

Visitors to London Zoo were treated yesterday to an impromptu cabaret. The gentleman pictured above put on a display of limb bending which would "not have disgraced Houdini," according to one witness.

The photograph was taken by Mr. Hideo Akura, a sheet-metal worker from Osaka. Mr. Akura, whose wife was delivered of a baby girl yesterday afternoon, said, via an interpreter: "This man is amazing. We would like him in Japan for our game shows."

Zoo staff were called to the scene when a member of the public reported two men behaving indecently together. In fact the "two" were one. Further witnesses reported that the man ran off at a speed of fifty miles per hour.

To my great relief I was unidentifiable from the photograph, a result of Mr. Akura's incompetence and the fact that my face was crammed between my buttocks. I could not help noticing that, distorted as my body was, its lines retained an elegance that many would still envy. My spine, for example, though shaped like a *W*, looked typeset rather than scrawled.

I had hardly stopped admiring the photograph when I saw that I had made it into print twice:

EXPERTS BAFFLED BY ROAD SUBSIDENCE

Geologists and forensic experts were scratching their heads this morning about the cause of a major road subsidence in Pimlico, London.

Residents in the Cambridge Street area were without telephone connections and many were without water as the mysterious collapse has damaged underground piping.

Police were called to the scene late last night. There are not at this stage believed to be any suspicious circumstances.

The speed at which bad fortune seemed to be extending its parasitic tendrils stunned me. Mere hours had gone by since my symptoms had begun publicly to show themselves, yet already a sunrise industry was establishing itself. Herman Coprolite was first in the queue, but who next? If the *Telegraph* was carrying both stories, it was certain that the tabloids would have them, too. I wondered what warped interpretation *The Sun* and the *Star* were putting on things but realized that for once it would have been difficult for them to have invented anything more perverse than the truth. It couldn't be long before I was discovered as the missing link. I imagined hordes of proles making their goggle-eyed way to my door, and wished to God that I had been given some useful power, such as that of destruction. I did not think that the inquisitive would pester me for long, once they had learned that the finale to my act was their own demise. I remembered a time when an airliner had crashed near to my parents' home, killing three hundred, that people had arrived with their families and actually pitched tents, the better to savor the carnage. My mother was outraged: that people could have the audacity to pitch tents on "our" land; but my father found the perfect solution to the problem. Even though the land wasn't his, he charged the gawpers rent.

Work was an unfaceable prospect. There were certain to be one or two hawk-eyed creeps who would spot me in the newspaper. One particular new copywriter called Giles something had made me his role model and tiresomely begun to copy my style. My style is, of course, uncopyable but young Giles would have recognized my trousers, since he had probably just bought himself a pair. There was also the matter of Elephants' Graveyard, which wasn't quite ready to serve up to Belden. There are accounts on which it is possible to work despite difficult circumstances but something like Elephants' Graveyard demands that the trivia muscles are limber; and my trivia muscles had polio.

Angry that there was nobody else to blame for the absence of a phone line I stomped to the bedroom and dressed carelessly, something I could not remember ever having done before. Even last year, when the bozo record producer in the flat beneath mine had caused a fire and a 3 A.M. evacuation, I had risked death by taking the time to select a decent outfit, rather than appear on the pavement like some-body from a transit camp.

Having closed my front door and looked left and right twenty times, as though about to cross a motorway, I came face-to-face with Mrs. Estroy-Jones. She was still wearing her kimono, clogged like a toffee that had rolled under a bed. When she saw me she screwed her hands into little claws, her eyes into sooty slits, and hissed at me.

"Morning, Mrs. Estroy-Jones!" I chirped. She hissed again. I hissed back.

"Cheerio!" I said, and continued down the service stairs. She contin-ued her inexplicable way up them.

In the street my hole was a superstar. It had a fan club, the public. Gawping, wondering. It had cosmetic surgeons, the men from the wa-ter company and the phone company, trying to make it beautiful again. And most of all it had its freeloaders: the media. At least thirty of them were scratching another day's living from a hole in the ground. They formed a society all by themselves, like a baboon colony. First there were the outcasts, the reviled: newspaper reporters, snapping around the fringes, slyly awaiting their opportunities to rush in and snatch a mouthful of the big meat. Then there were the venerable but toothless members of baboon society, the radio reporters, allowed a share of the leavings by the new generation, the television teams. The first, from the BBC, was being fronted by a startling siren called Ami Leysdown. I had been trying to get to meet her for months, to see if she lived up to her name, but without any luck. Marcus claimed to have had her. I doubted it. She looked to me like a woman who needed a lot of manning, the kind who would not notice if Marcus inserted his entire body into hers, let alone his legendary cocktail sausage.

The second television team was from TV-AM. To my dismay it was fronted by a friend of mine, James Custer. The lustful seconds I had spent on Ami were time enough for him to have homed in on me. I turned to go—too late.

71

"Nick!" he called, "Just the man I wanted!" and was upon me in two strides.

"Hello, James," I said. My hands crab-scuttled about my person in an attempt to hide the clothes.

"Nick, you old sod! You look a bit dog-eared. *Green and brown?* Didn't know that was what the posers were wearing. Still . . ." He grinned without malice.

"I've been kept up all night by this noise," I lied. "I was too tired to dress properly."

He laughed. "That's perfect. Give us a quick interview?"

"No, James, I will not. I'm not appearing on network television in a green jacket and brown trousers."

"Go on, Nick. Don't be a wet blanket. Besides, the morons who watch TV-AM won't notice."

"Nope."

"Please? None of the other residents'll speak to us."

"Sensible them."

"Be a sport. I've got a live link in forty seconds. We can't have the third shot of the hole this morning, they'll fire me."

I thought that unlikely, since James's father is the biggest shareholder in TV-AM.

"Tell you what, old chum," he went on, "give me a few words and I'll introduce you to old Imay Laydown over there. I know you're after her, your eyes were out on springs a minute ago."

"Were they?"

James looked oddly at me. "Well, not literally."

"Oh," I said.

"Are you feeling OK, Nick?" asked James, placing his hand on my shoulder.

"Just tired. Just tired." I looked at Ami. She was outrageous. "All right, James, I'll do the interview. But can you ask your cameraman to shoot us in close-up?"

"Anything," he said.

"Ten seconds!" shouted a technician, and I was on live television, with unbrushed hair, a green jacket, and brown trousers. Perhaps the viewers couldn't see them. But I knew they were there.

"Hello, Peter," said James to the camera, his entire presence changing, from straight-spined ex–public schoolboy to something altogether looser. "Well as you can all see I'm here at the hole."

The cameraman panned to the hole. Somebody in the studio, some tenth-rate comedian, must have made an innuendo about the hole, for James said to camera, "That's right, Bernie, I think it *would* need a lot of *stuffing*! Anyway, I've got someone here with me who witnessed last night's events. Good morning, Mr. Taig."

"Good morning, Mr. Custer," I said.

"Ha ha!" went James, for no apparent reason. "Now you saw just what happened last night?"

"Well, not exactly, no. I heard a loud noise and came down to investigate. When I arrived the hole was already here."

James spoke to the camera again. "*Too* right, Bernie! I wish all holes were like that, too!" He turned back to me. "So you didn't see what happened. But have you got any theories of your own?"

"Only dull ones, I'm afraid. It looks to me like a simple case of sub-sid—"

"Him!! That man is the culprit! And here is the evidence!"

Mrs. Estroy-Jones stood just out of shot (though not for long) holding aloft my binoculars and newspaper. How stupid of me not to have realized why she was creeping up the service stairs! I gave James an imploring look but he is much too good a journalist to let such opportunities pass. He turned from me and poked the microphone at Mrs. Estroy-Jones.

"Good morning, madam. You have a theory?"

"A theory?" she asked with hauteur, "a theory? A *fact*. That man there, Taig. He threw something from the roof last night which caused this destruction. Here in my hands I hold the evidence that will send him to the gibbet!"

"I see," said James, stroking the bridge of his nose. "Those look like a pair of binoculars and a newspaper to me, madam. How exactly are they incriminating?"

73

Mrs. Estroy-Jones ate air for a couple of seconds.

"Why, do you not see? He used the binoculars to choose the spot where he could cause most damage. I understand these things, I am an army widow. He is an evil and destructive ruffian, and I shall not rest till he swings!"

James was beginning to laugh.

"And the newspapers? What was he doing with the newspaper?"

Mrs. Estroy-Jones looked confused. Her fingers trembled over her eyes.

"Yes, Bernie," said James to the studio comedian, "I think we have, too," and took the microphone away from Mrs. E-J. "Well, were you on the roof, Mr. Taig?"

"Yes, I was, as a matter of fact. To watch the lunar eclipse."

James paused and looked at me like a cat might at a broken bird.

"I thought it would be something like that. Thanks. And now back to you in the studio, Peter."

Mrs. Estroy-Jones had taken her evidence to one of the policemen. He appeared to be taking her seriously.

"Who is that old loony?" asked James.

"It's complicated. She thinks I killed her cat."

"And what *were* you doing on the roof, really?"

"I told you. Watching the lunar eclipse."

James smirked. "Pull the other one, sunshine," he said, still in his television character. I gave him a "remember-your-background" look.

"I suppose it's none of my business, though," he said in his real voice. "Come on, I'll introduce you to Laydown."

In the corner of my eye I saw Mrs. E-J scything toward me, towing the policeman by the cord on his radio.

"Another time, James. I'll have to go," I said, and ran.

"Maybe on Saturday at Marcus's party?" he called after me.

"Maybe," I called back. As I turned the corner Mrs. E-J and her captive policeman had begun to give chase.

I was almost at Victoria Station before finding a working telephone. It was one of the new alfresco ones, made more so by some creative

74

vandalism. I dialed Christian, miraculously getting the ringing tone after only four attempts.

"Nicky!" he yelled, inevitably through a mouthful of food. "You've just been on telly! There I was, scoffing down me Alpen and up popped me old mucker. Vivian was right, weren't she? It was you made that hole in the street?"

"I didn't know you were on first-name terms with the old cow."

"She ain't an old cow, she's my mate."

"Look, Christian. Don't harass me, I can't take it."

"All right. Here, I liked your clothes."

"You would. Listen, I can't come to work today. Can you make some excuse for me?"

"Oh, no!" he wailed, "Have you hurt yourself? Shall I come round? Me moped's all charged up, honest. I've got bandages."

"No, I'm fine. It's just . . . well, I'm not fine. But I'm not hurt. I couldn't face Elephants' Graveyard, that's all."

"If you're sure you're sure. I don't know, though, Nicky. You might have done yourself a mischief and not know it. Now an uncle of mine, he fell out of bed once and banged his head. Dead in a week. Brain hemorrhage. Go on, let us come round."

"Have I called the right number here? You are Christian Kidd, not my mother?"

"All right, all right. I won't come round. I haven't cooked Rory his breakfast yet, anyway."

"So you'll make my excuses?"

"Yup. I'll tell Belden you've overstretched yourself."

"Very funny. Thanks. I'll call you later. Oh, and give my hate to Rory. Bye."

Christian's genuine concern for my welfare brought on a fresh attack of self-pity. As I shouldered my way through the office-bound crowds, huddled up like an oppressed mill worker, I found it necessary to give myself what my nanny used to call "a good ticking-off." It wasn't as if I had never faced adversity before. There was the time when I thought that I had made Diana Hannay pregnant, for example, when I was seventeen. There had been probings, samplings, sweat-

75

drenched weeks before the truth was discovered. She was pregnant. But I'd coped, hadn't I, I'd come through? After all, it was *my* father who'd lent me the money for the abortion. Then there had been the time when Dickon Dunbarr had given me that kilo of cocaine to hide from those Colombian hit men. When they'd come knocking at my door had I not done the decent thing? Had I given them the *whole* kilo? Of course not. And I certainly did not tell them where Dickon was hiding. Not beyond the general area, anyway. I mean, Eaton Square's a pretty big place. Or how about last year, when I'd found myself lost in the South Bronx at three in the morning? Had I panicked, gone yeller? Of course not. I'd simply walked up to the nearest youth and asked whether, if I gave him the contents of my wallet, he would escort me to the subway. And he, after some haggling during which I agreed to give him my jacket, too, had. So you see, Taig, life has presented you with problems in the past and you, by dint of natural good breeding, cour-age, and a superior bearing, have dealt with them. Turning into a liv-ing cartoon is just another of those problems which to you are trifling. You will deal with it. Won't you?

Thoughts like those buttressed my bravery until I reached Cam-bridge Street, but the crowd about the hole showed me that my pres-ent problems were of a different magnitude. I pressed myself against the railings and oozed behind the backs of the onlookers. They were too interested in the hole to notice me, yet I felt their threat as I slid along, sweat turning my spine into a column of ants. As I drew close to my building somebody tapped me on the shoulder. I barked in anguish and my hair literally stood on end as I turned to face my tormentor.

"That's novel," said Lucy, pointing at my hair. "I didn't think you'd embrace the punk ethic so late in life."

I reached up. My locks stood like knitting needles in my scalp.

"Shit, I can't take much more of this. Get inside, quick," I said, pushing her ahead of me through the door.

The rigid hair flopped down the moment we gained the safety of the lobby, just in time to prevent it being seen by Calvin. When the espe-cially favored cross his threshold Calvin insists upon operating the lift

—or at least, miming it, the lift being automatic. Lucy is one of the chosen. Calvin gave his goldest grin.

"Top of the mornin'" he brogued, fakely since he has never been closer to Oireland than Kilburn.

"Good morning to you, too, Calvin," said Lucy, meaning it.

During the journey I clutched my unpredictable body while Calvin made his usual sad attempts to chat Lucy up. He even did his petit-four impression for *me* as he whisked back the lift doors with a clumsy flourish. Lucy cooed farewells, stopping just short of blowing kisses.

"You should change your name to Esmerelda," I said to her loudly as Calvin was closing the doors.

"Don't start, Nick," she said. "Calvin's got a bent spine, not a hunchback. And at least he's human. God, I'm sorry, I didn't mean that."

I let us into my flat. It was good to see her, a relief. I suddenly felt almost sick with horniness, but knew I'd have to work subtly for its reward.

"So you know?" I asked. From a bulging carrier bag she produced a copy of *The Sun*. "What are you doing with that?"

"I'm hardly likely to be reading it, am I? Look."

She opened it. Beneath the headline NOW GET OUT OF THAT!!!! was the same photograph that the *Telegraph* had carried.

"At least Mr. Akura's having a good time," I said.

"What?"

"Doesn't matter. How did you know it was me?"

"I just knew. And look . . ." She opened another page. The paper was running a competition to find other "contortionists." WHO'S THE BIGGEST BENDER?, they wished to know, and were offering five thousand pounds prize money. I feigned hurt.

"Why are you here anyway?" I said, toeing the doormat in my best little-boy-lost fashion. "I thought you never wanted to see me again."

"You great twit. I love you. I'm sorry about last Saturday, but you can't blame me, can you? It was a pretty fantastic story. What am I saying? It still is a completely unbelievable story. And then . . . what on earth is going on?"

"I really, really wish I knew, little Luce. Something's happening to my body, I . . . it's ludicrous." I gave my upper lip a heartbreaking pre-sob tremble. Lucy took the bait.

"Poor, poor darling," she said, holding my chin, kissing the end of my nose. "Tell me everything." I sniffed and took her hand.

"Later," I said, leading her to the bedroom. "Later."

∘∘∘∘∘∘∘∘∘∘∘ S E V E N ∘∘∘∘∘∘∘∘∘∘∘

"**W**ell!" said Lucy, running her finger around my left nipple, "You didn't tell me you could do *that.*"

I won't describe what *that* was. Let's just say that in cartoon terms my performance was nine tenths Woody Woodpecker and one tenth He-Man, Master of the Universe.

"I didn't know I could," I said. "Despite what you accused me of doing last Saturday with Victoria Smale I haven't touched another human being since you."

She rolled over onto her stomach and traced her finger on the floral pillowcase with exaggerated interest.

"Nick, please, please don't get angry, please don't think I disbelieve you, because I don't . . . but you realize what's happening to you isn't possible? People just don't turn into other things, least of all cartoons."

I tried hard not to feel angry but my voice was packed with it all the same.

"What do you suggest, then?"

"I don't know. Hypnosis? Hysteria?"

"Don't you think I've been through all those things? Don't you think I want that to be true? But it *is* happening, isn't it? Even if the photos in the papers weren't of me, and even if that hole outside was a perfectly normal case of road subsidence, you've just seen the evidence first hand. Haven't you?"

"I suppose I have," she said, turning away.

"You *suppose?* Lucy, if I spent twenty years studying under a yogi and another twenty in a troupe of acrobats I couldn't possibly have . . ."

She turned back, anxiety squalling in her eyes.

"But I don't want to believe it. I don't. I'm *scared.*"

"And what do you think *I* am? I'm terrified."

We stared, each the other's victim.

"God!" she exclaimed. "I'm being so selfish," and she wrapped me up tight to her breast. We lay like that for a time, Lucy breathing calmly but giving the game away with her pounding heart. Then she started to giggle. It was good to hear but still I asked her why.

"I'm thinking about how you hung the duvet off your prick. It was just so funny."

"Evidently," I said, unheard through the titter attack.

"And then when you bent over the bedside table and . . . oh, goodness." She reached for a tissue to wipe her streaming eyes. "It's no good," she said, blowing the laughter from her nostrils, "I do believe it but I can't take it seriously. It's too ridiculous."

"Oh, I don't expect to be taken seriously, just so long as you believe me. And you do?"

"Yes, I do."

"So you're sure you wouldn't like to make absolutely certain?"

She laughed again. I held her gaze until she stopped.

"Maybe there *is* just the teeniest little doubt," she said.

Half an hour later, having proved my case beyond reasonable doubt, I found myself dizzy with hunger. Ludicrous amplified bellowings, like a cow in a cave, issued from my stomach. This new symptom started Lucy giggling again and she went out to the kitchen to cook for me. I followed and sat at the table, rumbling. It was a comfort that my illness needed feeding, it made it more homely—or at least, earthly. Lucy had brought provisions. Sausages; bacon; eggs; white bread: all manner of nutritionally dubious yet psychically filling foods emerged from her bag. I felt I'd never before seen her so much in her proper place, as she dealt expertly with the frying pan (I'd forgotten I possessed such a thing), tossed bread into the toaster, boiled the kettle and scrambled eggs simultaneously. She wore one of my shirts and I was hypnotized by the busy twitching of her cute bunny bottom, peeping out beneath the white cotton, and by the sound of her soft voice, drifting across on currents of smoky bacon. I realized then that I would probably have to make her happy and marry the lovely little thing.

"So, what do you think then?" she asked, placing breakfast before me.

"What? Sorry, I wasn't listening."

"Nick, if we're going to get you better you'll have to concentrate. I said we should get in touch with this friend of my father's, Dr. Anschluss. He's a specialist in nervous disorders."

"Who says I'm suffering from a nervous disorder?" I snapped. "This isn't *my bloody fault,* you know."

She touched my arm. "Not mental illness, neurological illness."

"Oh."

"And we've got to start somewhere, haven't we? Eat your breakfast."

She went to dress while I ate. When I'd finished she reappeared, led me back to bed, and tucked me in.

"Have a snooze, darling," she said, pushing back my fringe and kissing my forehead. "I'll look after you now."

· · · · ·

I had a strange dream when she went out to the phone box. We were just married. Naturally we looked fabulous. As we left for our honeymoon I expected to find my car covered in the usual paraphernalia but instead my best man (Christian, oddly) handed me a suit decorated in the way the car should have been and told me to put it on. I changed in front of all the guests then, gathering Lucy into my arms, took off into the sky. After a time Lucy told me to land. She then said, "Good-bye. I'll see you in the Maldives." I asked her why she couldn't come with me but she replied that I had to make the journey myself. I said that I didn't want to, but it was no good. The suit carried me off and I watched Lucy fade as I climbed higher and higher with, it seemed, no control over my destination. Then I awoke. Lucy sat on the bed with tea and biscuits. She was really enjoying herself.

"What did Anschluss say?" I asked.

"He said it sounds fascinating and he'll see you next Monday. Well, actually he said, 'It zounds vascinatink, I'll zee heem next Murnday.' "

"I don't believe it, a joke psychiatrist."

"I've told you—he's *not* a psychiatrist, he's a neurologist. And he can't help being Austrian, pig."

"Why next Monday? It's ages."

"Don't know. He's very eminent. There's probably dozens of people who've turned into cartoons that he's got to see before you."

"Himself chief among them from the sound of it," I said. Lucy gave one of her "You're a bastard but I can't help loving you" sighs and handed me another biscuit.

· · · · ·

Monday seemed a dangerously long way off. God knew what could happen between me, the world, and next Monday. But Lucy, of course, had planned ahead. She had already called ZZD and her own employers, written a shopping list, and designed the entire week's meals. I had no need at all to leave the building, except on Saturday for Marcus's annual party.

Marcus's party is one of the few events that must be attended if possible; so much so that one of his unofficial nicknames is the Great Fatsby. Such is its exclusivity that one could not display the invitation on the mantelpiece, in case people thought one proud. Or worse, stole it. He always hires somewhere that captures perfectly the mood of the time. In 1983, the year when money got class, it was an entire floor of London's most expensive hotel that had had the honor of containing us. But in 1984 we were pulling money's leg, so the party was in a disused railway arch at London Bridge. The rats we found most amusing, especially when the female star of a television sitcom was attacked by them. Marcus had real winos to serve the drinks. To make it funnier he had the tramps publicly deloused before allowing them to serve us. In '85 Marcus was working in America, so we had a dinner in his absence. In '86 he hired a giant marquee. Not particularly original, except that it was erected in Hackney, on the country's most notoriously deprived housing estate. Marcus called the party "Laugh on the Dole." We certainly did, but the quantities of policemen needed to suppress the ensuing riot didn't. One of them was almost killed, which spoiled things a little. Last year it had been a tea warehouse on the river next to Tower Bridge and this year promised to be the most perfect of all. Marcus had sued a pinko newspaper magnate for criminal libel, won huge damages, and invested the money on the stock market, with insider information. Estimates of his fortune vary but certainly he had bought himself a two-million-pound mansion in Kensington and that was this year's party venue. I certainly could not have thought of a place that better summed up 1988.

The reason for the party is not, of course, for people to enjoy themselves. Anybody in a position to be asked has long ago lost all capacity for having anything so crass as a "good time." The reason for going is to have a useful and productive time. For a start every reporter from every society and gossip page is there. I have usually managed to get my picture into print at least twice and this year I was determined to have my name underneath. Also this year, for the first time, a documentary was being made about it. There was a television crew last year, too, but only to record a short section for yet another program about London's nightlife. When it was transmitted the tone was disapproving. "Look, viewers," it was saying, "look at these spoiled bastards. Thank Christ you're not like them, eh?" In reality the guy who made it is a good friend of Marcus. His puritanical commentary could not have been more wry.

My prime requirement of this year's party was to get a new job. All the top creative directors would be there and I'd laid my plans weeks before. I intended to spend no more than an hour seeing and being seen, then grab Don Stamp, head of the hottest shop in town, impress him with free toot, and virtually sign on the dotted line there and then.

Lucy had long ago stopped trying to avoid The Party. She knows how important it is to take a woman. They're part of the kit, they say "Yes, I've got it all, too, thanks." She made an attempt to stop us *both* from going, on account of my illness, but that only strengthened my hand. I

needed her there more than ever in case something dreadful happened. She had to agree.

· · · · ·

The week passed almost without incident. In the continued absence of
telephone connections caused by my hole, Herman Coprolite was denied easy access. He did attempt to appear in person, but Lucy's love
affair with Calvin meant that the lobby door was guarded ferociously
by the twisted leprechaun. My illness, too, seemed to disappear, except when Lucy and I made love. Her simple soul was particularly
entranced by my ability to screw her from another room. She continued mothering me and I saw that her job with Oxfam was a mere
substitute, a conduit to drain her huge desire to love and care for *me*. I
felt stupid for not having realized it before. Marriage was what the girl
needed, not a career. I made up my mind to propose to her on the
following Sunday, when I would be popping with generosity after Marcus's party. The thought of the gift I was about to bestow kept an
enigmatic smile upon my lips for the whole week.

· · · · ·

I cannot remember more enjoying dressing for a party than on that
Saturday night. In fact the process began in late afternoon when I
shooed Lucy back to her own flat to forestall any argument over mirrors. Having drawn all the curtains and selected some appropriate
music I ran my first bath. It is crucial to bathe twice for important
occasions. One would not, after all, allow guests to dine from unrinsed
plates. First comes the long soak and exfoliation by means of washing
grains and sackcloth bath mitt; then the tepid, pore-tightening second
bath. Showering is not at all the thing to do in such circumstances,
denying as it does the essential contact with the physical self. One
needs time to take it in, to understand its possibilities for power.

In my first bath, having exfoliated, I prerasaged, then shaved. Two
different razors are required. The first, a twin-bladed disposable, is for
the general facial area but a cutthroat is what's needed around the
ears, to avoid the Polish border effect.

Emerging from the second bath, my skin snapped tight to my muscles, I meditated briefly before beginning the construction of my hair-

style. Many people believe that the path to great-looking hair is an expensive cut, but that is only partly true. The real prerequisite is good hair. Many are the times I have sat at my barber's next to some sad case whose "hair" would shame a coconut with alopecia, listening while they demand a style that would be difficult enough to create in *stone*. Naturally, this disability does not afflict me; my hair is an ebony fountain which needs the merest advice from scissors. I have it cut short at the back and sides, with a longer fringe which I am free to scrunch and gel into provocative fronds over my eyes or to sweep back if the mood takes me. The latter style was my choice for the party. One looks far better on camera with the hair off the face, provided one's forehead is a smooth expanse of alabaster, not sweet potato.

I knelt at the side of my restored Victorian bath, as though worshipping at a claw-footed idol. Taking the brass shower from its rest (can you believe that some people are tasteless enough to have them gold-plated?) I adjusted the water temperature with a nursemaid's care: too hot and the hair can be dull and unmanageable, too cold and it is impossible to rinse properly. Choosing from the range of shampoos that I have custom made and then decant into crystal I tipped a walnut-sized blob of creamy goodness into my palm. It is critically important how long one massages for; too little and the scalp isn't stimulated, too much and one can suffer the shame of greasiness within the hour. I find that singing the first two verses of "You're the Top" times things precisely.

Mild crisis intervened, having rinsed, when I could not remember whether I'd conditioned my hair last time I washed it. Cursing, I wrapped a towel about my head and went to consult my Filofax. To my intense self-loathing I discovered that I had not even *washed* my heroic mane for five days. It had been twice that long since it had seen conditioner. What I needed was a hot-oil sachet but I knew there was none in the flat. Miserably I went back to the bathroom and had to be satisfied with the regular sort of conditioner, which I decided to leave on for twice as long as usual. I apologized profoundly to my hair as I rubbed the fluid in, coaxing and tempting it with promises that never again would I be so thoughtless. It worked. After toweling to the damp

85

stage I could see I had been forgiven, that it was ready to do my bidding.

The quantity of gel to use is a matter of extreme precision. Most people use too much, too quickly, and the result is like a varnished sea lion. A little, gradually, is the secret. Beginning at the back with a smear for general control I worked forward strand by strand, licking my locks with the taming substance. Selecting two of my mahogany and bristle brushes from their rack I swept back in an airy parabola, then with a surgeon's accuracy and the smaller brush attached a few wayward wisps to the luscious confection. I stood back and admired what I had created. Classic, timeless, with no hint of the spiv.

"Well done, Nicholas," I said aloud. The gorgeous creature in the mirror flashed me his teeth.

My teeth, in truth, are somewhat vulgar, beaming Arthurianly as they tend to across darkened rooms, but what to do, what to do? I have searched chemists for some dentifrice that might subdue their fluorescence but all products are for those with the contrary problem. Many are the whispered conjectures as to the veracity of my teeth, but I have learned to live with the gossip. Those privileged with an invitation to run their tongues around them know that they have encountered reality. I restrict my treatment of them to the medicinal: a floss, a probe with my Plaqueattacka, then leave well alone. I also avoid all mouthwashes, the first resort of the orally decadent, preferring instead to remove old food from my dental interstices before it can putrefy.

After the hurdles of my toilet had been cleared I reached the home straight. Generally I disapprove of the use of cosmetics by men. I do not include in that statement adolescents, for whose attempts to conceal their pomegranate acne beneath lurid orange lotions one feels a degree of sympathy. But grown men, except those cruelly underprovided for by that mutha, Nature, should avoid makeup. Unless, like me, they know how to apply it. The key, the matrix, for those wishing to improve their technique, is this: first put it on, then *almost* take it off. I begin with a fine line of mid-brown kohl beneath the lower lash line. The common mistake is to apply it inside the lid margin, which effectively halves the size of one's eyes while simultaneously making one look like a transsexual lizard. After that apply some coffee-colored eye shadow (the sort without feminizing twinkly bits) to the lid, with a smear of lighter color just beneath the brow bone. Then, with a large brush, dust some blusher (in a bricky shade, *not* red and *definitely* not rose-pink) *below* the cheekbones, assuming we have them. Finally, take a tissue and wipe off to the point where it appears that we have removed it all. Believe me, we won't have. Lipstick, lipgloss, and foundations are to be avoided at all costs, unless the aim is to look like a drag queen. I can absolutely guarantee my method, which has helped to have women at my feet for the past ten years.

I had spent three days musing upon my choice of clothes for the evening and now I cracked open my wardrobe like a lucky Egyptologist. A suit, it had to be a suit, for the same reason that my hair had to be swept back from my face. I flipped through the rack as if through a record collection, letting the clothes call up the past. The crumpled gray satin from Yasmine Zod that I wore to my first job interview; the safari pastiche from Danny Tanner, still bearing faint bloodstains from the fight I was forced to have with the yobbo who tried to close the doors on me when I was late submitting my Telecom share application; the black Yo-Yo Toyota which I have never liked but women love for its lack of impeding buttons. My choice for the party was a dark blue pinstriped Carlo Sabbini. Its subtle references (shoulder, lapel) to the 1940s were rescued from the retro by the playful contemporary device of misaligning the buttons and their holes. It would show the world that, while meaning business, I was sufficiently relaxed to mock the very idea. A pinstriped shirt added to the intention, containing as it did two large holes that exposed the raunchy raisins of my nipples. A tie? Of course, thin and formal, my genuine old-school. But tied in a Windsor, that knot so beloved of treacherous wideboys since the duke himself. Not, of course, that I consider myself among their number. Next I chose a classic pair of black Church's brogues, to show that there was a solid foundation to the playfulness exhibited from the ankles up. Finally a piece of jewelry, the skeleton of a baby vampire bat, set in acrylic resin. On my lapel it gave just the right amount of shock to the outfit. It would cause the initial attention necessary if people were to look at the rest of me. Some fools believe that old chestnut "a well-dressed man's clothes are not noticed for ten minutes." They are dull cowards. A truly well-dressed man is noticed *immediately*, and ten minutes later he is the center of attention.

It was done. Inside my excitement ran a cold channel, almost like bereavement. Now that the preparation was over another time of such innocent pleasure could be many months away. The feeling passed and I half ran from mirror to mirror, greedy to gauge my effect against different backdrops, beneath various lights. In the bathroom, brightly lit against the tiles, I was almost frightening. Hyperreal. In the hall the shadows cast by the overhead light hid the cold fire of my eyes within inviting hollows. In the drawing-room mirror, softly lit, and framed by tasteful things, I was a monster of Romance, flashing dark then bright; angel, mortal; irresistible, repellent; everything, nothing; the alpha and omega of Charm. I hugged myself to myself and spun around and around, holding in my bliss, jealous of it yet so in love I thought I would burst. Tears of joy began to make their itchy way around my eyes and I stopped myself, dead. Tears would ruin everything—not least my eyeliner.

Lucy rang the bell. It seemed so common, so cheap to share myself but I knew that I must. It was already ten o'clock so I went straight downstairs. When I opened the door Lucy gasped.

"Nick," she said, "you look marvelous."

As we walked the short distance to my Avant I looked at Lucy's chic black dress, classy flat shoes, understated pearl earrings, and I simply had to admit it to her.

"You know," I said as I drove the car smoothly away in the direction of Kensington, "I do."

W hen I was a child my sister contracted meningitis. My parents, grateful for her eventual recovery, went first to church and then to Hamley's, where they bought the most magnificent dolls' house I have ever seen outside a museum. My envy was pustular. Not because I wanted a dolls' house, but because I wanted something that said "I'm rich" with equal clarity. My show of pleasure at Katia's good fortune was quickly seen through and Mother admonished her to share the gift with me. But I didn't want to *share* it, I wanted to find fault with it, to spoil its perfection. I could not. The closer I looked the more impeccable its beauty became. The harder I tried to prove its worthlessness the greater was its worth. Finally I burned it. In fact I talked Katia into burning it by suggesting that a fire in the mansion was the perfect way to test my radio-controlled fire tender. I did not tell her that I'd filled its water tank with lighter fuel.

Now, as we turned the corner in Marcus's drive I saw that someone had rebuilt the dolls' house at one-hundred magnification, and that this time there was not even the possibility of sharing it, much less of burning it down.

"Gosh," said Lucy with irritating wonder, "I didn't know Marcus was *that* rich."

No, I thought, neither did I, but said instead, "Mortgaged up to the eyes, of course," which was probably untrue.

"All the same. *Gosh.*"

"Yes, all right, gosh. Gosh, gosh, gosh. But do try to close your mouth before we go in, it's so infra dig to look impressed."

"I'm not impressed, I'm appalled. Why does he need it all?"

"I don't think *need* figures in the equation," I said condescendingly.

"It bloody well should," she replied, and we drove the last few yards in silence.

Marcus had not had the façade decorated in any way for the occasion. No fairy lights, rose-twined pergolas, or bunting detracted from the statement the house made. If giant neon letters had been flashing from the roof, the presence of Wealth could not have been advertised more clearly. All the interior lights blazed through undrawn curtains and I could not help feeling respect for Marcus's subtle manipulation of avarice. The showcase can be yours, if the price is right! A sudden feeling that it never would be made my chest tighten.

"Come on," I said angrily as I slipped my car into a gap between *two* Ferrari Testa Rossas, "let's show Marcus what money can't buy."

"Let's just try to enjoy ourselves," said Lucy as though English were a foreign language.

"I don't have any trouble at all doing that. It's your little problem. You're the one who stands there all evening like a guide dog for the morally blind. I *like* my friends."

"Do you?"

"Oh, stow it," I said, and walked off.

· · · · ·

Although it was not yet ten-thirty many had arrived before us. Even the novices knew that this was not the usual quick-lay stopover, to be stumbled into at midnight, hollering for the john. The beehive noise that fanned through the open front door was not quite conversation, but the whirring of three hundred minds in the act of calculation. Everybody wanted to get something from this party and if they didn't then that could only be because they already had everything. It was those in the latter group whom I noticed first, as we stood in the hall and our arrival was announced over concealed loudspeakers.

Near to us, like a slight silver queen on the marble chessboard of the

hall floor, stood Merlina Megatherium, billionairess and famed anorexic. She had taken starvation to the level of art when she featured
in an exhibition in New York the previous year. While sitting for a week
in a gallery on the Lower East Side, eating nothing and drinking only
water, talented black and Puerto Rican youths had sprayed graffiti
such as DIE, RICH BITCH! DIE, MOTHERFUCKER! on the walls around her. They
say the queues stretched two blocks—Merlina's friends, mainly.

"Isn't that Merlina Megathingy?" asked Lucy like a tourist.

"Yes," I replied tightly. "Try not to be so obvious."

"God, she's thin. I can see her veins."

Merlina swiveled her head on its bony stalk and smiled at us. If she
had heard Lucy's remark she'd taken it as a compliment. Her companion looked angry at having lost her attention for a moment. It was
Herman Coprolite.

Lucy looked panic-stricken. "Nick, it's Herman Coprolite! Quick, before he sees you!"

"Stop flapping, will you? He's never met me in person. And he won't,
either, unless your squawking gives us away."

I didn't need to hear this conversation to know what he was saying
to Merlina. To have her on his books would raise him to the exalted
rank of internationally celebrated celebrity celebrator. But I knew his
courtship would fail, because his clients all do it for the money and
that is something not lacking in Merlina's life. Any chance he may
have had evaporated when he plucked a canapé from a passing tray
and popped it into his mouth. I could not believe that a sharp busi-
nessman had failed to do his research: Merlina's disgust at food is so
complete that she gives dinner parties where she appears only on a
video monitor at the head of the table. As he ate the canapé I watched
Merlina's hands flutter in panic before she rushed for the stairs, presumably to vomit. Coprolite shrugged and moved away. As he passed
me I held his gaze, with no flicker of recognition.

Merlina's nauseated flight upstairs drew my attention to a modern
triumvirate at the first landing. The first was Paddington Sh'Aim, the
world's most powerful communications baron. His political views,
voiced loudly in his many "newspapers," are so extreme that he advo-

cates the reintroduction not only of hanging but drawing and quarter-ing, too. His deep brown jaw moved up and down like the lid of an expensive suitcase as he talked to the second man. He was Eddie Custer, father of James who had interviewed me for TV-AM. Unlike James (Winchester and Trinity Hall), Eddie is a self-made man. Physi-cally, it is easy to believe. Five feet five (tall), five feet four (wide), his head apparently borrowed from another species then put on upside down, and in the back of his neck a deep cleft, as though he couldn't quite reach around to tie the sutures. After an early life of crime petty in its rewards but not in its violence he earned ten years in Pentonville where he took an economics degree and learned that it wasn't neces-sary to draw blood when robbing people. He now owns three television companies (not officially, of course), the country's second-largest su-permarket chain, an airline, and about half the property in London that hasn't already been nabbed by the queen or the duke of Westmin-ster. His politics and his ambitions parallel those of Paddington Sh'Aim and their mutual enmity makes the rivalries of Mafiosi look like lovers' tiffs. The fact that they were talking to each other would have been impossible to believe, were it not for the third man. He was Paul Somerleyton, the government minister with final say about who would get satellite broadcasting rights. In theory no monopoly could exist but in practice the rewards would be going either to Sh'Aim or to Custer. None of the three held a drink as they stood in tight formation, too close to fight yet too far apart to cooperate.

"Now who's staring?" asked Lucy, waving her hand in front of my eyes. "Please could you get me a drink? You know how tense these people make me."

"Why? They're not interested in you."

"Please, Nick, could you just get us some drinks?"

I went resentfully to find a waiter. This was my world, these people were my friends. Who the hell was Lucy to condemn them? What made her friends any better? Failure, that was all that bound them together. Don't tell me they actually enjoyed being paid peanuts to wipe the arses of abused children or do Voluntary Service Oversees in diseased

African villages. I was amazed to think that only a few hours previously I had wanted to marry Lucy.

When I discovered one of the black serving boys whom Marcus had hired and dressed so wittily in rags I took my anger out on him. It was appalling, having to walk a hundred yards for a drink. What did he think he was getting paid for? And I bet he was claiming unemployment benefit. It was disgraceful.

As I weaved my way back through the bonhomie of my people I caught the eye of lovely little Ami Leysdown, dressed so erotically in a blue lurex sheath that I wanted to pee. She smiled over the rim of her glass and I chalked her up for later.

Lucy still stood dumpily in the same spot when I returned.

"Thanks," she said, adding "for nothing" with her eyes.

"What exactly is the problem?" I asked.

"There isn't one. I only asked for a drink, for God's sake. Is that unreasonable?"

"It's not just that. I thought you might have made an effort. Just for an hour or two. You know how much this means to me."

"Yes, I do, and I am making an effort. It's you who's been impossible, ever since you saw the house. It's not my fault if you're envious of Marcus and it's not fair to blame me."

"Me, envious of Marcus? What nonsense. It's you who's envious."

"OK, I'm envious. Happy now? Perhaps we should circulate a bit before we do something *vulgar.*"

"Fine," I said and prepared to move off. A fanfare stopped me in my tracks. Marcus was making his entrance.

Marcus always enters his parties with some hugely amusing flourish. When the party had been in the railway arch he had arrived in one of those miniature steam trains on rubber tires, dressed in British Rail uniform. He then collected our invitations, which were in the form of railway tickets (marked "First Class to Success"), and anybody without one was ejected, or "thrown from the train." When the party had been in the marquee on the council estate we were all terrified when a gang of armed skinheads had gatecrashed. Marcus had set it up, of course, and arrived dressed as Hitler to pacify them with a Nuremberg-type speech. It was brilliantly funny. This time he had excelled himself.

From the top of the stairs came a procession, led by a brass ensemble playing the Grand March from *Aïda*. Behind was a group of twenty or so of the black serving boys in their rags. At the rear, in a sedan chair, was Marcus himself, dressed in thousands of pieces of gold leaf and nothing else. The troupe halted at the top landing and then the boys began clambering over one another, pressing their bodies groin to groin, wrapping shiny black thighs around sweaty black necks. Even in the blasé aquarium of Marcus's party the atmosphere was suddenly awkward. Pedophile cabaret was perhaps too much. A relieved sigh came from the audience when it became apparent that the boys were actually using their bodies to form letters of the alphabet.

"What does it say?" shouted someone. Marcus looked a little worried but managed an uncharacteristic bit of wit.

"I don't know," he shouted back, "the coons all look the bloody same to me!"

There was much laughter and applause.

"It *says*," he went on, "The Gilded Youth!"

The brass ensemble struck up again and Marcus was carried through our midst. People cried out, or touched him for luck. When he reached me he leaned down and spoke.

"Nicholas, don't forget I want you to meet my friend Miranda. Come to the folly in the garden in twenty minutes."

He moved on, leaving me in a blessed afterglow of pride, as the cheering continued. When he'd disappeared from the room I turned to Lucy. She had gone, leaving her half-full glass on the spot where she'd stood. I thought about chasing after her but there was no point: I'd been seen coming in with her, she'd fulfilled her purpose. It wasn't my fault that she had no sense of humor. I picked up her glass, drank the contents, and went to find Ami.

94 {

In a corner of the main drawing room I saw Ami's blue dress twinkling. Lurex is well named: I made for it like a pike. On the way I was stopped by Christian. As usual he was dressed in clothes I would not donate to the gardener.

"Nicky!" he said in his aggravating maternal-faggy way. "I've been so worried about you."

"No need to worry about me, Christian. Couldn't be better."

"Honest? What about—*you know*, then?" he asked with sugary concern and an am-dram wink.

" 'You know,' as you put it, is fine. Gone."

"I'll be blowed. Did you see the doc, then?"

"No, I did not," I said tightly.

"I still think you should. It could be dangerous. You could have a relapse. You *should* see the doc."

"For Christ's sake. I'm fine. I got *better*. And at this moment the only thing bothering me is you. You're blocking my view of that raunchy little tart, Ami Leysdown."

"All right," he said, sounding hurt, which made him even less appealing. "Where's Lucy?"

"I don't know. She pissed off. The best party in town wasn't good enough for her."

"I know how she feels. This place is full of wankers. I only came here for Rory's sake."

Lucy's display of disapproval had already exhausted my tolerance. There was none left for Christian.

"No," I snapped, "let's be honest. You, Rory, and Lucy are only here because of *me*. If you didn't know me you wouldn't be asked, and then all you can do is carp. It's a shame you're queer, you and Lucy would make a nice pair. Why don't you go and find her? She was last seen making her way to Clapham wearing a hair shirt. Come to think of it, your taste in clothes is pretty similar."

A man, a real man, might have hit me then. Anger of some sort was appropriate, I wanted it. Christian just unpeeled another layer of passivity.

"I'm sorry, Nicky. I was worried, that's all. I'm sorry. I'll see you, then," he said and drifted off. I really wanted to hit him.

Ami was talking with two other women. One was Roz Rezza, hostess of *Talking Dirty*, the world's first postpunk housework show. The other was Marlene Kake, born-again feminist and authoress of the midlife

sexual crisis guide, *Your Secret Vagina*. I could see that I'd be a welcome intrusion. As I approached Ami looked at the floor, smiled privately, and turned away from her companions. The blue dress was so
tight I could see her pubic mound; her nipples strained at the thin
material like the snouts of little sex animals. She looked me up and
down frankly.

"I like your brooch." Her real voice was less fluffy than I'd wanted it
to be.

"Thank you. It's a bat, or it was a bat."

"Oh, I do hope it wasn't killed specially!" she said, half ironically.

"I hope so too," I replied. "I'm a firm believer in beauty without cru-
elty. Though I must say, your beauty is definitely doing cruel things to
me at the moment."

She gurgled into her champagne and smiled.

"James warned me you were a smoothie."

"Warned you? Oh dear, I hope I'm not too smooth. I can be rough,
when the occasion demands," I went on. She looked down into her
glass and then, weightedly, at me. The little tease.

"What's happened about the mystery subsidence in Cambridge
Street? Did you get your hole sorted out?" she asked, lapping her
tongue down into her drink, like Bambi. With a cunt.

"Yeah," I drawled. "What about yours?"

She looked into my eyes brazenly. My touch of crudity had hit the
spot, as I knew it would. I fought down the smile that always spreads
when I smell success and moved in closer; our eyelashes almost
touched as I waited for her inevitable response.

"Tell me, Nick," she said scentedly, "tell me. Where do you buy your
eyeliner?"

Marlene and Roz turned their heads. I was far too embarrassed to be
tongue-tied.

96

"Er, I don't usually wear it. Special occasion, you know. I borrowed
it, actually."

"Mmm, yes. Weren't you with someone when you came in?" Why do
women *do* that? What did Lucy mean to Ami? I went to take a swig of

my drink but the glass was empty. It was my opportunity for a dignified escape but I ignored it and carried on.

"Nobody special. And besides, I'm not with anybody now, am I?"

"No," she said, "you're not," and turned back to the others. They
went into a gossip scrum almost immediately.

"Bitch," I said, but more at a waiter than Ami. He took it in his stride
and handed me a glass of champagne. I almost thanked him.

· · · · ·

Half a bottle later I'd regained my wind and was making my way to the
garden, the folly, and the mysterious Miranda whom Marcus so much
wanted me to meet. Poor Ami, she wasn't to know I was one of the
chosen. In the conservatory I saw Rory McKaine, looking particularly
like a caricature of a rugby-club bore. The muscles on his thick neck
crept down the collar of his tweed jacket; red heat radiated from his
open-pored features and he held, of all things, a pipe. Crumbs of food
sat on the drink-wetted promontory of his chin, falling off occasionally
like edible dandruff, as he shouted at his companions.

"So, then," he bawled, "I unzipped m'fly, whipped out the old agony
column, and she said, 'If you think I'm taking *that* thing all the way up,
you can pay the doctor's bill!!' "

Christ, was he still pretending to be straight? Surely, after his last
arrest there wasn't anybody who didn't know the truth. I tried to slip
around behind him and out into the garden but some feral sixth sense
possessed by beasts like McKaine alerted him to my presence. He
wheeled around, breathing blasts of raw hormone directly up my nostrils, and brayed at me,

"Nicko Taigo!," then paused, as though that were a witticism. When I
failed to do whatever I was meant to he belted me in the stomach,
hard. Not viciously, merely in "fun." I half expected him to follow
through with that other piece of body language so beloved of his kind:
the eye-watering squeeze of the balls, but Rory, fierce polisher of his
tarnished machismo, is careful never to touch another man's genitalia. Publicly, at least.

97

"Heeey! Nicko!" he spittled, "we're! going! to! have! a! bumpering!
contest!"

"Bumpering" is a mindless public-school party game. The aim is to drink enough alcohol to kill an elephant in as little time as possible. Played by schoolboys it is forgivable. I did it myself. But when thirty-year-old men do it one wonders why they can't afford proper drugs. Now Rory was suggesting I join him and his friends (who all looked exactly like him, differing only in height, like organ pipes) in a bout of bumpering. I would willingly have let Ami humiliate me again before taking part in such a ritual.

"No thanks, Rory. Really. There's somebody I have to see in the garden."

His eyes rolled. He scared me a little.

"Bumpah! Bumpah!" he chanted. "BUMPAH! BUMPAH!"

"Stick it up your jumpah," I said and nipped through the door.

"Party poopah, party poopah!" shouted Rory and the organ pipes before exploding into nitrous laughter at their own funniness.

Considering the warmth of the evening the garden was sparsely populated. The ingrained metropolitanism of Marcus's guests, the fact that most of them would panic if unable to touch a wall, explained it. The vastness of the house had still not prepared me for the garden. Estate agents in South Kensington feel equitable describing a garden as "spacious" if its dimensions are such that all the occupants of the house are able simultaneously to lie down in it. Here, Marcus could have laid down his whole house, with room to spare. It seemed endless. Or rather, they did, for there were two separate parts. The first, abutting the house, was formal. Its Euclidean lines spoke of a designer with a deep fear of Nature. The lawn and flower beds cut such crisp angles to each other that the difference between them seemed merely one of color, not texture. Even the plants looked like elements of an equation, fiercely clipped and trained out of their chaotic tendencies.

The second garden, visible over a scolded hedge, was almost a wild wood. Through the mesh of trees and tastefully chosen weeds I could see light coming from the folly.

The champagne (Moët, surprisingly) had begun its work and I walked toward the wood suffused with certitude. True, Lucy had walked out, but I was rather glad of that. She cramped me. My feelings earlier in the week had only been the ramblings of dependency. Really, it was time we diverged. Lucy needed someone more ordinary and I needed someone more, yes, extraordinary. I'd deal with it when I next saw her. Out to dinner first, buy her a present. Do the decent thing.

I had handled Ami wrongly, there was no denying it, but my mistake had been in the interpretation of the facts, not the facts themselves. I had assumed she was starving for it when really she was only hungry. It didn't matter. I would catch her again later, do something lovably inept like knock over a table. She'd get hungrier all right. And in the meantime there was Miranda.

Most important was the complete absence of my curious little illness. It had been two days since anything had happened, and that had only been when making love. Whatever it was, it had passed. I remained intrigued about it but no longer frightened. I thought that perhaps I would keep the appointment with Doctor Anschluss next Monday—I rather liked the idea of being an item in *Nature*. But I knew, I could feel in my bones, that the illness had lost its grip on me. To prove the point I stood on my hand and pulled. Nothing. I poked at my previously plastic features. They stayed put. With a hiccup of happiness I ran the length of the lawn and into the wild garden. When I reached the folly I knew beyond doubt that I had regained the sweet freedom of normality. My run had produced no special effects at all. No flywheeling, no Roadrunner imitations. I was cured.

· · · · ·

There was no door on the folly so I walked straight in. There were about twelve people inside, most of whom I did not know. Know, that is, to talk to. I recognized most of them instantly. Five were members of the rock group Mission Insensible. They are one of the last bands to target their product directly at the teenage market before it finally disappears into advertising folklore. Their unique selling proposition is angst, that adolescents' commonwealth, which they have taken to new depths of tortured introspection. Their lead singer (though he prefers the term "galvanizer") calls himself Paean. His real name is Errol Plank. Onstage it is his habit to wail and tear at his flesh while singing his tales of alienation, misunderstanding, and love-gone-bad. Then, in a monologue that rises in its self-pitying intensity he tells his young consumers that he's had enough, that he cannot take this sad, sordid world a minute more, that yes, he's going to kill himself. Right here, right now, onstage. When the concert hall is a swilling troughful of ecstasy the bouncers allow some of the hysterical kids to climb onstage and "save" Paean, even as he is thrusting the barrel of his (fake) Magnum into his throat. The show finishes with no encore, the better to allow Paean to count the money that has bought him three houses and the ability to purchase cocaine as if it were salt.

A skiable heap of the very same drug sat on a low wooden table in the center of the folly. People were partaking of it like sherbet. Merlina Megatherium had recovered from her vomiting and sat next to the table, snorting through a silver tube like a mosquito. I wondered if this food wasn't a little on the solid side for her. Another member of Mission Insensible sat behind her, rubbing amateurishly at her approximate tits. She seemed unconcerned. There were three girls, pretty in a Woolworth way, attached to the other members of the band. None of them looked awed, like groupies are supposed to. Commerce was in their eyes.

In a corner, on a cushion, squatted the preposterously fat film director, Jason Sells. In the garden setting he seemed almost to grow before my eyes, like a forced pumpkin, and he was the only person to have brought a supply of food with him to the folly. Half a truckload of it sat on the floor and Jason reached out with alternate hands in a continuous feeding pattern. Slices of Parma ham went in alongside chocolate mousse; strawberry framboise with the claw of a lobster, shell and all. The factory mouth processed tirelessly. I was amazed that Merlina remained in the room but her eyes were so crossed that they had almost changed places. She was too coked to care. Beneath Jason's kaftan there was movement; a dismayingly handsome young man with peaky features emerged, wiping his lips. Jason did not say thanks, but managed an eloquent fart. The youth took a strawberry and moved over to the cocaine alp.

In the pharmacentric tabernacle even Marcus wasn't talking, an event rarer than the party itself. He sat on the opposite side of the

100 {

room, shimmering in his gold leaf. To my disgust he was nude beneath the costume. Like tinned herring roe, his soft gray body peeped out in places, and I saw for the first time that the tales of his equipment were true. I honestly have seen meatier clitori. His soggy face was a mask of indolent stupidity as he stared at the white mound on the table. Anjelica, the girl he'd brought to dinner at my flat, had been dumped and a new one was in tow. She was about twice as tall as Marcus (six feet or so) and easily the most fantastic creature I had ever seen. Her hair was dark beyond black—an irregular hole in the air through which it seemed one could peer into another universe. Her lips were plump red bordello cushions, comforting and erotic at once. Her eyes, larger than any I had ever seen, were of a violet so intensely luminous it seemed to shoot straight from a prism. Appropriately she took no drugs. She seemed in no need of chemically-induced escape from a world that she had probably never inhabited in any usual sense. This, I hoped, was Miranda; and it was she who first noticed me standing in the doorway.

"So, you've found the oasis too?" she said in a soft, mildly foreign bass. Marcus focused his face and squinted at me.

"Nicholas," he slurred, "you've arrived. Have some smack, do."

So *that* was what it was. I had wondered why there had been an absence of cocaine's grandiloquent prattle. Heroin is not me at all. It makes people dumber, not smarter, and it makes me throw up. They say that that stops with regular use but then you throw up if you *don't* take any and that's called a smack habit. I didn't know what to reply. I needed to stay sharp if I was going to nail Don Stamp. On the other hand I didn't want to look foolish, or anger Marcus.

"Actually, Marcus, I'm pretty out of it already. I won't, thanks all the same."

"Nicholas!" he piped like a panto dame, "I will not have the new puritanism rearing its shaven head in my gazebo! Now have some smacky. It's on the house. Well, it's on the table actually, but it's free all the same."

} 101

His jokes had not improved under the influence of heroin but everybody laughed, as they always do. Except The Woman, who trapped me in the violet beams.

"I don't do smack, either," she said. "We'll be puritans together."

"Suit yourselves," said Marcus. "What's the world coming to when you can't give things away?"

"You've given enough away this evening," I said. "This party is more than generous. I don't want to help you break the bank any more than it has been."

A couple of members of Mission Insensible laughed. Marcus lifted up his head.

"You're extremely thick, Nicholas. A bit of smack won't break *my* bank. I *deal* the stuff, cretin."

I must have shown my shock for Marcus gasped sarcastically and pulled his face into a mime of surprise.

"You didn't think I bought this house with my salary from *Simply Trilling*, did you?" He snorted. "How dense can you be?"

"But I thought . . . the libel suit . . ."

"Libel suit. That's funny. This party cost more than I made from that scam."

Most of the occupants of the folly chuckled. I cast wildly around in my mind for a smart reply to Marcus's disclosure, but none came. To make things worse I felt my face take on a doltish expression. Then, before Marcus could make fresh sport with my ignorance, The Woman saved me again.

"I'm Miranda," she said. It was appropriate. I could believe that her father was Prospero. Some kind of magic had been worked.

"Hello, Miranda. I'm Nick."

Marcus puffed his cheeks at me. "Such naice mannahs on the boy," he sniggered, then squeezed Miranda's neck. "Mandy-Wandy just flew in from . . . Transylvania."

Only Marcus could have had the arrogance to diminish such a creature by calling her Mandy-Wandy and fondling her like a horse. He was oblivious to the gross incongruity between what God had given to each of them: she a goddess and he, barely a piglet.

"Mandy's been driving me *mad* to introduce her to a boy with black hair and blue eyes," continued Marcus. "And here you are, Nick. It's like a miracle."

"Yes," said Miranda, "like a miracle."

Something in her voice was draining all intention from me. Some power was traveling down a tunnel between her eyes and mine: the power of lust. Lucy, Ami, all the women I'd ever had or wanted, disappeared in a watery mist. At last I'd found the woman God intended me for.

"So Miranda," I said, easing up now I knew what was going on, "why are you in England?"

"To finish something I started," she replied.

"Something you started? You sound determined."

"I am. When I want something I *have* it, Nick."

It was so perfect. I wanted to lift her up, carry her away then and there, into our golden future.

"And what is it you want?" I asked, letting my tongue linger in the corner of my mouth for one articulate second. Miranda smiled—she seemed on the point of enticing me into the garden—but Marcus's crackling voice broke the spell.

"Oh go on, Mand. Put him out of his misery, the mite. Show him."

Keeping me trapped in the violet rays she slid one hand down to the hem of her green dress, which seemed itself to be made from some unearthly material. With a movement that began slowly but finished with a jerk she raised the cloth above her navel. I don't know what I was expecting to see. Perhaps a gun tucked into a suspender belt— evidence of some score that Miranda intended to settle—or maybe a pregnant belly, a child conceived illicitly to which she was going to give secret birth. What I did see, brashly dangling between the fantasy thighs, was a penis. A penis.

There was a silent second while those in the room took a deep draft of my misery. With one great foul belch they laughed it back at me. It lacked the seesaw innocence of human laughter; it was just a noise, a hurricane battering at my clapboard pride. To make things much worse I grinned and said, "Almost had me fooled there, har har," which raised such a gust of malice I almost fell over. There was no

desire to share the joke, there never had been. I'd been set up. I almost
suggested that Miranda should donate his/her offal to Marcus, since
his need was the greater, but an instinct for self-preservation stopped
me. Instead, with my smile still strapped inanely to the front of my
face, I backed out of the folly. Walking quickly away with my head
down I heard Marcus call my name. His tone sounded remorseful. I
stopped and turned to see him standing in the doorway, glittering under the moonlight.

"Yes?" I said, forgivingly. He smiled at me. I knew he would apologize.

"Don't forget you owe me for a coke spoon, you fucker."

· · · · ·

Lumpy dance music had started on the other side of the house while I
had been away. The windows in the conservatory sang in sympathy
with each slab-happy vibration. To me it sounded like a lament. A full
and unattended glass of champagne drew me to one of the white iron-
work tables, where I sat down for a drink. My thoughts were stacked
like jackstraws; I couldn't decide which one to move first, for fear that
the whole rickety construction might collapse. So Marcus was a smack
dealer. I felt stupid for never suspecting his perverse wealth. Mysterious riches had simply seemed appropriate to the myth. When I looked
at the story about it all deriving from his libel suit I saw that it had
never rung true. But I had wanted it to be so. I wondered why, and I
wondered why I had never been let in on the secret.

I thought about leaving the party, perhaps with an affronted flourish
at the way I'd been treated, but there was still my career stratagem to
be deployed, and if that went well, Ami Leysdown remained unscaled.
All I needed was an injection of self-esteem. I felt in my breast pocket
to check that my self-esteem was still there. It was: a gram of extra-
virgin toot. I sipped at the champagne, grateful for the cordon it had
thrown around my sensibility, then drained the glass and went to find
somewhere to snort myself back to reality.

Finding a suitable place to do the coke proved difficult. Other devo-
tees had colonized all the bathrooms and lavatories. I was not going to
toot up in public. Like driving a Rolls-Royce it's considered vulgar but

nobody misses the opportunity for a free ride. I started on the bedrooms. One of the ten had to be available. Inside the first a couple
copulated hairily. To my disappointment I knew neither of them. In
bedroom two were another couple. The girl, whom I had never seen
before, looked about twelve years old. She sat on the edge of the bed,
her feet hardly touching the carpet, her knees knocking, crying. The
man was Oscar Michaels, author of the year's most fashionable and
filthy play, *2gether 4ever*. It concerned a middle-aged man and a very
young girl, whose love is misunderstood and results in mutual suicide.
From the tableau in the bedroom I could see that act one had been
played out but that the girl was having second thoughts about the
finale. Michaels knelt by the bed, wiping her tears with the back of his
hand. He turned at my entrance, his face composed halfway between
apology and anger. When he saw that I had no more right to be there
than he the apologetic aspect vanished.

"Knock! Knock!" he said, waving me away. The child on the bed
looked to me for escape. But I didn't need somebody else's problems.

"Very literary," I replied, and closed the door.

The next bedroom was locked and silent, the occupants either exhausted or involved in rituals too depraved for words. I was surprised
that this party, at the cutting edge of sophistication, should include so
many guests of such basic tastes. It had never seemed so in previous
years, but there had never been bedrooms before. I found an empty
one eventually, too small for any advanced sexual workouts. It was
paneled in ash, a somewhat quiet wood considering Marcus's love for
the chichi. Against one wall was a single bed, also of ash, shaped like a
harem slipper. The bedcover was made from many hundreds of pieces
of brightly colored silk, individually sewn together. I felt a fresh wound
of envy at Marcus's financial ability to lay in such labor-intensive heir-
looms.

I laid two perfect parallel lines of coke on the glass-topped bedside
table. Rolling up the crisp twenty-pound note I had brought for the
purpose, I bent down and ran my nose along the road to sanity. The
mild, stinging flak salted my nasal membrane and I lay back in antici-
pation. It came, as perfectly as usual; a refrigerator door opened in my

tropical head. What had been the big deal back there in the folly? I'd no idea. Who'd been humiliated? Search me, matey. Some other dickhead, not Nicholas Taig, London's brightest copywriter, lothario, and bon vivant; envied by the weak, adored by the strong. I went to leave the room but turned back. There was something I needed to do. With my bladder.

Steam rose with pleasing pungency from Marcus's heirloom. I grinned and zipped up my fly, only regretting I'd crapped before leaving my flat. Now *where* was that *bastard* Don Stamp. He was about to give me a new job, one that might just, if it was lucky, deserve my talent.

Don was in the hall, his bony arse propped against a Chippendale table. Like many viciously rude people he's partial to an audience, and he was entertaining one now. Not with jokes or anecdotes, but with conjuring tricks. He's very good at them—was once a professional and now uses them in place of conversation.

As I approached he was in the act of removing a string of sausages from the cleavage of Mrs. Paddington Sh'Aim. I knew it was dangerous to interrupt in midtrick, but he ran the best shop in town, I wanted a new job, and I had a quarter of cocaine plastered to my brain. So I walked right up.

"Don, hi."

"Who the fuck are you?" he spat, removing a last oily chipolata from the tittering Mrs. Sh'Aim.

"Nick Taig," I replied airily. "We met a couple of months ago at Stavely's?"

"Yeah? So fucking what?" His long body, topped with a sharp wedge of a head, gave him the simply brutal appearance of a stone-age axe.

"So I thought I'd say hello."

"Yeah?" He ran his eyes over my clothes and made noises like a geiger counter. "What you doing with a fucking dead mouse on your coat?"

"It's a bat, actually. Do you like it?"

"Do I what? Looks like something my cat coughed up. I suppose you do look an even bigger wanker than the rest of the wankers round here. Probably a compliment in your book."

"Thank you," I said with a gay little laugh.

"Look, what you after? I'm busy."

I smiled around at his little audience, who seemed almost as annoyed by my intrusion as Don himself.

"So," he repeated "what you *after?*"

I abandoned badinage and summoned my call-a-spade-a-spade voice.

"OK. A job."

Don laughed. It sounded like a match being struck.

"You must be joking. I wouldn't give a job to some tosser who can't do his buttons up straight and wears dead bats on his coat. Fuck off."

I laughed again but could not stop a knot of desperation forming in the pit of my stomach.

"As it happens," he went on, "I can offer you a job. I need someone to come and clean my bog twice a week. I'll offer you that."

I ignored him.

"I'm with ZZD at the moment . . ."

"Right, in that case I wouldn't even let you clean my bog."

"Come on, Don. I've done some good work."

He shifted himself from the table and stood up. I hadn't realized how tall he was.

"Shall I tell you the truth? I'm not interested in your poxing work. I'm sick to the back teeth with little wankers on the make. I stand here all night, not hurting a fly, and all the time I get bothered by gits like you. If I *wanted* new blood I'd go looking for it. I've never heard of you, that's how good your fucking 'good work' is."

I felt my smile wear off, along with the best of the coke. I could tell the audience was beginning to hope for a bit of violence to go with the conjuring tricks.

"Not all good work wins awards, Don. I did the Pan-World Airlines commercial."

"That pile of horseshit? With the singing seats? Great way to sell an airline, great. Who'd wanna sit in a seat with a mouth? It might bite your arse. Good campaigns are s'posed to have legs, not fucking *teeth.*"

"All right, if you didn't like that, I did the Benkson Industrial Equipment campaign, too."

"The one where you butchered *South Pacific?* You wrote the words for that? I don't know how you've got the brass neck to stand there and brag you're the talentless little snot who wrote 'There Is Nothing Like a Crane.' I tell you, if I was Oscar Hammerstein's widow I'd spend some of my old man's dough having you put out of my misery. Get lost."

The cocaine had definitely disappeared, leaving me a chemical Cinderella. Another time I might have relied on anger to see me through the next moments, but events—no, I had to be honest—*people* had conspired to use up all my fight.

"I can't help it if ZZD wants me to do a certain type of work."

"Don't go blaming ZZD, son. Akron's a mate of mine. You should be grateful a scumbag like you gets work anywhere."

"Please, please, please. I only want a job," I thought. The realization that I might have to go home with nothing to show but my wounds filled me with desperation.

"Look," I said with a grin so fake it hurt to pull, "perhaps now is the wrong time. I'll bring my book around to you next week."

Don's eyes suddenly narrowed in the axe head. People began to titter. I couldn't believe my weakness was so visible. Then, for some reason I developed a sudden and dreadful earache. I decided to give up; it was too much to take, the Fates were against me. Insult, humiliation, failure, and now pain. I knew when to retreat. Don tipped his head back, as though preparing to split my skull with his nose. I had never seen somebody so poised with hate.

"Don't try upstaging *me,*" he hissed. I had no idea what he meant.
"Sorry?"

"This," he said, reaching out to my left ear. *"This!"*

108 } I put my fingers there and my bowels slid with sudden fear. Something warm, soft, and wet had emerged. Oh, Christ, Christ, Christ. Please, not now. Anytime but not now. Don pulled at the soft thing, which came away from my ear with the pain of a prematurely picked

scab. He held it out for me to see. A chain of marshmallow balls was linked to a sac of the same material. At first it didn't seem to be anything except disgusting; then it floated upward and spread out and I knew exactly what it was. I had produced from my ear, in physical form, a large cartoon thought balloon. Written across it in wet black letters were the words,

PLEASE, PLEASE, PLEASE. I ONLY WANT A JOB

Don reached out for the balloon before it could float away, crushed it into a soggy ball, and dropped it in my drink.

"I saw him palm that, five minutes ago," he said very loudly to his audience. "These bloody amateurs!" Then he passed his hands through the air and produced two doves. They must have been in his jacket all night.

"Now, that's real conjuring," he said. "So why don't you fuck off and try getting a job at the circus?"

The Nick Taig who had pirate-swaggered into Marcus's party might have turned things to his advantage, but he'd left me alone at some earlier point. The creature who remained could barely summon the energy to shuffle away. As he went, people huddled and remarked. And when he reached the front door he noticed three of the black serving boys, propped up against one another in a tripod of hilarity; and he knew how it felt to be outside society.

ᵒᵒᵒᵒᵒᵒᵒᵒᵒᵒᵒᵒ N I N E ᵒᵒᵒᵒᵒᵒᵒᵒᵒᵒᵒᵒ

T he sky steamhammered summer thunder on the roof of my getaway car. I was unsure quite what I was getawaying to, but movement was comforting in itself. My illness, I realized, had only been recce-ing its objective for the last week. Now it had mounted D-day. Each fresh thought blooped from my ear, just as it had at the party, and soon my car was filling with miniature blimps advertising the contents of my head. For a time I pushed them into the back, then under the seats, but very quickly the entire vehicle was stuffed, leaving me the tiniest of gaps through which to see. When the rain started, in great snotty sheets that the ancient wipers couldn't clear, I pulled into a side street and stopped the engine.

Standing in the rain at midnight, shepherding my own thoughts from the car and watching them float away over London, I teetered on the very edge of reality. Like a novice diver I felt the pull of a new dimension and for a moment it seemed that I might leap into it, never to return. Only the writing on the thought bubbles prevented me: the driveling stream of self-pitying mundanities fixed me in the real world.

110 {

GOD HELP ME, GOD HELP ME, PLEASE GOD HELP ME and **WHY ME? WHAT HAVE I EVER DONE?** (Yes, *that* one) and **GONE, GONE! ALL THAT GLORY AND GOODNESS. GONE.** *(What?)*. And, for no discernible reason at all, **ONCE IN ROYAL DAVID'S CITY, STOOD A LOWLY CATTLE SHED.**

Engrossed in my thoughts, as it were, I did not hear the approach of a young couple. Despite the monsoon conditions, upper-class thrift compelled them to stop.

"What marvelous balloons!" said the woman from behind the waterfall plunging off her umbrella. "Can I have some for the brats, if you're just throwing them away?"

"I'd really rather you . . ." But it was too late; she had already pulled one through. I saw, just before it disappeared, that it bore an artless couplet on the subject of Marcus's pudendum and what I'd like to do to it. The woman saw, too.

"Oh!" she squeaked, and attempted a worldly laugh.

"What is it, darling?" said her husband, ducking with a grin from beneath his brolly and under hers, keen to share the joke. Unlike his wife he knew the difference between honest dirt and plain filth.

"Not very funny," he said, as though that had been my intention. "There are children, you know."

The spurned thought balloon popped out, wobbling cheekily into the air, and the couple walked smartly off, their heels tutting on the wet pavement.

"Tut-tut, Nicholas," I echoed, and continued to empty my car of thoughts.

· · · · ·

The blinding rain stopped with a shudder, just as I set free the last balloon. I had thought myself to be near Hyde Park but now saw that I was in Bywater Street, off the King's Road. It was alarming to wonder what my mind had been doing when I thought it was driving me home. Bywater Street—John Le Carré had made it the home of George Smiley. Perhaps if I just knocked on his door he might tell me whether the Russians were to blame for my misfortune; though I doubted he would take seriously a character of such obvious fictionality.

My sopping suit now started steaming, with that dirty smell which even the cleanest clothes have when wet. I reached into my pocket for cigarettes but the rain had done a thorough job and I retrieved only a handful of soggy Shredded Wheat. But I bared my teeth in triumph at the Fates, for there was a fresh pack in the car, and matches, too.

I could almost have been a normal person, leaning against his car and enjoying the pleasure of a cigarette on a summer's night. Ah, how easy it is to dismiss the power of nicotine, I thought, as I lay back across the hood. What a powerful drug it is, I thought, as I stared at the stars. And how very relaxing, I thought, as I slithered to the pavement. And what the hell am I doing on the pavement? I thought, as I tried to move and found I could not.

I lay there for a moment, boned. Then, with the return of anxious misery, I was dragged from the ground on unseen strings. It was a reflex to feel relieved at regaining erect status, and I was promptly dropped again by my sadistic puppeteer. It went on for a minute at least, with me standing up, feeling relieved, falling over; standing up, feeling relieved, falling over. Only when fear and tension were a steady state was I allowed to remain upright, clinging winded and white-knuckled to my car as if it were a Zimmer frame. Balloons flowed freely from my ear, filling the air. From a distance it would have looked as though somebody was celebrating something in Bywater Street. Perhaps somebody was, but it wasn't me.

Four people turned the corner, two hundred years away. What I wanted to do was befriend them, tell them my tale, laugh at it with them, with the humans. What I did, though, was to jump into my car and drive away. Only one of the four looked at me as I sped past. The others were too busy reading my thoughts.

· · · · ·

By 3 A.M. I'd done a lot of thinking. I knew that I had because my drawing-room ceiling was obscured by clouds. They were all telling me the same thing: the cat would soon be out of the bag, among the pigeons, and playing the ukulele. Even if people had believed Don Stamp's "exposure" of me I could not avoid attention for long: conjurer or freak of nature, I was bloody good entertainment.

I had to escape. Home to my parents was tempting but for how long would that be safe? Even before the media Gestapo unearthed me my father would probably have sold the TV rights; and my health-crazed mother would not want something with infective potential beneath her roof. I nestled for a while with the telephone in the crook of my neck

and the Filofax splayed upon my thigh but my finger could do no walking. The people I knew did not want involvement, only association. If I
had been a little more famous, a little more rich, a little more *pertinent,*
then I might have been worth the inconvenience. I did dial Christian,
but the line was broken; and when I went to call Lucy I stopped, realizing that that line was pretty much broken, too.

· · · · ·

I awoke next morning, still in the chair, and listened for a moment to
the pounding in my head before realizing that the noise was coming
from the front door. Without stopping to consider the wisdom of doing
so, I opened it. Herman Coprolite stood there grinning, a crocodile-
skin attaché case in his left hand and a bunch of flowers in his right.

"How ya doin', Nick? How's tricks? Hah ha ha!"

I stared at the huge bouquet in its funerary cellophane.

"For you," continued Herman as he bailiffed his way past me. "Your
first night flowers! Stand back and let me throw them at your feet."

"Good morning, Mr. Coprolite. This is my flat. Do come in."

"Herman, *Herman.*"

All too bloody Herman, I thought. He stumped through into the
drawing room and I followed, his guest. My thought balloons had all
lost their gas and now carpeted the floor like the evidence of a safe-sex
orgy. Coprolite's simian form doubled in a burlesque of mirthfulness.
Tears of hilarity squirted down his cheeks.

"Too much, too much! How d'ya make 'em? Christ, what an act.
What an act! Whadd'ya do, get some surgery inside of your ears? They
gotta be like suitcases. I wish to sweet Jesus they'd bring back variety!
Ladeees and Gennelmeen," he shouted at an imaginary dress circle, "a
star is born!" and thrust the crackling flowers into my arms. I said
nothing, but my mind decided to. A balloon popped from my ear.

"OK Nick, no need to get personal," said Coprolite. I looked at the
bubble. **FUCK OFF, YOU IGNORANT FAT YID,** it said.

"Mr. Coprolite, you don't understand. This isn't an act, it's an affliction, a sickness. I have absolutely no control over it whatsoever."

He pulled another of his silent-movie faces to register amazement.

"Wow! Even better. A real freak. You're made, boy, made!"

113

I stared at him. There was no malice on his bacony features. In me he saw a property and the potential to raise good rent—it was an equation as natural and immutable as $E = mc^2$.

"Is it, like, just the earhole number," he went on, "or is there more? Tell me there's more."

Nothing mattered anymore; I felt a rush of candor.

"Well, up to now my fingers have grown to a length of two feet; my left leg to fifteen; I've jumped off a five-story building without coming to any harm—though I can't say the same for the pavement—my chin has caved in, and my nose has popped out; my body has stretched, it's contracted, it's been tied into knots; I do a very respectable impression of the Roadrunner and my cock, Coprolite, since I'm sure you'd hate to be spared any detail, my cock can be just what it fucking well *chooses*, be that a pneumatic drill, a cucumber, or a pogo stick. In short I seem to be the world's only living cartoon and I've no desire to do a promotional tour. So kindly go away and leave me alone."

My outburst was obviously pretty small beer in comparison with the histrionics of his regular clients. He took it calmly.

"OK, so say I leave you alone. Do you think I'm the only"—he picked up my most recent balloon and quoted—"ignorant fat yid who's gonna come calling? News travels fast, boy. I'll give it till tomorrow."

"You'll give what till tomorrow?"

"Till you won't be able to walk down your own front stoop without getting mobbed. You ever seen a big bunch of morons feeling nosey?"

"I think I can deal with the morons, Coprolite. Perhaps I could start by asking you to leave? For the last time."

"Oh yeah? Come here." He went to the window, beckoning me to follow. "See that car down there, the red Toyota? And see that guy sitting in it? Well he ain't got a flat, and he ain't outa gas neither. He's from the *News of the World*. And see those two guys standing there by the church? They're from *The People*. And as far as I know the queen's mother ain't visiting these condos today. See what I mean?"

"What nonsense!" I exclaimed. "You're bullshitting. Go back to selling encyclopedias door to door, or whatever it was you used to do."

"You know," he laughed, "you're up the creek without a paddle—

way, way up—but you won't give an inch. Am I asking so very much, really? If I wanted I could throw you to the lions. I don't need the dough, I don't need you at all. I've asked around, and you're a rotten little asshole by most accounts, so I might be doing the world a favor if I left you to the dogs. But what am I doing instead? I'm doing *you* a favor. So why the fucking attitude problem?"

"*. . . a rotten little asshole by most accounts . . .*" Coprolite almost snared me with that, conjuring as it did all the previous evening's dereliction. I needed an ally, someone who at least resembled a friend. But I could not let it be him.

"I am not a complete stranger to the tactics of the salesman." I sneered. "I'm in the same line of business myself, in a less seedy way than you, of course. First you try the hungry hustler act on me. Then you soften me with the fatherly concern and now you're following through with pretended indifference. A good performance, very polished. You could almost turn pro. But let me make myself clear, once and for all: you are not going to close this deal. I am not buying aluminum replacement windows today, thank you."

I felt that my speech had the ring of finality and went to sit down. Coprolite, however, was just getting into his stride. He followed me, waving the crocodile-skin attaché case under my nose.

"How much you pulling down, Nick? In a good year? Twenty grand? Twenty-two?"

"I do not have 'good years,' Coprolite. I'm salaried. And as for how much I 'pull down,' that is none of your damned business."

"OK, so about twenty grand. You'd tell me straight out if it was worth shouting about. Now this case here," he said, pointing at it although it was only a foot from my eyes, "has got more dough in it than you'd make in a good *decade*. I want you to have it, as a token of goodwill, a little taster."

"Go away, go away!" I shouted, jumping up and waving my arms. "I'm not interested! Can't you see? I have *principles*. Do you even know what they are?"

He popped the catches on the case and more cash than I had ever seen congregated in one place cascaded to the floor. There was so much that I could smell its seaweedy odor from where I stood. I felt a whipping pain in my eyes and as I clutched at them there issued from my head the loud and distinct "Ding!" of a bell.

"*So!*" yelled Coprolite triumphantly, "You've got *principles*, huh? I really hate to use old gags but I think we know just what you are. Now we can haggle over the price."

I ran to the mirror. Where moments before had been my eyes there now flashed bright green pound signs. Coprolite's assumption was understandable but wrong. I didn't want the money, or money at all. I only wanted my old life back. When I turned away from the mirror he was smirking. He wasn't after I hit him.

It was the punch of a lifetime. My arm flew across the room without my having to walk there and my fist swelled to the size of a pumpkin on the way. It connected with all points of Coprolite's face simultaneously and threw him six feet to the far wall. It seemed a little unfair that he should have had to take the force of all my anger and resentment but I felt exhilarated just the same. He lay, boiled and mashed and snoring loudly.

I began picking up the money. With typical theatricality he had removed the paper binders that had organized the fifties into neat bundles of one thousand pounds. I counted as I gathered. It was comforting, like a capstan song. "One thousand . . . two thousand . . . three thousand . . ." The trivial speed at which it increased was alarming to the son of a merchant banker. "Nine thousand . . . ten . . ." I'd reached eighteen when Coprolite came alive like a creature frozen for ten millennia, grunting and coughing bloody lumps. He sat up with assistance from his low center of gravity and examined with disinterest the gory gobbets on his shirt.

"I've changed my mind, Nick."

"Good."

"Yeah, you don't need me. What you need is a fight promoter. Now a good pal of mine just happens to be . . ."

I started to laugh.

"What's so damn funny?" he asked.

"I'm simply trying to work out whether you're a man who doesn't bear grudges or a man without pride. I just knocked you out. Those are your teeth on your shirt. Doesn't that matter?"

"Sure it matters," he grinned gappily. "The prices my dentist charges, it matters. But where does pride come in?"

I sighed. The man was a scoundrel.

"Listen. I ain't always been forty pounds overweight in a thousand-dollar suit. I grew up in the Warsaw Ghetto. You heard of the Warsaw Ghetto?"

"We have an education system in this country," I sniffed.

"OK, so maybe you know a little. Now learn something. I was around eight years old when they shut us in. There was some real food at first, for a month or so. Then there was rat. I swallowed my pride along with the rat and the rat tasted a whole lot better."

"Spare me the homily, Coprolite. You sound like a miniseries. I suppose you'll finish on a gag?"

"No," he said with sudden force, "*you* sound like a miniseries. You and half your fucking countrymen. You think we're pretty crass, us Yanks, huh? Pretty shallow? It's the other way around. Only shallow men can sneer at love and pain and call that subtlety. You English ain't refined—you're just plain *scared*. Feelings? Whoa, no thanks! You'd rather shit your pants in public. So I'll finish my story, OK? I'll tell you how there soon wasn't any rats to be had. So people started eating other things—things we didn't talk about, things worse than rat. Pride did stop us from admitting it to ourselves, but it didn't stop us from eating. And the ones too proud, died. We survived. Now you think I should stand up and fight 'cos a kid half my age whipped me? I know pride."

He gathered his teeth into his handkerchief and asked if he could use my bathroom. Feeling foolish I went to make coffee. We drank it in silence, Herman eyeing me from time to time, without his previous mercantile appraisal. He seemed to want to help, and I wanted to ask it of him, but something stopped me. Not mistrust—at least I would know where I stood under his protection; and not my unwillingness to become a public property—that seemed to be happening whether I

117

liked it or not; and not even my typical distaste for people such as him. Something else stopped me. Pride, I suppose.

The silence grew too heavy, and Herman lightened it with scurrilous anecdotes of the famous, including one about a celebrated actress's apple-pie fixation and her consequent use of cinnamon during love-making. It was strange, after being the butt of others' laughter, to have somebody entertain me, and for no other reward than simple human pleasure. I felt sorry when he rose to leave.

At the door he made one last attempt on me.

"You sure you won't change your mind?" I shook my head. "Look, I'll just leave you this itty-bitty case. Maybe you won't be able to reach a cash machine . . . OK, OK, I give up."

"I'm sorry about your teeth. Did you collect them all?"

"No problem. They're fake anyway. I'll get the bastard to snap 'em back in. I'll say it was faulty workmanship. Bye, kid. You still got my number?"

"Yes, Herman. I've got your number."

· · · · ·

As the day wore on and the men loitering outside did not go away but instead were joined by others I realized that Herman had not been bullshitting. I wondered how the press had heard so quickly. None of the guests who had seen my performance at the party could have imagined the truth. Herman was far too savvy to risk the goose that might yet lay golden eggs and besides, the reporters had arrived when he, too, thought that I was nothing more than a cabaret artist. Only Lucy and Christian had known the truth, and neither of them was malicious enough to do such a thing, even to somebody as worthy as me. There was nobody else. Except, of course, of *course*, it was that backslapping bumboy, Rory. Christian, always incapable of bearing another's burden, would certainly have told him, and McKaine, equally incapable of interesting anybody in his own dreary life, would have told everybody else. For several minutes I forgot my predicament and lost myself in a fantasy of revenge which culminated in the stran-gulation of Rory with his own beloved jockstrap.

At about three o'clock I was thrown into a cartoon panic when two

118

reporters slipped into the building as a resident was leaving. My heart tented my chest, threatening burst buttons with every beat, and my flat was filled with its amplified booming. Sweat squirted from all bodily exits and I ran from room to room like a large and frightened garden sprinkler. They came to my door and clattered on it while I lurked leakily in the kitchen. Somebody must have interrupted them, for I soon heard well-practiced footfalls disappearing down the hall, releasing me from terror mere seconds before I drowned in my own perspiration.

· · · · ·

By late afternoon I had reconciled myself to a siege. There was sufficient of Lucy's shopping to sustain me for several days, by which time the Hounds of Wapping were sure to have rekenneled. I was quite looking forward to the battle of wits, or halfwits in their case. Then I noticed the lack of one essential supply, without which I could not exist another hour, much less three days. There was only one cigarette left in the flat. To calm my rising panic it was immediately lit and sucked to a husk in one neurotic lungful. Moments later I was a tramp in my own home, scrabbling through ashtrays and wastebins on a desperate foray for anything that looked as though it might once have been related to a tobacco plant.

After five minutes' hectic rootling I dumped my spoils on the kitchen table. Among the coffee grounds, burst teabags, and other brown detritus mistaken for tobacco nestled sixteen fine, fine dog ends. I laid them in a line. Connected, even by a microsurgeon, they would have formed no more than two healthy cigarettes. Connected by a vibrating addict on the point of going cold turkey they were hardly worth the bother. I did bother, of course, jealously emptying the poisonous half inches into a breakfast bowl with the absorbed concentration of an artisan. I felt proud of my pungent heap, as though I had actually created something. All I had created was a fresh problem: how to fashion the raw material into a smokable whole. I tried to roll it inside a strip of newspaper, but without glue to seal the edge I got no more than a mouthful of burning air and lacerating tobacco shards. I made a pipe from aluminum foil, which worked for a time, before the heat was conducted along the stem to roast my lips. The last indignity, before I abandoned hope, saw me crouched over the burning breakfast bowl, a towel draped around my head, gasping at a cloud of mixed toxins in the hope that one of them was nicotine.

It didn't seem to be. When my eyes had stopped streaming, and the smell of burning hair faded a little, my craving took on vampirish proportions. I paced and slavered and scoured my brain for an answer to the problem. Aside from Tom next door and Mrs. Estroy-Jones I knew nobody in the building. I had never wanted to know any of them, they were all too much like poor imitations of me for my liking. Or theirs. Tom was away on another weekend seminar at the outer limits of alternative medicine, exploring the efficacy of live frogs as a cure for herpes or somesuch nonsense; which left me with not a friend in the world. My only course was to go myself, in disguise.

I never thought I would find myself regretting my distinctive dress sense. All my clothes shouted my presence and there was not a single hat to pull over my eyes. There were sunglasses, a drawerful, but sunglasses are worn to make one conspicuously anonymous and would have drawn the hacks in an instant. There were some of Lucy's clothes but drag was out of the question; my life was doing a grand job of imitating farce without further assistance from me.

On the point of abandoning artfulness and making a crude run for it I remembered that the stairwells were being repainted. Calvin had whined to me about having to share his rooftop bunker with the painters' overalls. I was on the roof in seconds. Knowing Calvin's suspicious nature I was surprised to find the bunker unlocked. Inside it resembled a cross between Hitler's and a porno bookstore but there were the overalls and, joy, a painter's peaked cap.

I returned to my flat just long enough to rake my hair forward plebeianly, pull the cap down low, and collect two fifty-pound notes that had strayed from Herman's fold. Striding self-confidently into the sunlight I was the prototype of Working Man. The Scarlet Pimpernel would have smiled approvingly to see me saunter, with just the right degree of round-shoulderedness, past the mumbling reporters. Not one of them so much as looked at me.

If I had been a drowning man, and my cigarette an aqualung, I could not have clamped it to my mouth with more gratitude, nor drawn on its vital contents with more bliss. To add to this inspirational ecstasy, the brand was Marlboro, not Park Drive. Akron Darkly's diktats seemed to belong to another world entirely, and at that moment I was glad it was so.

After the storms of the previous night the air smelled deliciously laundered; the sky flapped like freedom's own flag; portly bees were going about their summery business and I, moved by the corny perfection of it all, began to whistle. I never whistle, barrow boys do that, but it was the right thing to do, it added the final verisimilitude to my disguise. None of the reporters stirred when I walked past again. I actually smiled at two of them, and one began walking over. I could not have cared less.

"Got a light, mate?" he asked.

I certainly had, John.

"You working in the building then?" he went on.

Yur, guv'nor, I was.

"Seen anything of the geezer in number twenty-seven?"

No, me old china, I hadn't. I *was* enjoying myself. So much for the gundog nostrils of the investigative reporter.

"You must be looking for grief, grafting on a Sunday. Off the cards, is it?"

Ah. What the hell did "off the cards" mean? I guessed I was probably off them.

"Oh, right," said the hack, who suddenly seemed less dim, "so you're not just in the painting and decorating game?"

"Er, no," I stammered, my accent performing an alarming glissando up the social scale, "I do a touch of . . . window cleaning, too."

"Hear that, Marty?" he called to his colleague. "He does a touch of window cleaning, *too.*"

The "too" was spoken with masterly sarcasm. I felt a perspiration faucet open in the center of my back.

"Well, ain't that interesting," said Marty, producing from behind a wall a camera with such a ludicrously long lens it might have concealed a rocket launcher. The first reporter took a painful grip of my wrist. "You're Nick Taig!" he informed me.

"Let go of me, you wanker!" I yelled. "This is assault!"

He was curiously unbothered by such niceties and tried to hold me in a photogenic pose while Marty crouched down with his extremely candid camera. Perhaps punching Herman had exhausted my pugilistic potential because for some reason I chose not to clout my assailant but to run instead. The human terrier maintained his grip on my wrist but the rest of me moved off swiftly. A translucent strip of flesh stretched like gum between myself and the reporter, thirty yards distant. He hollered at the photographer to do his job but he was still adjusting controls on the overfed lens. Before a single shot was taken the reporter lost his hold and sprawled to the ground with a satisfying crack, cursing his colleague even as he fell. The skin rejoined my wrist, adding momentum; I was around the corner and out of sight in a second.

· · · · ·

I had been squatting like a ski jumper behind a bush in Hugh Mews for twenty minutes and my thigh muscles felt on fire. I would not have chosen such a place, especially since the bush was about as much use as a fig leaf to a tumescent whale, but the reporters had shown more competence in the chase than the catch and I hadn't the luxury of choice. Twice they had sniffed up and down Hugh Mews while I wriggled on my haunches behind the miniature bush. I would certainly have been discovered, were it not for their bizarre practice of shouting to each other the whole time. "Anything?" one would call. "Nope. Anything with you?" the other would answer. It was as though they were frightened of me. Their noisy camaraderie concealed my desperate rustles and I remained undiscovered—at least, by them.

The owner of the bush and its adjacent mews house banged on his front window. He was Chinese. I pointed innocently at myself. He pointed at the end of the mews. I pointed at myself once more. He struggled with the security key and threw open the window.

"Go away! I call police. You go way!"

The Chinese look as though they were born to be angry, don't they? I went way.

· · · · ·

Despite the danger I could not resist returning to Cambridge Street. The number of journalists had grown since my departure. I wondered what the collective noun for them might be. An insensitivity? A bastard? Or something more technical: a font, or an ozalid? I settled for a cirrhosis.

The cirrhosis of journalists was pacing abstractedly like bored zoo creatures. Each had his (they were all male) own means of entertainment. Some wore Walkmans; others chain-smoked; others gossiped, and one, to my breathless surprise, read a newspaper. They made a sad spectacle, obeying instincts beyond their understanding. I felt rather sorry for them, born without the benison of privilege and now selling their time and decency for the advantage of some billionaire megalomaniac like Paddington Sh'Aim. I felt like turning myself in to aid those less fortunate than myself before remembering that I was still looking at the kind of people who knock on doors at six in the morning to ask such sensitive questions as ". . . and how did you feel, Mrs. Smith, when you had to identify the dismembered body of your little Stacey?"

123

I could tell that it would be some time before I saw the inside of my flat again. Taking one last wistful look I turned and walked in the direction of Victoria Station. I did not look back. In my condition turning into a pillar of salt was a genuine possibility.

· · · · ·

My painter's outfit and the need to husband my cash had excluded me from any smart establishment in SW1, so I had taken a table in LocoBurger, British Rail's answer to McDonald's. I marveled at the resilience of the working-class intestine. All around were noisy, happy folk, sucking at shakes with the color controls turned too high, or munching on burgers like cheap upholstery. The deadly vivacious girl behind the counter had served me just as if I were a real painter, even though I had chimed my order in a World Service baritone. Unlike my local shopkeeper, who had grudgingly given me the Marlboro on credit because he couldn't change a big note, LocoBurger's tills were bursting with junk money. There was no flicker of surprise at an ordinary man producing a fifty.

I had always imagined myself an adventurer. At school I was first to sign for rock climbing, canoeing, caving, and woman hunting. At university it was I who'd led undergraduate missions impossible, to place the bursar's bicycle up a tree; to put diuretics in the lecturers' wine; to drive down to London and score coke. Later it was I who first vacationed in Turkey, almost before it was plumbed in; I who skied backward at Val d'Isères; I who led our frequent escapes from restaurants when we didn't feel like paying. Now I realized that my cherished swashbuckling had been as tame and organized as a kindergarten sports day. All my life's "adventures" had been a piggyback race, with me the passenger of convention. Now, for the first time, I was on my own. I didn't even know how to eat a cheeseburger.

For an hour or so I milled aimlessly on the booming concourses of Victoria Station, watching the clattering destination boards fan their selections like cardsharps and fantasizing vaguely about escape. In a spirit of irony I bought a copy of *Options* magazine and read about the array of syndromes afflicting the modern woman. Toxic-shock syndrome; premenstrual syndrome; postviral syndrome. Nothing, though, about abject-misery syndrome, or utterly-hopeless-situation syndrome, so I gave the magazine to a woman who looked as though she might benefit, and kept my options to myself. At six o'clock convention did rescue me. I went to a pub.

The pub had less atmosphere than the moon on a bank-holiday Monday. Despite an abundance of toadstool-like tables the few patrons were standing. From their green canvas bags and the amateur topiary of their haircuts I guessed that most of them were army lads returning to barracks. They looked scared and tearful, like prep-school boys half their age, all fairly fresh from parental rejection. None of them made conversation; bravado was taking all their concentration. Instead they watched vacantly the Olympian television suspended above the door, or played on the numerous slot machines, arrayed like cities of light against the far wall.

I'd pulled off the fifty-pound-note trick with the desiccated landlord, who had considered ejecting me but generously relented and given me my drinks on tab until he had sufficient change. I took my pint of bitter and went to sit in the field of plastic toadstools. Without much surprise or consternation I watched myself appear on the local news. They showed a photo of me at work, which I knew must have been supplied by McKaine because I remembered Christian taking it; and the one of me at London Zoo. I didn't hear why I was being featured— for being missing or just because I was newsy. The lads at the bar watched uninterestedly. I pulled my cap down lower and peered into my bitter.

· · · · ·

"What about that then, eh? What about that?"

The person asking the question was also digging me in the ribs. I turned to see whether he was bigger than me, and if not, to tell him where to go. It was the most extraordinary tramp I had ever seen. He was a mobile museum of twentieth-century fashion. A stoved-in Derby hat; a collarless shirt (with one cracked pearl stud still in place); a purple and black suedette jacket with a Peter Pan collar, worn as a waistcoat, over which was a shocking pink teddy-boy drape coat; high-waist blue loonpants and a pair of bile-green boots with stack heels.

Astonishment canceled irritation. There was I, creeping in shadows in fear of my freakishness, and here was somebody celebrating his.

"I said: what about that then?" he went on in a perky rat-tat. "Some geezer's gone an' turned into a cartoon, they reckon. What about that, then?"

"Amazing," I replied unexcitedly.

" 'Course, you never can tell these days, can you, what with that radiation whatsit off that Cherno-wossname? My old mate Ashtray, now he told me there's cows up Scotland what's got three udders!"

"Mmm," I said, remembering LocoBurger. "I think I just drank some of their milk."

"Go on! Mind you, now Ashtray, 'e does like his drink. So there's no tellin'. I mean, *last* week 'e reckons he sees Madam Thatcher 'erself down Whitehall, 'avin it away in the back of a motor vehicle. Now that don't strike me as likely. I mean, she's got three 'ouses, ain't she? She don't need to get her leg over in public."

I admitted that the prospect of the prime minister practicing coitus automobilus seemed remote.

"Ah, but that's the drink talkin', see? No, I reckon it was 'er stand-in. She must get right cheesed-off, makin' out she's Thatcher all day long. I don't blame 'er lookin' for a bit of light relief. Anyway, son, what you drinkin'?"

I was somewhat taken aback. Winos aren't supposed to offer people drinks. They beg ten-pence pieces (or fifties, these days) from you for "cups of tea." I insisted that he let me buy the drinks.

"No, you only got that fifty, ain't you? I saw you up the bar. The guvnor won't wear that one again. Shirty old ponce. What's your poison?"

I asked for another pint of bitter. He returned with what looked like a quadruple Scotch.

"There you go! Drop o' Scotch. Do you the world o' good. You're no bitter drinker."

126

"Well, Mr. . . ."

"Benedict Sweet. Ridiculous innit? Call me Benny. Or Sweety if you don't mind a smack in the gob."

"Benny. Thank you. Though what an alc—a gentleman of the road is doing standing me a giant Scotch, I don't know."

"Like the look of you, don't I? Anyway, who says I'm a tramp? I'm a bleedin' oil millionaire, inni? You just knock it back. You look like you need it."

I guzzled the Scotch while Benny sipped at his. Aside from his attire he was an ordinary-looking man, unimpressive. I guessed his height, without the elevator heels, at about five feet four, and slight with it. A jockey's build. He had tiny hands—atrophied almost, though not de-formed—and surprisingly clean nails. His face, what was discernible of it behind a thick piebald beard and long gray hair, was preteen neat. It was a powerless face, but not a weak one. His skin had a postmeno-pausal transparency, with many fine blood vessels glowing beneath the surface, and his teeth were small and sharp. But his eyes were far from ordinary. They were an everyday color, a sort of brown, and of an everyday size and shape, but they were so clean. When people fight for youth, with the knife and the cream, nothing can be done to scrub the past from their eyes. Benny's eyes looked as though they had just been born. I put his age at about seventy.

" 'Ere," he said, peering beneath the peak of my cap. "I know you, dunni?"

I had thought that he wasn't the prying type. His sudden recognition of me as the human cartoon upset me more than a simple fear of exposure. I felt the human race had let me down again.

"No, you don't know me," I said.

"I do. I bloody do."

"You don't. You bloody don't," I replied, making to stand up.

"No, don't go," he said, touching my arm, "I don't mean nothin'. S'just I never forget a face. You was at a party down by London Bridge. 1984 it would've been. Wasn't you?"

The thought that this kind old man was among those publicly de-loused for our entertainment at Marcus's 1984 party winded me with shame.

127

"Yes, I was," was all I could say.

"There y'are, see. I never forget a face. 'Nother Scotch?"

· · · · ·

No more was said about the party. I sensed the pointlessness of apologizing and resisted the urge to lie about my presence there. Benny seemed content to let the mere fact of my attendance speak for itself. Now that we were no longer strangers the potential for intimacy was gone, and our conversation moved into the kind of trivial backwater usually reserved for those on much more familiar terms. We spoke until closing time, of politics and people, theories and things, cucumbers and cars, but of ourselves not at all. Benny's voice modulated over the Scotch, from its original inquisitive Cockney staccato to something unplaceable. A sudden American intonation, then perhaps South African, and then pure Home Counties—as though his voice were blowing around the globe on the trade winds of his past. Whenever there came a lull in our talk he would sit and smile at me like a fond old nurse.

At eleven the landlord announced, for positively the last time, that we were no longer welcome. I hadn't noticed that we ever had been. I decided against telling Benny of my homelessness, since I felt sure he would have pressed me into spending the night in some itchy hostel. I expressed my sorrow that we would never see each other again.

"We might do," he said. "You never know when you could need your old mate Benny. I'll leave you me card."

I laughed and went to speak to the landlord about my bill from the beginning of the evening.

"Oh, Benny saw to that," he said. When I turned, Benny was gone. I went to our table to collect my cigarettes and there, shining on the Formica, was a pink calling card, saying

BENEDICT E. SWEET, TRAVELER.

And there was a telephone number, too.

ooooooooooo E L E V E N ooooooooooo

I had been staring at the ceiling for a good—no, a bad—half hour. Although quite an interesting ceiling (more for its peanut-butter encrustation of nicotine and intriguing selection of dried foods than its Edwardian moldings) I was actually staring at it as a defense against having to think about anything else. The room, at the Oresteia Ho-ho-hotel, smelled of a thousand sadnesses before mine: a room to weep in, to fight in, to shame in, to die in. A mechanical womb, where Life had no constituency; its fluids all diesel and electricity; the furniture so starved and poor it seemed hardly there at all; the scrawny woodwork covered in the aimless gougings of the unspirited vandal. I wondered about those people now, people who wasted their vitality on staying alive, on clinging to the rock face without hope of a summit. I was beginning to count myself among them. Nick Taig? Wasn't he rude to me at a party, once?

· · · · ·

Upon my arrival the previous evening I had tried the fifty-pound-note trick, but the receptionist had had no trouble with my change. There wasn't any. When I'd expressed mild surprise at the price of a room in what was only one step up from an actual flophouse he had snatched the key from my hand and hung it back on its hook. "Try Victoria Station. Very cheap. Room service very bad," he'd said, and then petulantly placed a NO VACANCIES sign on the desk between us. The ensuing

courtship had almost reached the stage of proposal before he'd relented and given me the key. When I'd reached my room the telephone
had been ringing. It was him. "Room service!" he'd chuckled. "Nighty-
night." And then, instead of "good-bye," "No charge!" No charge? The
room itself had totted up a five-star bill on my soul's account.

· · · · ·

I lay in bed for another half hour, shrouded in the mean sheet which
smelled clean but felt dirty. Shrink-wrapped for a pauper's grave. I
ransacked my memory for comfort but it was useless. People like me
never salt away the past, we don't believe we'll ever need it. Only the
present remained, daring me to deal with it. Lucy had made an appointment with the strange-sounding Dr. Anschluss. Much as I did
not want to be examined by some Viennese quack I saw it as my last
chance before I would have to become a client of Herman Coprolite
and another chattering guest on the *Wogan* show.

Not everything was against me that morning, for directory inquiries
had answered after mere minutes and then, tirelessly, managed to
locate Dr. Anschluss in the Harley Street area. His receptionist had
known my name straight away, and "invited" me for eleven o'clock. It
was hard to tell whether she used the word euphemistically or just
because Anschluss's clients were not the type of people ever to be told
what to do.

In the taxi (unavoidable, I felt, despite my scurrying resources) I
made the mistake of entertaining myself with paranoia. What if that
woman there, in the blue Renault next to us at the lights, were to work
for *The Sun*? What if the cabbie, glancing with such professional un-
concern in his rearview mirror, were to recognize me and broadcast
the fact on his radio? It was a game I'd played a thousand times before
—when secretly meeting some woman; when doing a presentation for
clients; whenever I could toy with the idea of failure or detection. But
now the rules were changed, and the game took full opportunity for
revenge. Suddenly it was making suggestions without my permission,
and by the time we reached Harley Street I was too twitchy to get out.
The kindly cabbie had to assist me, by demanding his fare and pointing out that the meter was still running.

The interior of the house had been vandalized far more comprehen-
sively than my room at the Oresteia, and by people who should have
known better. Its arrogant suggestion of power reminded me of the
offices of Zane, Zane, Darkly. Marble again, everywhere it could safely
be located; and leather furniture so distended it looked as though the
animals had simply been left to rot and fill with death's gases. Death,
really, was the key to the place, despite its avowed function as a tem-
ple to life everlasting. I wondered how it was that the clients of such a
place had come to a pitch of self-delusion so intense they believed
mortality to be optional. I climbed the stairs, through galleries of mortality. The first, a palette of jaundice, from pale butter to spring daffo-
dil; the second, Modernists: anorexic girls and their stern mothers; the
third, avant-garde sculpture: the bone sick, knotted in their chairs;
and on the fourth, my floor: nobody except the receptionist.

She was sitting behind a computer, writing in a ledger. Unlike her
peers on the previous floors, she was middle-aged and wore a crispy
uniform. Anschluss had bought in some seriousness. When she saw
my overalls she put down her pen, affronted that a mere workman
would taint her antisepsis. I removed my cap.

"Oh, *Mr.* Taig. I'm so sorry. Do sit down."

"Thank you, I'd rather stand," I replied, my taxi paranoia still playing its game.

"As you wish. The doctor *is* expecting you. He's just . . . he won't be
a moment. Can I make you comfortable in any way?"

"No, really. Thank you."

A Niagaran lavatory flush announced both the reason for Anschluss's absence and his arrival. Lucy's rendition of his accent had
seemed unlikely enough, but he had gone the whole way and followed
through with his physical appearance. He could not have looked more
like the popular notion of the nutty mittel-European professor. His
eyes swam behind aquarium glass and his hair was a mass of white
wire, magnetically attracted by the ceiling.

"Gut mornink, Niklaus. I may call you Niklaus? You are vair popular
boy at ze moment. Come, come," he said, indicating with a shake of his
crackling hair that I should follow. The receptionist seemed close to

laughing at her boss. I was much nearer, and pressed my hands over my ears to stop any honesty emerging. Anschluss did not walk, he slid, pushing his dinghyesque shoes over the green carpet like a skier on grass. He stopped every yard to give me an encouraging smile, as if to ensure I was keeping up with his pantherish speed. I managed, somehow, and we arrived by teatime at his consulting room.

Anschluss sat in a tweedy wing chair, staring at me through the submarine glasses and running his hands up his anemone hair.

"Vy," he asked "vy hef you your fingies in your earse?"

"Oh," I said, removing them, "sorry. I'm a little nervous."

"Goot, goot," he chuckled. "Vair vould ve neurowlogists be if pipple veren't nervous?"

I laughed for him. "It's kind of you to see me, Dr. Anschluss. You're my last hope. I *can* hope, can't I?"

"Ve ken all hop. If ve do not hop, ve havn't a leg to stand on."

I laughed loudly at that. Anschluss looked puzzled.

"I sink," he said, pressing his temples as if to prove it, "I sink ve shell start vis some rutteen qvestions, if thet vould not be too doll?"

"Not at all. I could happily put up with a lifetime's dullness after the last few days."

"Goot! So, ven did you virst notice any zymptoms?"

"Just over a week ago, I think."

"Ah-hmm. End?"

"And . . ." I told him about the waste disposal. I told him about the hospital. I told him about Nelson and my leg; and the zoo and the hole in Cambridge Street and sex with Lucy, and the party. Reporting it to the doctor, as though it were any other illness, should have made it seem more real but it did not. As I went on I felt increasingly estranged from the teller of the tale. He was somebody I didn't want to know: a barroom bore, a subway psychotic, another fucking fruitcake I'd cross the street to avoid. Anschluss sat nodding in a manner that suggested my case made a pretty average Murnday murning.

When I'd finished he was in a trance. It didn't seem a thoughtful trance, or a bored one, but rather one that suggested he hadn't any idea what to ask next. He looked at his watch as though it contained an answer. I smiled encouragingly, which had no effect.

"So there it is," I said, crossing my arms and trying to look finished. Anschluss remained absent. "That's about it, really. What's your opinion, doctor?"

"Opinion?" The question seemed to frighten him. "I do not yet hef one. Let us continue. Niklaus, hef you ever fentazized about repping your mutter?"

"Dr. Anschluss. I mean no disrespect when I say this, but I doubt that anybody has ever fantasized about raping my mother. And besides, how could it possibly be connected with my ailment?"

"Anysink might be connected to any ozzer sink. Vor example, do you vorry about ze shep of your pee-knees?"

"My pee-knees? Oh, that. No. It's pretty penis-shaped, I think. Except recently, of course."

"Aha! Zen you hef a goot look at ze ozzer boys' pee-knees-ease?"

"Not especially close, no. One can't but know these things."

"True. Remove your cloze and mount my couch."

I undid the buttons on the overalls. At navel level I realized I was about to experience the popular nightmare of ponging at the doctor's. It had been almost three days since I'd had an intimate wash, and my odor was now more *low-* than *de la* Renta. Anschluss smiled genially, as though all his clients smelled like pet food.

"My underwear, too?" I asked hopefully, wondering which particular Stockhausenian olfactory chord would be struck when *they* came off.

"No, keep zem on," he replied, shuffling across to his couch and covering it with paper from an oversized lavatory roll on the wall. "Come and lie down here."

His examination was strange. He didn't have the usual doctors' knack of inflicting pain without pressure, and he stayed prudishly away from my genitalia, when most doctors make an immediate and bracing sortie to that area. It was while he was examining (for the second inexplicable time) my knees that I noticed he wore a wig. Vanity, even in the hopeless, is understandable, but why would anyone choose to wear a wig like a frozen porcupine? By the time he told me to

133

dress I was feeling a trifle suspicious. His next questions added to my sense of foreboding.

"You lif alone, Niklaus?"

"Yes."

"Qvite, qvite alone?"

"Not all the time, no. I have a girlfriend."

"And vot is she called?"

"But I . . . you . . ."

"Yes?"

"She's called Lucy," I answered, noticing that the windows were barred.

"Loozy. And hef you told her all this?"

"Yes. All of it. She knows that I'm here this morning. She'll be expecting to see me later."

"And so she shell."

Anschluss continued his fanzine questions while my unease grew. Did I have any favorite foods, or any I particularly disliked? Did I prefer a firm or a soft bed? Did any natural fibers make me itch? Which brand of shaving foam, toothpaste, soap did I use? I had no idea why he wanted the information, but a firm belief it had nothing to do with neurology. I had once before seen one of his breed when, as a teenager, I developed a series of ballistic facial tics that had caused me to fire food at my parents' dinner guests. That neurologist had made me stand on one leg and recite the Lord's Prayer, blindfolded, while tickling me with a feather. There had been nothing wrong with me except puberty, though my mother had refused to believe this and sued him. He won. Now Anschluss was behaving like my biographer. His accent really was too yogurty. Thirty years' practice in Harley Street ought to have diluted it.

He had just started on his third question concerning my most beloved ice cream when I interrupted, "Excuse me, Dr. Anschluss, but do you have any idea what's the matter with me?" He looked startled.

"Em . . . em . . . vill you excuse me a moment?" he said, and shuffled toward the door faster than he ought to have done.

I suppose I should have taken the opportunity to escape while it existed, but curiosity had the better of me. The room itself offered no clues; it was as bland as a bank manager's. Anschluss was either an impostor or an anal retentive on the grand scale. I went around to his side of the repro desk and opened the top drawer. There was nothing in it, except some blank paper and beneath, a magazine called *King-Size Hanging Breasts.* Inappropriately the photos of the deformed women, with their separate breasts, unleashed my libido. I had to remind myself vocally that masturbation was *not* the most pressing issue before I could continue my search. The second drawer was bare but the third contained a tape recorder, running. Its presence was not proof of anything but its make, I felt, was. It was a Nagra, an extremely expensive type used by film crews (which was how I knew of it), millionaire birdwatchers, and surveillance professionals. A doctor had no reason for such a sensitive piece of equipment—as an alternative to notepad and pen an ordinary cassette recorder would have been sufficient.

A light began to flicker on the telephone. Without hesitation I picked up the handset and pressed the appropriate button.

". . . all I'm saying," said a Norfolk accent, "is get here quick. You said eleven. It's eleven-thirty."

"We're stuck in traffic. Can I help it if your piss-ant town is two hundred years out of date?" came an American voice.

"I don't care about your problems, Edsel. All I know is that I can't keep up this 'zo ven hef you hed zis experience before, Niklaus?' cobblers for much longer. It wasn't part of the bargain."

"I thought you were an actor? For Chrissakes, what do we pay you guys for? Act, Langley, *act.*"

"Actors, Mr. Edsel, need scripts," sniffed "Dr. Anschluss."

"Well, that's showbiz," replied the American, and cut the connection.

There was no way of escaping the room without being seen, and nowhere I could hide, except for a large stationery cabinet. I knew it couldn't conceal me for long, but it was better than nothing, so I opened it. To my intense annoyance it was already occupied. A man I took to be the real Doctor Anschluss (pinstripe suit and steel glasses—much more like it) stood bound and gagged, stuffed diagonally across

135

the cabinet. He made the usual anxious mumbling noises people do when discovered bound and gagged, so I began tearing at his bonds. When I removed the gag he gasped for air.

"Dr. Anschluss?" I asked, expecting gratitude.

"You idiot! Tie me up again zis moment!"

"Pardon? *Why?*"

"Becoz I don't know who zose madmen are, but I'm not gettink kilt for *your* zake! Tie me up, do you hear?"

I only had time to stuff him back in the cabinet and slam the door before "Dr. Anschluss" came back. He had all but given up his act. He was a small man, and quite old—I could easily have knocked him unconscious and made my escape. He seemed almost to want me to; it would have been revenge on his paymasters. But I did not escape. I didn't even think about it. Instead I smiled stupidly and sat in my chair, staring at the old ham with his powdery fright wig and (now I thought about it) Plasticene nose.

"Bloody Yanks," said Radio Norwich.

"Uh?" I went.

"Nozzing, nozzing," he replied half-heartedly.

"Uh," said the slumped retard, and the two of us lapsed into apathetic silence. I knew that something unpleasant was going to happen. It didn't matter. One bunch of bastards or another was going to get its hands on me and that was that. There was nowhere to run because my illness would go with me; *that* was the thing I needed to escape. At that moment I was willing to trade freedom for a good sleep.

It might have been two minutes, it might have been two hours, but at some point the intercom buzzed. "Anschluss" gave it a relieved prod.

"Oh, Dr. Anschluss," said the receptionist hintingly, "would you like some *coffee?*"

"Oh yes," he replied, abandoning all pretense, "send them in."

The two men who came through the door had obviously been to the same theatrical costumier as the fake doctor. I could not believe that undercover agents, even American ones, would willingly wear Burberries. They did, though—and they'd turned up the collars, too. Trilby

hats and sunglasses were absent but I had the feeling they were available if necessary. They were both young—twenty-two at the oldest,
and still wore their boastful American puppy fat around the jowls.
They entered the room with much sweaty bravado, their hands osten-
tatiously tucked inside the raincoats, but my passivity threw them
and they looked for guidance at the old actor. He waved his hand at
me.

"There's your man. I don't think he'll be any trouble."

I didn't think I was going to be any trouble either. The boys came
crouching toward me, rubbing together their fingertips as if tempting a
kitten. Then, far too late, my adrenaline decided to flow. Up I leaped.
The two Burberries looked pleased and withdrew their hands from
within the coats. Only one actually had a gun.

"Shoot! Shoot!" cried the gunless boy. Despite it being barred I ran
to the window and gave it a rattle as the gun went off with a disappointing ping and something stung my left buttock. "Anschluss"
screamed and jumped from his chair. The guns contained not bullets
but stun darts and the first had glanced off my arse, pranging the poor
old actor. He hopped about for just long enough to enrich my vocabu-
lary of East Anglian profanities before plopping to the carpet, the dart
standing perpendicular in his right thigh.

There was one still second when we all looked at the stricken man,
then the game was on again. I continued my futile attack on the window, straining my neck to watch the antics of the Burberries as
though seeing the dart would somehow protect me from it. For the first
time I wished my illness had made an appearance but it had chosen to
desert me. Another dart whistled past my ear and stuck in the trunk of
a yucca.

"You klutz, Edsel! Give me the goddamn gun," demanded the other
boy.

"Don't tell me what to do, Merk. That's insubordination."

"Purl-*ease!* You can't shoot straight!"

"Can too!"

"Cannot!"

"Can too, can too, can *too!*"

137

"Cannot, cannot, cannot. Give me that fucking GUN-UNH!"

It certainly did look like Merk's assessment of his colleague's marksmanship was right. He tried to extract the dart from his neck but was already half-unconscious and his body fell neatly onto "Anschluss." It was just me and Edsel. He came at me with his knees bent and his arms outstretched, the gun pointing off to the right.

"Your colleague did have a point, you know," I said.

"What?"

"Your gun's pointing the wrong way."

He looked at his weapon and I took the chance to duck past him toward the open door. Yet another dart sailed across my bows and into the doorframe. Instead of continuing I spun around to confront Edsel —a mistake, because something heavy came down on my head. It wasn't enough to knock me out but it did knock me down, stunned. The starchy receptionist had clocked me with her percolator. Despite my almost total immobility young Edsel swaggered over and fired a dart into my leg with an expression of pride at his own skill.

"Oh good *shot,*" said the receptionist.

"Yeah," replied Edsel, and the woman rolled her eyes at me.

My own eyes were the last things to fade away. They were still half-open when four men dressed as janitors came in. And they were still open just enough for me to see, before unconsciousness fell, that they intended to transport me from the building in a brown paper bag marked CONFIDENTIAL WASTE.

· · · · ·

Perhaps I was still somewhat drugged, or perhaps I had lost all capacity for surprise, but when I awoke, in a chintzy little room with oak beams and whitewashed walls, I felt no alarm and made no attempt to get out of bed. I knew that my situation had to be more unhappy than it appeared, but for the moment I wriggled cosily on the edge of sleep, refusing to let the future intrude. After a time there were footsteps, then a rattle at the door handle. I began to snore like a fat man.

"Tea?" asked a voice so light and threatless that I stopped acting and immediately sat up. A young man was staring at me, with murderous intensity. *"Tea,"* he stated, his face blackening with strain, his forehead a snakes' nest of pulsing veins.

"Yes. Yes please," I replied, wishing I'd never opened my eyes.

"Fucking well take it, then!" he coughed through clenched teeth.

"But where is it?" I asked, helplessly.

"Christ, open your fucking eyes, you pratt!" he gasped, with what seemed his last breath. I wanted to please, but he was carrying no tea. Then I looked up. Three feet above my head there floated in midair a bone china teacup. The saucer was tilted at forty-five degrees, and steepening. It began to rattle geriatrically and I snatched it just in time. The young man fell to his knees.

"Jesus, Jesus. You bastard, you bloody bastard. I can't keep it up there for ever," he panted, clutching at the bedclothes. I gave him a hand. He levered himself upright and promptly drank my tea.

"Sorry—fuck, sorry. I'll get you another one."

"It's all right," I rasped, "I wasn't really thirsty. You have a rest."

He tried, but was not the kind of person to whom rest came easily, if at all. He twitched and grimaced and picked at his face as he chased his breath. His otherwise pleasant, somewhat concave features were spoiled by a spray of self-inflicted bloodspots, mingled (around the chin) with acne's Alamo.

"I'm . . ."

". . . Nick, yeah? Melvin." He poked his arm forward and gave my hand a brisk shake. "Christ, I'm knackered. They'd do me if they found out I was wasting it on you." I had never heard anyone speak so fast.

"Wasting what?"

"Don't be thick, Nick. Tele-fucking-kinetic energy. What else?"

"Oh, of *course*. What else?"

"What else do you think your tea was doing in the air? A fucking flypast?"

His machine-gun charm disarmed me, as did his boyishly liberal use of swear words. He made me feel like a dormitory conspirator. "Look," I said, "I'm sorry if I seem a little green, but the last thing I remember is being put into a brown paper bag. It's a bit confusing."

139

"Did that one, did they? Went to visit some specialist, did you? He looked a bit iffy, yeah? Did that one on me, didn't they? You was lucky. Sometimes they take you out of your bed. Imagine that! *Night night, Mum. Night night, Dad.* Then: Bosh! You wake up in here. Fuck that. You wouldn't know if you was dreaming, would you?"

"I don't know if I am dreaming. Am I dreaming?"

" 'Course you ain't dreaming!" he said, in a tone of bewildered pity.

"Then what the hell *am* I doing?" I yelled. It was not unreasonable of me to wonder about my situation. Melvin pressed me back into the pillows.

"All right, don't shout! You're all right, you're all right. I'll tell you, won't I? They call this Rose Cottage. It's a research place."

He stopped, as though that were all I needed to know.

"And?"

"What else do you want me to say, then?"

"Who are 'they'?"

"Dunno, really. NATO, I reckon. Yeah, NATO. The North Atlantic . . ."

"Yes, yes, I know what it stands for. And *what* do they research?"

"We're back to that tea again, ain't we? How many blokes do you know can do that? Us. They research us, don't they?"

"Do they? And who are 'us'?"

"Here, you're one 'n' all. Else they wouldn't've brung you, would they? A weirdo, mate. We're all fucking weirdos. What sort are you?"

"You wouldn't believe me if I told you."

"Try me. You wait till you get a load of old Mavis. She is *well* weird. So what about it?"

"Well, I seem to be a sort of human cartoon," I said, and waited for a reaction.

"Sounds good, sounds good," was all I got. He stood up and looked out of the window. I would have joined him, but I was scared I might see nothing but the inside of a film projector. Mad scientists; NATO skulduggery; a boy with telekinetic power—I'd seen it all before. It was Saturday morning pictures. Perhaps my illness had been a staging post between reality and this: life in two dimensions, trapped forever on the Moviola of some diabolic film editor.

"Melvin?" I asked. "Is this real?"

"Do what? 'Course it's fucking real. What else could it be?"

"Almost anything *except* real . . ."

"You're a fucking nutter, you are. Don't I *look* real?"

"Yes, but . . . would you mind if I touched you?"

" 'Ere!" he said, as I reached out. "You a poofter?"

"Of course I'm not."

"Keep your paws off, then. Have this. This is real. It's your new watch."

"What was wrong with my old one?" I asked as he handed me a cheap Japanese model.

"Had the day and date, didn't it? Put this one on."

"We're prisoners here, aren't we?" I asked, as I snapped the watch-band around my wrist. Melvin looked astounded, in that way young boys do when their mothers can't learn how to program the video recorder.

"I don't reckon you're awake yet."

"No," I sighed. "Neither do I."

· · · · ·

There was a tap at the door. A girl wearing a tartan skirt came in.

"What do *you* want?" asked Melvin.

"I'm supposed to make him feel at home, too. We both got the morning off, Melvin."

"Well, he's tired, ain't he? He's too tired to have you pestering him."

"I don't want to pester him, just make him feel at home."

"*Oh* yes. I know what you want to do."

"Melvin! Introduce us."

"Nick Cassy Cassy Nick," said Melvin sulkily.

"My name is not Cassy," she said without pique. "It's Alison."

"Yeah, but we call you Cassy because you're no fucking good, are you, *Cassy*?"

"Stop swearing, Melvin. You're horrible enough as it is. Hello, Nick."

"Morning, Alison. And what kind of weirdo are you?"

"She can't do fucking anything," interrupted Melvin, adding a desultory "fucking." Alison crossed her arms tolerantly.

"I can predict the future."

"That's impressive," I said.

Melvin snorted. "Go on, Cassy, tell him the truth. Go on. You can predict the future, *but*?"

"But it's not much use," she conceded.

"See, Nick, Cassy's a bit pathetic. All she can predict is what's gonna happen to the royal fucking family. If you wanna know what color dress Princess Di'll be wearing when she opens some cancer unit, Cassy's your girl. If you wanna know when Fergie'll get put up the duff again, ask our Cassy. If you really need to know when old Phil the Greek will put his foot in it with the wogs, go and see Cassy. But if you wanna know something *decent,* like if there's gonna be a nuclear fucking *war* in the near future, she's absolutely fucking *useless!*"

"That's not fair, Melvin," said Alison. "It's not always the royals. Not always."

"Like when not, eh? Like when?"

"Like now, for instance. You're going to break your leg in three places in two weeks' time."

"Well, fuck *you,*" said Melvin and walked out.

"There! I'm not completely useless, am I?" she smiled. It was a good smile, with teeth almost as embarrassingly ceramic as mine. Her face, though somewhat lost behind an abundance of badly cut black hair, was attractive; the features heavy and Mediterranean, the coloring English. She did look the part of the half-hearted seer.

"Shall I show you around?" she asked.

"Yes, please. What shall I wear?"

"Haven't you looked in the wardrobe yet? They're bound to have got you lots of horrible clothes—they specialize in those, as you can see." She gave me a catwalker's twirl; the frumpy tartan skirt remained bonded to her thighs.

"Oh, I don't know. You look all right," I lied. She peered out from behind her fringe, challenging me to ratify the insincerity. "OK," I admitted, "they're awful."

142 {

"Just you wait," she said. "I bet they've got you something just as delightful."

She was right. For some reason my captors had marked me down as a gentleman farmer. Tweeds, moleskins, brogues, Wellingtons—all the countryside combat kit.

"Pooh!" said Alison. "It smells like an old pipe in here. They must've got this lot from some poor old widow. It *stinks.*"

"Excuse me," I said, "I've just remembered something," and dived under the bedclothes.

"Are you all right, Nick?"

"Yes, perfectly, thanks," I shouted, running my nose around those areas which ought by then to have smelled like a skunk's laundry basket. The discovery that I had been bathed and perfumed while unconscious was more disturbing than the smell itself would have been.

"So. *Are* you wearing any knickers?" she asked when I emerged.

"What? Oh, yes."

"That's all right, then. Put these on. They're the best I can manage." She handed me a plaid shirt and some brown corduroys, then turned her face to the wall. "I'm not shy," I said as I took them from her.

"You might not be," she said. "Come on—I'll take you on a tour."

· · · · ·

The American influence on Rose Cottage was in proportion to that country's influence on NATO itself. Its huge size matched the American idea of a "cottage," and the interior lacked that essential English ingredient: shabbiness. There must have been celebrations in antique stores from Sloane Square to Fulham Broadway on the day the decorators of Rose Cottage arrived with their Amex and their Diners. The bathrooms (of which there were five, i.e., four too many for any English home) had whirlpool baths. Tailored carpet, everywhere, deep enough for safari. I was surprised not to see it on the walls, but they had already been Laura Ashleyed to death; and the job-lot portraits of horses and dogs had, of all things, color-coordinated frames.

The top floor was divided, by locked doors, into three: Men, Women, and Scientists. I asked why. } 143

"To stop us fucking, of course. Gosh, sorry, it's that dreadful Melvin. He's so basic."

"But why would they want to stop you?"

"I don't know. Perhaps they're scared of what we might produce. Anyway, there's no danger of us doing it. Melvin is not a pretty sight, is he? And that's about as good as it gets, apart from one of the bofs who's quite sexy."

"I see. So you wouldn't mind boffing a boffin?"

"What?"

"Boffing—screwing. Boffin—scientist," I explained, wishing I'd never made such a feeble joke.

"Oh," said Alison, with an uncertain laugh, "of course. Anyway . . ."

"You were telling me why you don't do any . . ."

"Boffing?"

"Mmm."

"Yes, well, apart from anything, they can see everything we do. They've got cameras everywhere. Even our toothbrushes have got homing devices in them. So you see, the idea of sex with Melvin, while being watched by dirty old men, doesn't exactly amount to romance, does it?"

"No, I suppose not. Is Melvin in love with you, though?"

"I think he is. At least, he keeps showing me his willy every five minutes."

I laughed and followed her down the stairs.

Alison wasn't much of a tour guide. She whisked me from room to room, as though lingering would bring home the reality of imprisonment. I got a peek at two big sitting rooms, a dining room, a games room with a pool table and two electronic arcade machines ("They're for Melvin. The pratt," said Alison), and a conservatory. Whereas the Americanized interior had missed the point, the gardens had benefited from the treatment. It was a bit tarty, but its overpainting drew me to the door.

144 { "Don't do that," said Alison. "The alarms go off after four seconds. We can't go out unguarded."

"Bloody hell."

"You'll get used to it. Let's not stay here, it'll upset you. Come to the library, it's brill. They've got every book ever, except the ones about famous escapes."

On the way I asked where everybody was.

"They're all at work. The labs are in the stables—you get to them through that door there," she said, indicating a small door which I had assumed led to a broom cupboard. "It's locked right now. It's three-inch steel, you know, behind the wood. So's you can't hear the screams. That was a joke, by the way."

In the library, which was indeed crammed, Alison told me her story and something more of the business of Rose Cottage. She was twenty-one, the daughter of a printer and a schoolteacher, from some drear southeastern suburb of London. She had two sisters, Sue and Jenny, and a cat named Albert. Nothing about her childhood or early adolescence had been remotely unusual. The opposite, in fact. She told me how she, aged thirteen, would lie in bed and pray for a little mild anorexia, or a manageable amount of menstrual pain, or cumbersome breasts. Anything to give her a proper entrée to the Awkward Age. It wasn't as though she wanted any of the glittering prizes—a married boyfriend, or pregnancy—just a sorority badge. Then things did start to happen, but not of the type she wanted. She began to have strange dreams, always involving the royal family. Apparently the royals are the second-commonest cast members of our dreams, but Alison's dreams often involved royals who did not yet exist. She described the weirdness of knowing that Lady Diana Spencer and the prince of Wales would marry, long before they themselves did:

"I used to go and hang around outside that nursery school where she worked. I used to watch this girl, going home in the afternoon. Watch her and think *if only you knew.*"

When her life with the royal family came to occupy all her dream-time, and began to intrude on the days, she told her doctor. He had diagnosed adolescence and prescribed Aluvar. The drug only loosened her grip on the world and eventually her parents had insisted on referral to a psychiatrist. A committed Kleinian, the shrink had decided to blame everything on Alison's mother and put *her* into therapy instead. Alison then made the mistake, in an attempt to validate her experi-

145

ences, of telling the local newspaper hack about these visions. She backed up her tale with a detailed description of a visit by Princess Margaret to the opera, which was to take place the following week. As usual, she had been perfectly correct, down to the number of cigarettes smoked by HRH (the reporter had bribed a cleaner for the royal dog ends). And four days later she was abducted from outside her school.

"Do you know what really made me cross?" she asked. "What *still* makes me really cross? I've never found out whether I passed my A-levels. Isn't that daft?"

She laughed at this, but I felt no duty to partake of her forced jollity. With the knowledge that she had been at Rose Cottage for three years I found my last secret store of hope eaten by rats.

"But didn't anyone come looking for you?" I asked, punily.

"Oh, I imagine so. But look, people go missing all the time, don't they? There's a hoo-ha for a while, then the public lose interest, and then the police give you up as a bad job. Anyway, I'm sure there's some little arrangement in cases like this. There are more things in heaven and earth and MI5 . . . you know."

"Your parents, though?"

"I don't want to think about what my mum and dad—I just don't want to talk about that."

"Yes. I'm sorry."

"They do come unstuck every once in a while," she went on briskly. "Like last year. They took this nine-year-old. Becky, she was called. So, so sweet. She was telepathic—they're quite common. The trouble was, her mum was her receiver. Did you know that most telepaths can only really communicate with one other person? I can still see the bofs' faces when she said, 'My mummy says she'll be here tomorrow.' They couldn't get rid of her quick enough. It was dead funny. Really, *dead* funny."

When I failed to respond, she stood up and skipped across the room, to the uninviting books. There was much about her manner that spoke of an arrested development.

"Alison, don't you mind being a prisoner here?"

She was scanning a shelf, her back to me. Before answering she pulled out a headstone-sized edition of the *Decameron*, in the original. "Not really. I prefer it, in a way. At least here nobody thinks you're a loony. It's a pretty posh sort of a prison, after all. And when they're done with you, they will let you go, if you really want."

"Will they? This is wonderful. How do I apply?"

"Oh, just ask. There's a catch, though. You have to have a little operation."

"What kind of little operation?"

"I don't know what it's called. They sort of poke a pair of scissors in your head and have a good old snip. It makes you forget. Still interested?" she asked. Then she turned and gave me an apologetic, yet cruel, smile.

"No, I suppose not," I said. We looked at each other; the flimsy bravado vanished from her eyes and she lunked across the room with her granite *Decameron*. It made her seem very young.

"I could've gone ages ago. I'm of no military use whatever. I could make a fortune out of the newspapers."

"Yes, if all the journalists you'd put out of work didn't bump you off first."

She laughed. "Anyway, I've answered all the questions. What's your claim to fame?"

I was about to tell her when the bell rang for lunch.

· · · · ·

The door in the wall that Alison had shown me earlier was so small it forced the residents of Rose Cottage to emerge in crocodile.

"The bofs always come out first. This one's called Evens," said Alison, as a troll shouldered its way through the door. His standard of personal hygiene would have shamed a one-armed gibbon—I could almost see his smell. From the silage bin of his face there jutted a pipe, spouting napalm substitute.

"Yes, he is a bit icky," said Alison as I turned my face away from Evens, the worst thing since Medusa with a hangover.

147

Scientists two and three tried to exit together, and jammed face-to-face.

"It's bloody well happened again, Whitehead!" shouted the first, which was unnecessary, since the latter's ear was one inch from the former's mouth.

"If you weren't so damned pushy, Loewick, then it wouldn't, would it?"

"I am *not* pushy," said Loewick, pushing. "It was my *turn* today."

"Oh Mum, Mummy!" called Whitehead "Kevvy-Wevvy thayth that it'th hith turn today. Wah! Christ, you might be a brilliant physicist, Loewick, but you've got the emotional development of a lab rat." At this, Loewick stamped on Whitehead's toe, and he hopped yelling from the doorway. He was the only one among his colleagues who looked of an identifiable age, which I put close to mine. He was good looking, in an aquiline, 1930s way. Noël Coward would have sighed. He wore 501s—unlike his colleagues, who all seemed more messed than dressed.

Loewick, who now emerged complaining about the stupidity of narrow doors, the world in general, and other scientists in particular, was harder to like. His face resembled a dish of something steamed, with a couple of eyes poked in for a lark. Whitehead, obviously accustomed to him, now drew up his knuckles beneath an imaginary bosom and Bracknelled, "Now, Kevin! Behave yourself or there won't be any lunch!"

"Just watch it, Whitehead. Just. Watch. It," replied Loewick with an attempt at menace, before skulking off.

I don't know why, but I had expected the inmates of Rose Cottage all to be young. In fact they ranged from sixteen to sixty. First came two bingo dames, with matching pink cardigans, stretch slacks, slippers, and hair. In what was obviously a favorite routine they clutched one another, raised their noses, and said, "Aaah! Bisto!" before giggling off to the dining room. Next was a boy, about fifteen, so pale he might not have been there at all. He waited, shivering, for his companion, a brawny middle-aged man who looked as though he might have been a laborer. The two went into lunch with much mild joshing.

Next, and last of the residents, was another woman. She wore a red vinyl raincoat and sou'wester, and behind her she dragged a basket-work shopping trolley. Once through the door she produced from the trolley an umbrella that she put up, exclaiming, "Rain, rain, rain. All it ever bloody does is rain."

"That's Mavis," said Alison. "And don't laugh, because she's their star turn."

I was too surprised to laugh, especially since now a massive boot was coming through. It was attached to a man of the type bred only in America; a great sheet-steel, sun-visored gas guzzler of a man. He wore a gray, overtailored uniform and carried an automatic rifle. Having eased his body (bodies, really) through the door he went and stood to attention beneath one of the dog paintings. It was of a pointer, which I thought a nice juxtaposition. In the brief period when nothing blocked the doorway a light like film light shone out. Then through stepped a man who made the guard look puny, a huge paterfamilias, genial yet terrifying, like Moses down from the mountain.

"This is the boss," whispered Alison.

"Ah!" he boomed, managing somehow to make his voice echo in the carpeted hall, "Young Nicholas Taig! I trust little Alison has proved sufficient hostess this morn?" I could say nothing, only extend a flaccid bundle of fingers to be squeezed in his giant palm. He then patted me on the head, and I was transported back twenty years to the single Christmas when my father had dressed as Santa Claus. All I could think, as Alison and myself were swept off and Santa Moses cried, "To luncheon! To the repast!" was, "I wonder whether I'm getting a train set, or a new bike?"

M

avis, the woman with the shopping trolley, sat opposite me at lunch, still wearing her red vinyl raincoat and sou'wester. The guard stood at her back, holding aloft her umbrella. Occasionally she would poke her head out and take a weather check but always found it inclement and ducked back again. Nobody except me seemed to find this bizarre display amusing. Each time a smile nudged at the corners of my mouth the others would flash warning looks, or press their fingers to their lips, as if they were nervous of something.

Nobody spoke. Most sat with their hands in their laps, pretending interest in the tablecloth. I thought we might be preparing to say grace. Then Santa Moses, actually Professor Ryemann, stood up and rapped on the table with a soup ladle.

"Gentlemen . . . and ladies," he began in his extraordinary self-generated echo, "this day . . . is a joyful day; a day when our spirits can drink afresh at the fountain of conviviality. For among us comes a new friend, a fellow traveler on the mind's mystic motorway . . ."

"Oh Christ, he's off," said the scientist Whitehead, rather loudly. The professor ignored him.

"A motorway upon which you have all driven, or indeed, walked. And all found yourselves lost. Was it, you wondered in your extremity, junction thirty-four you should take? Or junction thirty-five? Or -six?

Well, no matter, my lost lambs, no matter. For the shepherd found you, and brought you here, to this spa of the senses, this service station of the soul, this, um . . ."

"Amen!" cried Whitehead. "Praise the Lord and pass the mulligatawny."

The professor, his skin thicker than the dullest vicar's, pressed on. "And now we have a new guest here, at Motel Mystico; a young man who, like so many of you, has suffered for being . . . for being what? Different, that is all. Different. But suffer no more shall he. For he has found the nipple and shall *suck*!"

"Hear, hear! Let's bloody suck, then. I'm starving to death," added Whitehead. It seemed to do the trick: Ryemann spoke his last sentence in a rush.

"And so, my friends, may I introduce . . . Nicholas Taig!"

There was some applause—polite but touching nonetheless. The laborer type stretched his arm across the table and shook my hand.

"Pleased to meet you. William Bulbrook here," he drawled aristocratically, which somewhat demolished my deductions. "And this," he went on, draping his arm around the sharp shoulders of the thin boy, "is Joe."

Poor Joe didn't seem to have the energy to breathe, let alone shake my hand. But he flapped his fingers like a wet glove and gave me a consumptive smile. I smiled back.

"You naughty man, Mr. Bulbrook. Aren't you going to introduce us?" said one of the bingo dames who'd done the Bisto-kids act.

"I'm so sorry, ladies. Nicholas, these are the Von Trapp sisters."

The dames cackled. "We're not *really* sisters," said the first.

"And we aren't called Von Trapp," said the second. "It's just that we're . . ."

"Quite, quite inseparable," said the first.

"And we sing selections from *The Sound of Music*," completed her friend. "It's where we met, you know. In the stalls of the Odeon, Bournemouth. I'd seen the film sixty-four times and Millie here was on her . . ."

"Ninety-eighth! And then we discovered we'd more in common than

151

a love for the musicals of Rodgers and Hammerstein, because we found that we were both . . ." Together they drew breath and yelled, "PSYCHIC!!" before merging into one mass of quivering pink pullover.

"Silly old bats," said Melvin from the other end of the table.

"And what particular direction do your gifts lie in?" I asked Millie, hoping that she hadn't thought Melvin's comment came from me.

"Direction?"

"Yes. What's your speciality?"

"Oh. Um . . . Um . . ."

"Mulligatawny?" interrupted her friend, thrusting the tureen beneath my nose. I ladled some soup into my bowl, wondering why it was that the inmates of Rose Cottage seemed so cagey about their talents.

"You were going to tell me what *you* do, Nick," said Alison.

"Ah, Alison!" boomed Professor Ryemann's church-organ voice. "A good question! Nicholas is a very special creature. Our first molecular randomizer. We have sought one of his kind for a very long time."

Although I resented being treated like a pinned butterfly it was a relief to have been labeled at last.

"You mean there's more than one of me?"

"We think so. We're almost certain the Other Side have had one for a while. But now," he beamed, "so do we."

"Ooh, it sounds ever so glamorous," said Millie. "What is it?"

"It's a nuisance, Millie, that's what. Bits of me change. I call it cartoonitis."

"Cartoonitis! I like that," laughed Millie.

"It's strictly inaccurate," offered Loewick, the scientist with the steamed face. "What's actually happening, at the subatomic level . . ."

"Oh shut it, Loewick," said Whitehead. "We don't have the faintest idea what's happening. We only got our hands on the poor sod yesterday. *You're* not clairvoyant, you know."

"And *you're* hardly a scientist," replied Loewick.

"Gentlemen, gentlemen please!" said Professor Ryemann. "This is hardly the example."

"Sorry," said Whitehead, introducing himself with a cool-dude flick of the wrist. "I'm John."

I duded back. "Hi."

"And I'm Loewick. But you can call me . . ."

"Madam," said Whitehead. We grinned at one another.

Loewick was not put off. "Kevin," he said.

· · · · ·

The mulligatawny was excellent. Definitely not a canned job. I wondered who'd cooked it. It seemed unlikely that those responsible for Rose Cottage, having taken so much trouble to be secretive, would risk employing civilian staff. The uniformed guards didn't look bright enough to understand can openers, much less recipe books; so I guessed that the domestic servants must have been recruited from government security agencies. I imagined some keen young spy, fresh from five years' training in the arts of surveillance, silent killing, and martini making, being told that his first big job was as a housemaid.

I was about to serve myself more soup when a horrible noise made me drop the ladle. It came from Mavis.

"Eeeeh! Eeeeh!" she wailed, pulling her sou'wester down around her ears and stamping her feet. "Eeeeeaah!"

Almost before the first scream ended everybody in the room had dived under the table leaving Mavis alone with me, the security guard, and the umbrella. Alison pulled at my trouser leg.

"EeeeeEEEEeeeAAgh!" went Mavis.

And from a cloudless sky, or in this case a cloudless dining-room ceiling, came a hailstorm of Biblical vehemence. For a second I was fixed there, fascinated, until a hailstone the size of a profiterole bopped me on the head and drove me to cover.

The scene beneath the table resembled some Luftwaffe-interrupted World War II wedding breakfast. As if to underscore this, Millie began to sing, "There'll be bluebirds over the white cliffs of Dover," in a crumbly contralto. John Whitehead was laughing himself hoarse. Melvin, I noted, took the opportunity to hold Alison's hand. Loewick was complaining again, this time about the folly of not carrying measuring instruments at all times. Through the noise of the storm Evens, the

153

trollish scientist, shouted his agreement. Pale Joe, who now seemed as translucent as sushi, pressed himself against William Bulbrook's Aran sweater.

"Calm down, Joe," said William. "Steady, old lad." But Joe grew more aerial until, like a pale flame, he disappeared entirely. So, that was his talent.

"Damn and blast!" said William, "He knows not to do that on an empty stomach."

The Von Trapp sisters now launched into "My Favorite Things" from *The Sound of Music.* "Raindrops on roses, and whiskers on kittens . . ."

Above us the storm raged on. Pulverized crockery rained continually; water from the melting hailstones saturated the carpet and began to encroach on our little island. Our brave singing was stopped at one point by a hailstone that must have been the size of an iceberg. It splintered the tabletop, letting water pour over Evens. From his reaction I could see it was the first shower he'd had all year. Throughout it all Professor Ryemann remained silent, his arms ineffectually outstretched, his white hair flying in the wind. Again he reminded me of Moses, without the same social connections.

The storm stopped as suddenly as it had started. A bolt of lightning, a scream, a thud, and it was over. Nobody moved.

"Bloody weather," we heard Mavis say. This was taken as a sign, and we crawled from beneath the table.

Mavis sat sipping mulligatawny. Uniquely, her soup bowl remained whole, as did she. Her umbrella was shredded on the floor, covering the face of the stricken guard. He lay unconscious or dead, in what remained of his uniform. A greasy plume of smoke drifting from beneath his shirt indicated where the lightning had earthed. Every piece of furniture was broken—the heavy green curtains were now grass skirts and even the wallpaper was missing in strips, as though a giant cat had sharpened her claws there. Professor Ryemann indicated the guard, who was carried out by Loewick and Evens, then turned to Mavis. I doubted even his puce oratory would be up to the task ahead.

Between dainty sips of soup Mavis paused and blinked at Ryemann, whose great white eyebrows writhed like live ermine.

"Mavis!" he said. "That was excellent. *Excellent.*"

Mavis smiled. "Lovely soup," she said, "but where's my brolly got to?"

A look of immature displeasure passed across her face and we held our collective breath. Even Ryemann, despite his reaction to the visitation of hailstones, looked a bit nervy.

"Where is my *brolly?*" she repeated, hitting the lonely soup bowl with her spoon. Joe, who had just reappeared, vanished once more. Alison was shaking her left leg like a sprinter limbering for the one-meter dash. With a crunch of splintering glass Loewick rushed into the room carrying a new umbrella. Mavis looked a lot calmer, but not as calm as the rest of us felt.

"Friends," said Ryemann, "I am afeared we shall be forced to continue our vittles in the library."

"Why?" asked Mavis wiping her bowl with a slice of perfectly dry bread. "Has the weather been bad again?"

A fresh security guard, almost indistinguishable from the fried one, served our second course in the library. Beige plastic TV-dinner trays were provided on which to balance our fine porcelain plates. There was little conversation, none of it about the weather. It amused me that the classic English topic should be so carefully avoided just when it was worth talking about. I answered many polite questions about my affliction (or my "power" as it was called) and I also answered a few shy glances from Alison. She was definitely fanciable, I decided. It was ages since I'd made love. In fact I wondered whether I had ever made what might really be called "love" to anyone at all. I thought of Lucy. Did she enjoy our lovemaking? I'd never really asked, except reflexively, and always answered to my own satisfaction. She *seemed* to enjoy it—but then women are good at seeming to enjoy things. When Alison next ventured a peek at me I felt myself blush.

155

The hailstorm had had a particularly bad effect on poor old Millie. She continued to give us excerpts from Rodgers and Hammerstein; a good selection, but with "Happy Talk" the dismal refrain. Pale Joe made a fleeting reappearance, during which William tried to feed him some lamb. But the events of the morning had been too much and he quickly slipped from sight once more. William was so upset by this that after lunch he implored me to join him in his room for a brandy.

"They thought, you see," said William, swirling his glass and staring into it, "that young Joe would be rather good for a spot of the old espionage, on account of the invisibility trick."

"I see," I said. William's room, like the man himself, was artlessly masculine. The soppy chintz remained, but a profusion of boyish things fought against it. Clothes (especially socks and underwear) were strewn everywhere; model aircraft, handcrafted in wood, perched on the flat surfaces. Others flew on cotton. Several cameras lay on the bed. I'd have taken him for a bachelor of the old school had it not been for the many framed pictures of the same athletic-looking woman which covered the wall by the window.

"Trouble with Joe is," he went on, "he's scared of his own bloody shadow. Well, he *is* his own bloody shadow, most of the time. So the chances of him parachuting into some Russian missile base are a bit thin. And not only that, there's another problem. He can make *himself* go invisible, and for some odd reason his clothes as well. But anything going in or out isn't—if you see what I mean. So even if he did manage to get into our imaginary missile base he'd be spotted—because the first time anything frightening happened he'd pee himself. Poor sausage."

"Isn't *anyone* here any use?" I asked.

"None whatsoever," laughed William. "Name me a name and I'll tell you their incompetence."

"Well, I already know about Alison."

"Totally useless. Couldn't predict tomorrow. Lovely girl, though. Who next?"

"The two old ladies?"

156 {

"Millie and Florrie? The idea there is that they can transfer their thoughts. Which they can. But they're both completely bats. I can't think that knowing who starred in the 1958 production of *The King and I* or how to crochet a matinée jacket would be of much use to NATO."

"But why can't they just tell them what to transmit?"

"Because it all gets a bit confused. Like them, dear old trouts. Just yesterday, for instance. The mad scientists asked Millie to send the opening lines of *Richard III* to Florrie. 'Now is the winter of our discontent' got through all right, but 'Made glorious summer by this son of York' came out as 'There's a bright golden haze on the meadow and I could just eat a nice bar of chocolate.' "

"Where did she get the bit about the bar of chocolate?"

"You know—Yorkie, the chocolate bar," he laughed. "You see? I can't see them transmitting the plans for battle stations in space, somehow, can you?"

I admitted that I couldn't.

"So, that only leaves Mavis," he continued.

"She can control the weather, I assume?"

"Oh no," he laughed. "I don't think Mad Mave can control anything. She's a materializer, she makes things appear from nowhere. That hailstorm was nothing. Last week she produced an entire minibus full of Frenchmen. One minute they were tootling along on their hols, the next they were here."

"Where?"

"On the billiard table downstairs, actually. God knows what Ryemann told them. Probably said it was a hallucination and blamed English food. She's great value, Mavis. Except when she conjures up wild animals, which she's got a bit of a soft spot for. Lions and tigers are all right—I advise you to keep a pork chop handy for them—but it's the slimy things I don't care for . . . snakes, scorpions. Make sure you check your shoes before you put them on in the morning."

"Thanks for the tip. So Mavis really is useful?"

"She would be, but she's mad as a coot. They keep her in the hope she'll learn how to control herself, but she never will. Still, it gives us a good laugh."

157

"And what about you? What's your incompetence?"

"Me? Oh, I'm not . . ."

He was cut short by the reappearance of Joe, who faded into view next to the window.

"Hello there! Have you been with us all the time?"

Joe nodded. I smiled at him, which must have been a little too aggressive, for the pattern of the wallpaper became visible through his torso.

"Come on, now," said William, "this is only Nick. Come and say hello."

"Hello," he said tinily.

"There's a good chap. Come and sit on the bed," entreated William. Joe flitted across the room to the bed. When he sat down, the mattress barely registered the impact.

"I wish I could do what you do," I whispered. "It would have come in very handy these last couple of weeks."

"Do you really?" he asked with a look almost like excitement.

"Yes, I do. I've been chased, photographed, hunted, humiliated. My, er—power is the opposite of invisible."

"Can you do it now?"

"I don't think so. It's not really up to me."

"Oh," he said. For a moment I thought he would cry, or vanish once more. I was reminded of a time when my one decent relative, Uncle Jim, had taken me badger spotting. Joe's was a gentle and intriguing presence, like the badgers'. I desperately wanted him to stay.

"Nothing to stop us trying, though," I said. "Grab my nose." Joe reached out and took a surprisingly firm grip. I told him to pull and my illness decided to perform. Soon my nose was three feet long. Joe was so excited that for the first time he appeared properly. He was still thin, but colored pink, not gray; and I could see that his real age was about twelve, not the fifteen or so I had thought. When I invited him to twang my anteater proboscis he did so with an openly boyish giggle.

My nose didn't stay protruded for long. It retracted into my face with a fartlike sound, which had Joe on the floor with laughter. William put his hand on my arm. When I looked at him his eyes were moist.

158 {

"You're a good man, Nick. Thank you. I haven't seen the boy like that for months. Didn't think I ever would again."

"It was no trouble," I said embarrassedly. To change the subject I asked again what his own particular power was.

"Haven't you worked it out yet? I haven't got a power—I'm Joe's old dad. Only him and me, you see, after the old girl popped her clogs. They came to pinch him one day from outside his school. But I'd gone to collect him, so I gave chase. And here we are. Been a year now."

"I'm terribly sorry, William, I didn't realize. I'm being stupid today—I think it's the aftereffects of the drug they slugged me with. So those pictures are of your wife?"

"That's her. Cracking, eh? Bloody cancer—they say it gets the healthiest ones quickest. Anyway, all gone now."

"When Joe was abducted—why didn't you call the police?"

"Well, because I knew something fishy was going on. Joe has always been able to do his trick, so I'd always worried that somebody else would find out. When I saw three men in suits bundle him into a Jaguar I just knew it wasn't an ordinary kidnapping, even in Chelsea. Besides, there'd've been no point in an ordinary kidnap. I'm not worth the money."

"You sound as though you are."

"That's Winchester for you. I'm not, though. I'm a carpenter, not a merchant banker. Couldn't stand the thought of spending my whole life with the same appalling people I'd been forced to go to school with . . . Why are you smiling?"

"You must know my father. He did choose to do that. Guy Taig?"

"Good grief! Gorgeous Guy! I bumped into him once a couple of years ago at The Oval. I was supporting the West Indians, just to be cussed, and he turned round and called me a nigger lover, very loudly. Dreadful man. Sorry, I'm a bit of a blunt old carpenter."

"No, that's him. Dreadful. What was he like at school?"

"Just as dreadful. We called him Slut."

"You'll be glad to know he hasn't changed."

"No, I'm not surprised. He wasn't popular at school. Such a snob. Like most of his sort. Wasn't his father an engine driver, or something?"

"Yes, and my grandmother was a cleaner."

"So they beggared themselves to send him to Winchester? Were they pleased with the result?"

"I don't know, really. He denied them. We only met twice."

"More horrible than I thought, then," said William. "Not to worry, though. I'm glad to see you haven't turned out the same."

I hid in my brandy glass, wondering what to say. Then a bell rang.

"And speaking of school," said William, "that's the start of the afternoon's torture. How high's your pain threshold?"

I must have looked startled, for William added, "Only joking, old thing. Only joking," and opened the door for me. I would have believed him, had it not been for Joe's sudden disappearance into the Twilight Zone.

◦◦◦◦◦◦◦◦ T H I R T E E N ◦◦◦◦◦◦◦◦

E xcept for underpants I was na-
ked. That didn't bother me. Attached to my anatomy, like rubber lam-
preys, were twenty-six (I'd counted) electrodes. That didn't bother me,
either. The two scientists conducting my first examination were
boiled-face Loewick and unwashed Evens. And that did.

The laboratory had plenty of hard high tech. I was sitting on some of
it: a chair made from a plastic that gripped me when I tried to move.
There were many machines, and then many more, to nursemaid them.
But there was also wallpaper with a repeat of dray horses, a battered
chesterfield, a Victorian plant stand with a computer on it, a mahogany pipe rack full of syringes, and a wind-up gramophone. These
things, I decided, were the British contribution to the enterprise.

Kevin Loewick's fish fingers continued attaching electrodes to the
few remaining bare patches of my skin. Thin wires trailed from my
body to the computer on the plant stand. There seemed no reason to
antagonize him on purpose, so I said, "I feel like Gulliver."

"What?" he asked blankly, gluing a sucker to my big toe.

"Gulliver, when the Lilliputians tie him down."

"Oh, yes. I saw that cartoon."

"It was a *book*, once."

"Was it? Don't read much," he said proudly. I went to cross my arms

161

in anger but the chair tightened its grip. I reversed my decision not to antagonize him.

Troll-like Evens, who had been in an anteroom, now entered the laboratory carrying a steel tray of veterinary-sized syringes. His foul pipe had been extinguished and stored in his beard. No doubt he thought it an endearing eccentricity.

"Nick, this is Stig," said Loewick. "I call him Stig because he's a bit like Stig of the Dump. Now there's a book I have read. Great stuff, really good. Have you?"

"Some time ago," I said. "About twenty years."

"My favorite," continued Loewick. "I always wanted to be like Stig—you know, no grown-ups telling you what to do, just living on a rubbish dump and getting dirty all day."

"Yes, yes, I said I'd read it, didn't I?" I interrupted, wondering if I was safe in the hands of a man who knew that *Stig of the Dump* was a book, but not *Gulliver's Travels*. Evens said nothing, so I reciprocated. Deliberately he rearranged the barbaric syringes, then gave me a scrutable smile.

"Right," said Loewick, attaching the last sucker to my left nipple, "shall we begin? Oh, by the way—are you cold?"

I was, in fact. Rose Cottage had been Scandinavianly air-conditioned: an American stipulation, no doubt. Despite its redundancy in England no Pentagon bigwig could have faced the humiliation of having an invading Russian army discover that the enemy couldn't afford to have their research establishments air-conditioned.

"Yes, I am cold."

"Right. Stig, turn up the 'stat a bit, would you?"

Evens didn't move.

"Stat's not working," he lied. I made terrible plans for him.

"Sorry, Nick. Still, we won't be long, OK?"

162 { Of course it wasn't, but together the muscular chair and the tray of syringes were enough to quash my objections. I nodded.

"So. Let's begin, shall we?" said Loewick.

"Yes, let's."

I looked at Loewick. He looked at me. After ten seconds he and Evens looked at each other.

"So let's begin," he said.

"Begin what?"

Loewick sighed. "The molecular randomization process, of course."

"Oh, *that*. I thought you knew. I can't control it."

Loewick looked at me as though I were a troublesome television, then stood up and adjusted one of the suckers on my thigh. I was surprised he didn't bang me on the head.

"It's true, Loewick. I can't *make* it happen. I'm not one of the Fantastic Four, you know."

"We got plenty of time," said Evens. His accent, if a modulated grunt can have an accent, was rural. Middle-Earth, I would have said. Loewick sat down again and the two of them watched me. Their lack of humanity was shocking: to them I was just a scientific curiosity, my species of no consequence. They were both the type who had started young, pulling the legs off spiders, and instead of growing out of it took biology degrees.

After five minutes Evens's right index finger disappeared up his nose. Abstractedly he let it off the leash for a good run. When it emerged it had found a friend, a bogey like a helping of mushy peas. After admiring it from several angles Evens slipped the green giant into his mouth. "Is this creature a man at all?" I wondered. It was my downfall.

"*Aha!!*" squeaked Loewick, jumping up to retrieve the balloon attached to my ear. "Data!"

IS THIS CREATURE A MAN AT ALL? had been written in copperplate, which I thought innovatory. Evens did not share the feeling, and doubtless would have said so, had his mouth not been full.

Loewick was very turned-on. He dashed to the computer monitor. The undulating bar chart might have been his first skinflick. His fingers flew almost artistically around the keyboard. When he was satisfied he took up his clipboard and came to sit by me.

"How common is this phenomenon?" he asked, crossing his legs.

163

"Fairly," I admitted. With denial exhausted as a stratagem I felt hopeless.

"I'm a scientist, Nick," he smiled. "How often is 'fairly'? Weekly? Daily? Hourly?"

"It isn't like that. It depends on the circumstances."

"The stimuli?"

"If you must."

"Well, I'm sure Stig's flattered he was your stimulus. Aren't you, Stig?"

Evens was attempting to stuff my thought balloon into a glass jar. He looked at me, but said nothing. Instead he snorted up the contents of his sinuses, with a noise like porridge in a plughole. He was really a very talented little stimulus; it took all my concentration to prevent a whole barrage of disgusted balloonlets flowing from my ear. But I didn't let it happen. I was determined not to make life easy for my tormentors.

· · · · ·

Half an hour later I still hadn't performed. Loewick and Evens remained impassively fascinated. By concentrating on the whitewashed ceiling I had managed to keep myself pure of thought, but the strain was tiring. It was like one of those nights when one crawls home loaded with enough alcohol to fly the Atlantic but refuses, for some reason, to throw up.

Loewick broke the silence by ordering Evens to make coffee. In a Tupperware-hostessy way Loewick asked how I took it, then handed me the mug with his little finger crooked. Into his own mug he dumped five spoonsful of sugar. As he tried to stir it he asked, "Your little performance at London Zoo . . . what prompted it, exactly?"

"Joy," I replied without hesitation.

Loewick reached for a file and consulted it. "I thought your special friend was called Lucy."

"Not Joy the woman's name, *Joy*. The abstract noun." Bloody hell.

"Joy," he said, as if for the first time in his life. "Why?"

He took up his pen, and I told him of my joy at being believed, at not feeling solitary and mad, at Christy's wondering pleasure in my strange abilities, and how these things had led me to leap from the steps in the elephant house.

"So what you're saying is that these things only happen when you're veryvery happy?"

"Yes," I lied, pointlessly.

"So how," he replied, "do you account for what happened earlier with Stig? Were you veryvery happy then?"

"No," I admitted.

Loewick smiled the smile of a bad scientist. He might have discovered radium, such was its self-congratulation.

"What I'd like to suggest, Nick, is that the molecular randomization process comes into effect at times of acute emotional stress. I'd like to suggest that. I feel that is the direction our studies should take. OK?"

I was hardly in a position to disagree, strung up like a cow in a milking parlor and halfway to hypothermia.

"OK," I muttered.

Loewick nodded to Evens. His big moment had come. Like some specialist chef, employed only for his meat-carving skill, he took up his metal tray and advanced. I'm not falling for that one, I thought—you're just trying to scare me into a performance. But they were not; Evens selected a hypodermic the size of a foot pump and slipped its military needle into my arm. He did it quite expertly, for a troll.

"Now, Nick," said Loewick while Evens filled me up, "I'm just going to slip this down your throat. Don't worry about a thing."

He produced a white plastic hosepipe that looked big enough to clear drains.

"Now, all we've done is given you a little dose of Somathex. It's a muscle relaxant. Quite harmless, but we do need to give you a bit of help breathing. Hence this," he said, jamming the pipe down my throat.

I found his equation of "quite harmless" with asphyxiation interesting. The machine that took over my breathing was too boisterous. It had obviously been set on "Pyrenean Mountain Villager," not "Urban Squash Player," and my lungs were alternately inflated like life rafts then popped like blisters.

165

"You might feel a bit strange in a minute," shouted Loewick through the noise of the respirator, as though it felt normal to be sitting naked and freezing, in a musclebound chair, with more wires than a switchboard and a vacuum cleaner down my throat. However, Loewick was as good as his word.

My feet went first. They just melted, like joke-shop candles, puddling onto the floor. There was no time for shock: my legs and torso soon followed. The chair tried to embrace me but I was a greased blancmange, slopping from its grasp. Last went my head, slapping down on the lardy lake that was once my body. The respiration tube stayed in place, but only for a moment; as the muscles of my mouth jellified I realized that I was about to become the first person ever to drown in himself. I began to choke. Just as it seemed too late, Evens came into view. With a video camera. He put it close to my face, the better to capture my dying moments.

"Is he still alive?" he shouted.

Loewick was leaping around his keyboard like the Phantom of the Opera. "Yes, all the readings are fine. It seems to have stabilized."

Stabilized? I could have been mayonnaise. I probably *was* mayonnaise. But Loewick was right: the drug had no further damage to do. The blancmange lived.

"Told you we shouldn't've used Somathex," said Evens. "What if he'd dropped off his perch?"

"Well, it didn't, did it? It only dropped off its chair. Now shut up and put that bloody camera down. I want some help measuring it."

Interesting, I thought, that I'd lost the right to the personal pronoun since becoming a blancmange. Didn't blancmanges have rights, too?

"I'll measure it and you input the data," said Loewick, extending a steel tape measure. Evens took a few last pictures of my indignity then went to the computer. My vital statistics, called across the room by Loewick with as much dribbly lust as any beauty-contest compere, sounded about right for a jellyfish with middle-age spread. My radius, I learned, was two meters; my depth two centimeters. I had become an oil slick. When they'd finished this part of the process, Loewick bent down close to where he assumed my ear was and shouted (into my left shoulder blade, in fact), "Now, if you can hear me, I just want you to know we're going to weigh you. OK?"

His insistence on tagging "OK" to the end of every sentence was driving me crazy. I imagined him using it on all his victims, as a little device to prove his humanity. "Now, Ratty," I could hear him saying to some poor pinned creature, "I'm just going to slice the top off your skull. OK?"

My ears were burning inside, presumably from the backlog of vitriolic balloons now trapped by my Camembert body. I had no intention of confining myself to sarcasm when (if) I became solid again. Both Loewick and Evens were going to feel the effect of a molecularly randomized left hook.

"We're just going to slip this underneath you," said Loewick, holding up a sheet of green canvas with brass eyelets around its perimeter. Everyone has seen the removal-of-the-tablecloth-without-breaking-the-crockery trick, but inserting the green canvas sheet was like doing it in reverse: a trickier proposition. It proved impossible to keep more than half of me on it. At one stage Evens's fingers accidentally slid up my flaccid bumhole—a new experience for me, and probably for him, too. With a disgusted grunt he withdrew his hand and stared at the dungy digits. I was surprised by this delicacy—after his earlier behavior I half expected him to suck them clean. Instead he went squealing to the sink, carrying his hand like an isotope.

This incident fueled their determination and I was soon loaded onto the sheet. Loewick fetched a small crane from another room and attached steel cables to the brass eyelets.

"We're hoisting you up now, OK?" he said. A motor burred and I left the ground. Since neither the sheet nor my body was rigid I immediately concentrated in the center, like a mozzarella.

"Seventy-six point three six kilos. Unchanged," said Loewick.

"Finished?" asked Evens. When Loewick said that he had, Evens took his pleasure by letting the brakes off suddenly. I splashed to the floor. "Whoops!" said the little sadist.

I thought then that the opportunity for revenge was at hand, for there was a return of solidity in my left leg. Within seconds I could

167

control half my limbs. I was going to get Evens and pull out his beard, hair by hair; I was going to take one of his harpoons, load it with boiling tar, and stick it in his . . .

But I had been preempted. Evens noticed my forming limbs.

"The Somathex is at half-life," he said. "Shall I prepare a new syringe?"

"No, that may not be wise. Five mils of Diazepam would be better, then we can get him straight to the tank."

The tank? What fresh hell was this? Evens hurried to his syringes to prepare another injection while I prayed for enough solidity to deliver one clean blow. He approached with his steel sting; I willed my arm to move; the needle nipped into the vein; I tensed my bicep. Too late. Although my body continued to take shape, the new drug put my mind in aspic, and I no longer cared what was done to me.

· · · · ·

It was a very good little boy who was helped up off the floor by his fwends Kevvy and Stig. He wanted to go pee-pees, so Kevvy unplugged all those nasty wires and things and took him to the wee-wee room, and didn't get angry with Nicky when he made some little splashes on the floor, 'cos he was a tired little thing, and after all, he had been so good, so very good. Then Kevvy and Nicky went back to the funny room with its pretty wallpaper with the big horses on, and Nicky sat in the big chair that cuddled him when he sat down and made him feel all cozy and snoozy, and he thought how lucky he was to have two such nice chums as Kevvy and Stig.

"Nick, don't fall asleep. We're not finished."

Kevvy was shaking him, and he had a funny look on his face. Nick giggled. He wanted to go bye-byes. Kevvy said there was just one more thing they had to do, and anyway it was a bit like bye-byes.

"You see, Nick, we're going to put you in a nice tank, full of warm water . . . very salty water, so's you float. And then we're going to put some little earplugs in, so your ears don't get all wet, and we're going to play you a funny sort of noise, and then we're going to close the lid so it's all lovely and dark and then we're going to leave you for a little while . . ."

Nicky didn't want to be left in a tank. It sounded scary.

"Don't worry," said Kevvy, "it's nice. It's a bit like being inside Mummy again." And when he said this Stig pulled a very strange face and laughed like Nicky's housemaster once did when he told him he was going to meet Mr. Birch, and Mr. Birch turned out to be a cane. Nick wasn't feeling so cozy anymore. The new drug was wearing off. His head hurt. He didn't want to go to the tank.

It certainly did not look much like Mummy, not even my own fearsome example. I wondered why the designers had drawn on such morbid visual antecedents. A coffin; an iron lung; an Iron Maiden—the tank resembled all these. Californians, I'm told, are keen to jump into them, but doubtless there will be Californians keen to jump into the San Andreas Fault when finally it yawns.

Like an undertaker showing off this season's collection, Loewick lifted the lid. Reaching into the blue water he produced a set of aluminum steps.

"Now, Nick, up we go! Up the courtesy stairs!"

I hesitated. With his pipe Evens prodded me onto the sharp steps. Loewick kept up his pediatric-nurse patter.

"Oops!" he said, "Silly me, nearly forgot!" And whisked my underpants down. Before I could cover myself, Evens had restrained my hands and Loewick produced a catheter. More jelly was squirted onto it.

"Can't have you weeing the bath now, can we?" he leered. And then those fingers, the fingers I wouldn't even allow to wash my car, were holding my generator and plumbing it in.

"I've had enough, Loewick. Let me go."

He seemed surprised by my return to maturity and raised his eyebrows at Evens who loitered unseen with yet another hypo. This time he jammed it in my thigh without aiming and Loewick took advantage of my pain by pushing me into the tank.

The Dead Sea was Perrier in comparison with the stuff in the tank. I bounced off the surface.

"There are eight hundred pounds of Epsom salts dissolved in there," Loewick informed me, "so don't drink any or you'll be up all night."

} 169

I wanted to murder him but the new drug scoffed my energy. I hardly twitched when he locked my wrists into padded restraints.

"These are just to stop you rolling over," he said. "OK?"

And at that point it really was. He slipped plugs in my ears. White noise, like the sound of distant applause, filled my head; the lid was closed and the light switched out. I was alone in the sensory-deprivation tank.

FOURTEEN

My time in the sensory-deprivation tank was a complete blank. In fact I emerged a grudging convert to its refreshing powers, despite the long immersion in salt water having transformed me into a bipedal scrotum.

Loewick and Evens were petulant about my poor performance. Loewick in particular seemed to want to dispose of me like another misconcocted formula.

"You're useless, I've decided," he said as I tried to unpucker my pachydermis with a bath towel.

"Perhaps it's you who's useless. Besides, I thought scientists pursued knowledge for the love of it."

"Not military scientists. We have goals."

"Goals, eh? Is that why you talk such balls?"

"Don't get clever with me, Nick. Stig's still got loads of full syringes, and they don't all contain nice muscle relaxants."

I hadn't seen this Loewick before: the well of viciousness beneath his simple cold incompetence. Here was a disturbing, childish criminality. He offered me a bathrobe with my initials embroidered upon it in blue.

"I'm terribly hungry," I said. "When's dinner?"

"You've missed dinner. There's probably something cold in your room."

175

"Thanks," I said, not stopping to confirm that they were finished with me.

· · · · ·

Another of Rose Cottage's amazing five-star feasts was laid out in my room: a real sideboard-groaner of a smorgasbord, and two bottles of excellent Chardonnay. It was somewhat wasted on me, since I was too hungry to relish anything and launched several prettily heaped slices of rye bread straight down my gullet like savory surfboards.

Over the wine I became thoughtful. If Loewick's opinion was correct, not simple pique, and I was of no military use, what would be done with me? That was obvious: the same thing as all the other "gifted" people at Rose Cottage. Luxurious imprisonment. The alternative, radical lobotomy, was more attractive. My past was already a fabulous country where I had once basked. Now I could not afford to go back, but it stayed in my mind to torment.

After two more glasses of Chardonnay I decided to escape Rose Cottage. Sober, I might have thought about the power (if not the efficiency) of the NATO machine; of how the people who had kidnapped me from central London were not likely to let me slip easily from their grasp; of how I would not go very far in the open country without outside help. But I was not sober, and I did have outside help. Benny Sweet.

I ransacked my room three times before satisfying myself that Benny's pink card was gone, but, tired and half-cut, I wasn't especially bothered. The second bottle of wine and a good forgetting session seemed as attractive then as escape. There were, after all, worse things than life imprisonment. Perhaps the Yanks would keep their perennial promise and withdraw from NATO. Then Rose Cottage would be forced to take in paying guests and I could get the first bus out.

· · · · ·

When I next opened my eyes, Alison was standing in the room, clutching a large piece of card to her chest. She, too, wore one of the monogrammed bathrobes, in coral pink. Against it her tamed Mediterranean looks were doubly exotic.

"I did knock. Honestly I did. I just wanted to give you this."

"That's all right. What is it?"

"Nothing, really. Just one of my piccies."

She handed me the card. There was a charcoal sketch of myself. Even I thought it flattering.

"I didn't know you did this. Thank you."

"Do you like it?"

"Yes, I do."

"There's lots more in my room. Want to come and look? Go on, it's not very homely in here, is it? Go on, say you'll come."

· · · · ·

Alison had almost managed to rid her room of the interior designers' ignorant attempts at personalization. The color-supp. pastoral of the walls was almost hidden by her pictures. All the residents of the house were represented, mostly in charcoal; there were still lifes and views of the grounds in watercolor, and many detailed pen-and-inks of the royal family.

"I am impressed," I said.

"Go on," she said with casual disbelief, "you've been at the booze."

"No, I am impressed. Why shouldn't I be?"

"Because you're not the type, are you? Not the type to be impressed by anything, really."

She said it without a trace of anger; a simple statement of fact. I was going to defend myself but there was no point. She was right. From Leonardo through Shakespeare to the Pan-World Airlines campaign ("That pile of horseshit with the singing seats" as Don Stamp had put it)—I saw them all as part of the same racket, the same scam, the same hoax. Let's make a monkey of the man in the street. He can't tell Stork from butter. Once, the senior creative at ZZD had given me a talk about the need for sincerity. "You've got to *believe* in it. *Make* yourself believe in it," he'd said, not seeing his sophistry.

"Have I offended you now?" she asked.

"No, no. You're right. But honestly, I do think they're good pictures."

"OK, I believe you. Thanks."

} 177

"Um, who framed them?"

"William. He used to be a carpenter."

"Yes, I know."

"Right. Well, we all try to do things for each other. Like my bed-spread. Millie crocheted that. Nice, isn't it?"

The bedspread was made from many colored squares of wool. I was reminded of the one at Marcus's, the one I'd peed on. That had been of a similar design, done in silk, and purchased. Alison's woolen one had probably cost little money, but a lot of time, effort, and, I supposed, love.

"Yes, it is nice."

"And I did her some piccies in return."

Piccies. Once, if I had been watching television with friends, and Alison had popped up on some local news program, we would have guffawed at her suburbanity, her lack of sophistication, probably even her haircut. Now I felt like laughing at myself.

"You're so posh, aren't you?" she asked.

"I suppose I am."

"I'm common. *Sarf* London. Not *Hemp*-stead, like you."

"Oh, I'm not Hampstead. Hampstead's not the thing at all. It's where the Yids live."

I realized then where her unusual looks came from, even as the casual jibe left my lips. She was dignified about it.

"I'm really tired," she said. "Time for bed. I'm glad you liked your picture."

I checked the impulse to backpedal and returned instead to my room. The remaining half-bottle of wine couldn't offer even a cheap seat to oblivion, so I was alone with myself. At first it was only my stupidity that I cursed, but then I saw that the problem was a lot worse. It wasn't so much what I had said, as why. Like a man discovering at the check-in desk that his passport is still at home, I scrabbled through my mind's baggage with increasingly pointless energy. There didn't seem to be a single thought, feeling, or opinion there that hadn't been planted by a third party. Race, class, religion, sexuality . . .

178 { Fucking hell, I was the piss-poorest end-of-pier comedian. A knee-jerk reactionary? I had St. Vitus's dance. Four legs—good; two legs—bad; no legs—really funny. Blacks? Drug-taking muggers, chuck 'em out. Women? Fine for fucking, go elsewhere for conversation. The poor?

Only had themselves to blame. And the Yids? Well, they live in Hampstead. And Eltham. I wanted to hurt myself. At least I could go back to Alison and face her anger.

She looked neutral when she opened the door.

"Hello, Nick. Did you forget something?"

"Yes, I did. Could I come in?"

She stood away politely, like an employee of the room's real occupant.

"So what did you forget?"

"I forgot to apologize."

"Apologize? What for?"

"For what I said, about Hampstead."

"I'm sure Hampstead won't mind," she said. Cool did not come naturally to her.

"I don't mean Hampstead, I mean I'm sorry for what I said about Jews."

"Yids, as it happens."

"Yes. I didn't realize."

"And if you had, you wouldn't have said anything, is that it?"

"Probably. But what I want to say is that I know I shouldn't have wanted to say it in the first place."

She looked skeptical.

"It's funny, being Jewish. People can't spot you, like they can with colored people, so they can't get their smiles ready. What is it people don't like about us, 'specially posh people? Does it really all go back to Jesus Christ?"

"I don't know. Nobody in my family likes the Jews. It's never been discussed why."

"But you work in advertising. That's full of Jewish people. You must know loads."

"Yes, I do. But not socially. I'm sorry for it now; I'm starting to be sorry for a lot of things just recently."

179

Alison's role as frigid sentinel to her racial pride relaxed a little. Her torso became less rigid; the bathrobe fell into folds where before it had been taut across her shoulders and breasts. I was excited to find that I could affect somebody with sincerity, and wondered why dissimulation had always been my natural first choice. I thought about my encounter with Herman Coprolite, and what he had said about people like me preferring to "shit their pants in public," rather than have a feeling. But he was only half right: I didn't mind feelings, so long as they weren't true. Worse, I'd considered those in clear communication with their hearts to be inferior, brute sentimentalists. How did this pitiful inversion happen? How did the world turn upside down?

She had to sit on the bed. The teenager was almost returned in her, and with it an awkwardness about being alone with me, and nothing but two tailored towels between us.

"I've got some wine in my room," I said. "Only half a bottle—I've been a bit greedy. Still, shall we share it?"

"I've only got a toothmug," she said.

"Couldn't we share the glass, too?"

She nodded and smiled, and was still smiling when I returned with the now-warm wine. I sat on the floor to pour it, not wanting to discomfort her by sitting on the bed. I handed her the glass, and like most women not accustomed to alcohol she acted drunk three seconds after the first sip.

"Lovely wine," she said questioningly.

"Sorry it's a bit warm. I'll have to ask for a fridge."

"Oh, I like it warm. Sensitive teeth."

She found this funny, and giggled, impossibly tipsy. "Shall I tell you something?"

"If you want."

"That picture of you."

"What about it?"

"I'll have to whisper." She leaned down and pressed her lips to my ear. "I did it six months ago. I'm getting much better with my predictions. But don't tell the bofs."

180 {

This set her off again and she tumbled from the bed. The loose robe opened slightly, exposing her left breast. To my surprise I looked away. Alison, emboldened by imaginary drunkenness, did nothing to adjust the towel—if anything, she opened it further. I had no doubt that I was being seduced, but could not take the easy advantage. She was behaving how she imagined a "Nick" woman would, and another time she might have been correct, but not then.

She lolled for a few seconds more, then sat up, pulling the robe suddenly tight, like a surprised bather. She seemed angry, but at which of us I wasn't sure. Without considering me she downed the wine in one gulp, then refilled the glass and guzzled again. Thus fortified she said, in an Annie Oakleyish voice, "Don't fancy me then, eh? Oh, well, sod it!"

This frontierswoman approach made me laugh. It was so full of nerve, so close to tears. She looked utterly nonplussed by my laughter, unsure whether to be tougher or to join me. Then she put her hand to her mouth and laughed. I thought it was because she had seen the joke, but when I looked down I saw it was for a different reason: my sexual feelings were advertising themselves through the gap in my bathrobe. It was probably the best commercial of my career.

A red light flickered on the walls of the room, refracting from the many pictures so that everything danced and shimmered in pink. I looked for the source but could not find it; then Alison said, "I think you're blushing."

She was right. The realization that my own cartoon-assisted blush was the source of the light only made me blush more, and for a moment the room lit up, as though the carpet had been rolled back to reveal a live volcano beneath.

"Yes, I think I am. Poor old Loewick and Evens. This is a new symptom, and they've missed it."

"It's quite pretty," said Alison, bringing her face close to mine. "I like it."

The blush, less fierce now, played on her black hair, coaxing red highlights. I felt the familiar approach of a smoothy line, but it was unrehearsed, unweighed for economy of effect. It just emerged—and through my lips, not my ear.

"It's the closest we'll come to firelight," I said, and kissed her.

· · · · ·

"Do you think I'm a slag?" she asked later.

"Why should I think that?"

"Didn't exactly take a lot of persuading, did I?"

"Neither did I."

"You're a bloke," she said. The gap that this statement opened in our delicate intimacy both spoiled and enhanced the moment. No woman known to me, in any sense, could ever have said such a thing. Persuasion was never an element in the equation, with yielding on the other side. Mutual taking—that was the thing; and it felt proper, even to me. Yet Alison's view, albeit wrong, was touching for what it represented. I wanted to talk about these things, but she carried on, "It was only my second time, though. Only my second time. And I liked it. I bloody well *loved* it."

She made a poor Jezebel, throwing back her head with controlled abandon. She rolled onto her front and angled her naked buttocks at me; for a moment I thought she was offering Sodom's Dish of the Day, as a final challenge to her own innocence. But then I saw she was crying.

"I've fancied you for months," she sobbed, "and I've waited for you to arrive, and now you have I just feel like I've spoiled everything."

"But why?"

"Oh, because I've forced myself on you, not given you the chance. I didn't want it to be like this, but I was scared, you see."

"Yes, I see. It's all right. You didn't force yourself on me."

"But you don't understand. I had no choice. You'll be gone tomorrow."

At first I thought this was part of some ships-in-the-night romantic fantasy, but then I grasped what she meant. "You mean literally, don't you?"

"Yep. I don't know how, exactly. All I've seen is that we'll be in the garden when it happens. But I know it's tomorrow."

182 {

She fixed me with a terrible look, knowing perfectly well that my every atom was screaming with elation, daring me to look saddened by our imminent separation. I couldn't. The grin set in like cement, even though I didn't want it to. Alison got on with her crying privately, while

I sat and stroked her hair, my heart and stomach squeezing their special juice into my veins so that most of me was already far away from Rose Cottage.

Eventually she juddered to a halt, sat up, and blew her nose extensively on a pastel Kleenex.

"I fancy a ciggy now," she said.

"I thought you didn't?"

"I've got a little stash, for emotional occasions. I've had them ever since I came here. We used to smoke them after school. They're in the bottom of the wardrobe, in a red shoebox."

I jumped up, shamefully grateful for the excuse, and truffled madly in the scented detritus. The red box took little discovering. I took it to her.

"This is my special safe place," she said in the same self-protective, childlike tone that had marked our first encounter. The box contained, among other things, a ghostly Polaroid of Alison and her family looking frostbitten on an English beach, a miniature of Bacardi, a lock of hair, some polished money, and a record of Spandau Ballet singing "True." She took the packet of Sobranie Cocktail and something caught my eye. In the bottom of the box lay Benny's pink calling card. She saw my startled expression and snatched the card, tucking it under her thigh as though I would miss her sleight of hand.

"Where did you get that from?" I asked, sounding stern without meaning to. She coiled away, the mauve Sobranie hanging in the corner of her mouth, like some fifties tart afraid of her pimp.

"Don't be angry, please. I just wanted a little part of you to keep, for me. I knew you'd be going away, so I stole it from your room. That bit of hair in the box is from Becky, the little kid I told you about. I only wanted a keepsake. Please don't be angry."

Her flesh was all goosed and her arms, wrapped tight around her, made nakedness a dangerous thing—like a hermit crab between homes. Tears dropped from her elbows. She looked about as lonely as a person can, and I had no words to fill such need. Again I took refuge in action, fetching the bathrobe and placing it around her shoulders. Then I sat and patted her hair stupidly, while she cried like a cello.

It wasn't me but someone else who brought Alison back from her private Atlantis. An anxious knocking at the door.

"Hold on, I'll just make myself decent," she called, wriggling into the bathrobe and scuttling to the door. I heard her sigh with relief, then draw quick breath once more as she realized that even though the midnight caller was friendly she, Alison, remained the custodian of a naked man.

"Millie," she said. "What's the matter?"

"Are you all right, dear?"

"Fine. Why?" Alison danced in the doorway, attempting to block Millie's line of sight.

"It's just . . . well, silly, really. Only me and Florrie, we had one of our *vibrations*, you see."

This sent me giggling. I stuffed a corner of pillow in my mouth.

"What sort of vibration, Millie?" asked Alison, signaling with her leg for me to keep quiet.

"Ooh, *terrible*, lovey. It started down here, then it went all up here, and down here. Terrible. I blamed those prawns at tea, but then we both said it together. 'Alison,' we said. Are you sure you're all right?"

I had half the pillow down my throat by then. Literally.

"Yes, thanks, Millie. I'm fine."

"Well, you don't look fine to me. You look like you've been crying. Nothing's been getting on top of you, has it?"

At this I guffawed with such force that the pillow shot from my mouth and hit Alison in the small of her back. She spun around, and Millie wasted no time popping her neat gray head through the gap.

"Oh. Have I interrupted something?"

Alison gestured frantically for me to cover myself, but I was laughing too much.

"Look, Millie, it's not like you think . . ."

"Isn't it?" asked the old lady with a new-fashioned look, "What a shame. It looked so much fun."

Alison gasped.

"I didn't take up the crochet till quite late in life, you know," said Millie as she retreated, chuckling.

Alison closed the door and leaned against it, panting like an escaped convict.

"Well!" she said, rather primly, then, "Well! Who'd have believed it? I just don't know what to do now."

"Don't you?"

"No."

"How about giving them another vibration?"

· · · · ·

I was the last to arrive at breakfast. I'd gone first to the library, where a security guard had told me breakfast was in the dining room. He had a copy of Nietzsche's *The Gay Science* on his sofa-sized thigh. I wondered whether he was reading it or just confusing his supermen and looking for the pictures.

All Mavis's storm damage had been mended; even the wallpaper was new. A pantomime hush fell when I sat down, unbroken except by the noise of cornflakes tumbling into my bowl. I caught Alison's eye as I reached for the milk. She looked like a woman who'd been doing all night exactly what she had been doing all night.

"Saturday today!" beamed Florrie, apropos nothing. "I wonder what ENSA will have laid on for us?"

"Well I, for one, am refusing to play croquet, ever again," said Millie. "Last time we played, Professor Ryemann *hit* me. I told him that playing was the thing, not winning. But he hit me again. Horrid man."

William Bulbrook chuckled. "He didn't exactly hit you, Millie. It was just a playful tap."

Millie went the color of her hair. "Mr. Bulbrook. Professor Ryemann is six feet four. I am five feet one. One man's playful tap is another woman's bruised sit-upon."

William chuckled again. "Morning, Nick. How did they treat you yesterday, my old fruit and nut? You look a bit green about the gills, if you don't mind me saying so."

"I thought you were joking when you asked me about my pain threshold. It was virtually torture in that lab. I'm covered in bruises, and I don't know what the drugs they gave me were, but they kept me up half the night."

I regretted these fibs the second they were out. Millie made great and noisy ceremony out of spooning kedgeree for Florrie; Alison almost snapped her toast with the pressure of buttering it; Melvin sniggered openly; and Joe, as a coda to this concerto of disbelief, made his head disappear.

"Bruising, eh?" said William.

"Yes. Um, where's Mavis this morning?"

"She has hers with the Frankensteins," said Melvin. "She's a right pain at breakfast time. Always making bloody disgusting things appear. Remember that time she made all them dead toads appear in the milk jug, Bill?

"Thank you, Melvin," said Alison. "It's just as revolting being reminded of it."

"Shut up, Lady fucking muck. How's *your* bruising?"

Alison chose to direct her angry expression at me, not Melvin.

"That was a bit uncalled for," I said.

"And you! You can get stuffed as well! Fucking my fucking bird, you toffee-nosed ponce. Who d'you think you are, anyway?"

"Your WHAT?" yelled Alison. "Melvin, I wouldn't let you into my nightmares, let alone into my body. You've got a dirty mouth and a dirty mind. And spots. Me and Nick were not 'fucking' last night, we were making love. And if you knew the difference, if there was a *chance* of you knowing the difference, then I might give you a kiss next Christmas. As it is, you'll be lucky if I pull your cracker."

She fluttered from the room like a beautiful and delicate kite, her hands and eyelids quivering. There was much rearranging of the cruets.

"What's eating *her?"* asked Melvin. Millie glowered at him. I wiped my mouth on a napkin, tossed it at him like a Regency ninny, then rose to follow Alison. Melvin was already pouring himself more Coco-Pops.

· · · · ·

I found her in the conservatory, staring out at the garden, dry-eyed. I pulled up one of the wicker chairs, upholstered in yet another careful chintz, and placed it so that our knees almost touched. For a time we sat silent. I lit two cigarettes, thinking that she would want one. This was surely one of her "emotional occasions." But I was wrong; she shook her head at the offer, and I ground the rejected tube on the flagstones, feeling useless. My moccasin gave off a singed whiff. Alison wrinkled her nose.

"Sorry about that. Smells horrible, doesn't it?"

She smiled, and I relaxed a little.

"I'm pregnant."

I didn't take in what she had said. "Oh," was my answer, if I gave one. Then I saw that her talent with the future altered everything.

"You're *what?*"

"It's all right. I have an abortion. I thought I should tell you, though."

"It isn't all right. It isn't all right at all. Why didn't you tell me before . . . before we did it?"

"I didn't know. It was only this morning that I saw it all. Not that it would have changed much. I already knew you were going away, didn't I?"

"But this changes everything. Suppose I don't want to go now? Suppose I don't want you to have an abortion?"

"You do, though. I've seen that. You *are* going today, and I *do* have an abortion. It's not worth discussing."

The sudden plasticity of tenses, the short-circuiting of alternatives, held me in a magnetic field till my cigarette burned down and the filter grew too hot to be ignored. Nothing seemed worth discussing, if Alison knew the outcome.

"So what happens now?" I asked, angry with frustration.

"I don't know everything, do I? We say good-bye, I suppose."

I cast around for something with which to call time's bluff. "Come with me."

"Don't be silly. I've told you what happens. And anyway, you don't love me."

She was right. I realized at that moment how much I did love Lucy, and how much I wanted to see her again. What had I done to deserve the generosity of these women? First Lucy and now Alison, giving of themselves to keep my soul aloft. I hung down my head, carelessly

187

noting that my neck was lengthening, till my faced pressed on the cold flags.

"Don't be sad, it's not your fault," she said, which just about finished me. I flopped to the floor, a penitent beanbag. She knelt down next to me, and from somewhere produced a smile.

"If you don't get up, I'll nick your ciggies. I do fancy one now."

So I heaved myself up and lit two more cigarettes. She smoked hers peacefully while I watched. And she didn't shed a tear.

●●●●●●●●●●● S I X T E E N ●●●●●●●●●●●

"**W**HEEE!" screamed Mavis. "I'm winning, I'm winning!"

"You're cheating, Mavis, that's what you're doing," said Millie. "Cheating!"

. We were in the garden, all of us. The scientists were losing to the freaks at quoits, thanks to Mavis who was indeed cheating. Rather than throw her quoits at the target she was stuffing them into her shopping trolley, then causing new ones to materialize in the winning position. Millie was the only person affronted by this absence of fair play: the rest of us were happy for the diversion, and the scientists were actually applauding. After missing his chance during the dining-room hailstorm Loewick had come prepared, with a necklace of cameralike measuring instruments. He was wearing shark-infested Bermuda shorts and a purple tie-dye T-shirt, out of which stuck limbs that looked as though they had just been used to stir paint. Altogether he resembled first-prize winner in a World's Most Obvious Tourist competition.

William was official scorekeeper, but his calculations could not be heard above Loewick, who squealed other figures from his dials each time Mavis produced a spectral quoit, and Evens, who noted them down then squealed new ones back at him. I had thought Mavis incapable of controlling her gift, and pointed this out to William, who'd told me so the day before.

"Nothing's changed, has it?" he replied.

"Well, she's making them quoits appear, isn't she? That looks like control to me."

"I suppose it *would* be. But they're not quoits, are they?"

"Aren't they?"

"No. They're snakes. Horribly poisonous ones, as it happens. But don't worry, they're too scared to bite anyone."

"What a comfort you are, Bill."

"Glad to be of help. Are you ready for your turn? The nutty professor's next, then you."

Professor Ryemann's throwing style was, in its way, more entertaining even than Mavis's. After curling his huge body in on itself like a hibernating bear, he sprang open, releasing the quoit, then stood with his arms outstretched Mosaically, as if waiting for the lawn to part before him. When his quoit had flown past the target and disappeared from sight he bellowed some ridiculous archaism, like "Zounds!" or "Odds-bodkins!" before stomping ground-tremblingly into the longer grass in search of his lost quoit.

I went to take my turn but Melvin had other plans. For him the lawn had become, after the fracas at breakfast, medieval lists; and like a latterday Lancelot he was going to use his skill to win back the hand of fair Maid Alison. It seemed an appropriate nom de guerre, in view of his troublesome skin. He barged me aside and knelt in front of his quoit. After throwing Alison a somewhat waterlogged smoldering look he began to concentrate on the little circle of rope. It rose and zig-zagged toward the target, but soon lost height. Melvin's face went blue, clashing with the stressed yellow peaks of his Himalayan acne. The quoit quivered mockingly.

"Forty-two point eight!" shouted Loewick.

"He hasn't scored yet," said William. Nor did he; the quoit fell to the grass, quickly followed by Melvin himself. Alison started to laugh, and Melvin gasped for air enough to insult her.

"Save your breath, Melvin," she said. "Fuck *me.* Is that what you're trying to say?"

He began to reply but fainted instead; nobody went to assist him. Alison's amusement was only skin-deep, and she turned onto her front to continue her solemn examination of the grass. "This afternoon . . . we'll be in the garden . . ." It was impossible. I had no plan, did not even know which direction led to freedom and which deeper into captivity. From where I stood, a dozen titanic security guards were visible, ringing the lawn. Lean black rifles hung from their shoulders. Who knew how many more were in reserve? I had no money, no transport; my only connection with the outside world was Benny Sweet's pink card, hidden in my underpants—though I wasn't sure he deserved the mystic power allotted by my imagination. Altogether I was certain that Alison's prediction was wrong. Perhaps I'd failed to spot a particularly cruel sense of humor.

"Wake up, Nick!" said William. "Your throw."

Carelessly I threw my quoit. To my surprise it hit the mark, disturbing one of Mavis's snakes. He hissed in the pissed-off manner anyone would if press-ganged from a peaceful Amazonian liana for quoit duty in rural England. William announced the new score: the scientists had no hope of catching us, so Ryemann took the opportunity to declare without too much dishonor.

"Ah, Fortuna smileth not upon the handmaidens of Einstein," he boomed. "The ingestion of portable potables and carryable comestibles would seem, now, a logical stratagem."

Mavis looked frustrated by this nonsense. I could sense a tantrum forming, with nowhere for us to shelter if it did.

"A picnic is what he means, Mavis," said John Whitehead, the blue-jeaned matinee-idol scientist.

"Why don't he bloody say so then?" asked Mavis reasonably.

"Because he's a mad old bastard," replied Whitehead in Ryemann's direction. Of the scientists he seemed the only one eligible to carry a certificate of mental good health, were such things required by law. Though I hadn't spoken to him at length we had exchanged many understanding raises of the eyebrows. I wondered how someone so

191

obviously of this world had come to work at Rose Cottage. While the picnic was being unpacked I decided to risk asking him.

"I can't tell you here, too many eager little ears. What about coming for a walk round the grounds? Professor?"

"Yes, lad?" Ryemann Tannoyed, though only six feet away.

"I thought I might show Nick around. He's not been on a tour yet."

"Splendid! Orientate, orientate," replied the ever-runic Ryemann, and went to dividing a game pie with a protractor and a machete. Whitehead grinned at me and led the way.

· · · · ·

I had wanted to pay close attention to the grounds, so that I would have some idea where to go, should Alison's prediction prove correct. In the event Whitehead's revelations were so startling that I was oblivious to my surroundings, except in the most general terms. We walked away from the lawn, through the long grass, and into some woods. Then Whitehead began to talk.

"The thing is, Nick, that I didn't exactly choose to come here. I was invited, like everybody else."

"Some party."

"Ah, well, the invitation wasn't exactly of the RSVP variety. I'm as much a prisoner here as you. More, really, because if I ever got out I'd soon find myself in an altogether less-agreeable establishment, courtesy of her majesty."

"I see. What have you done?"

"Nothing 'specially awful. I'm a very good chemist, but I didn't get a very good degree, so I didn't get a very good job, and so I started my own business."

"Sounds the perfect eighties enterprise. Did you get a development grant?"

"Well, not quite. It was a little factory. Just soft drugs, you know. No PCP or methadone, just acid, bombers, ecstasy. Saturday-night junk for Saturday night junkies. I still do, actually. Got to keep your hand in—want some speed?"

192

"No, no thanks. Drugs and my condition don't mix well."

"Just thought I'd ask. Anyway, when they caught me I got sentenced to fifteen years. Ever been inside a prison? They're not like they look on the telly. Honor among thieves seems to have died out, rather. Then I was visited by this little man who claimed to be from the prison education service, and I ended up here."

"For how long?"

"I don't ask. For the rest of my natural, I suspect. Unless I opt for the luxury lobotomy."

"Alison mentioned that. So it's true?"

"Definitely. They give it to all the military boys. They come here on a year's special posting from America, then when they go they're oper- ated on to clear their memories. It hardly seems necessary to me— most of them are so thick that a good shout in the ear would blow away any vestigial brain tissue. But you know the military, they do like to be thorough. Or thurrow, as they say."

We had come to a stream. On the far side was a fence made from an almost transparent mesh; it looked flimsy but lethal. Whitehead folded his long legs elegantly, like an undercarriage; I remained standing. My cartographic plans were shot to bits—I had no idea of which direction we had walked, or how far. Some water creature, a vole or a rat, popped through a hole in the bank. I felt violent toward it for its stu- pid, timorous freedom inside my prison.

"Are you all ex-cons here?" I asked.

"No, Professor Ryemann's merely a lunatic, in case you hadn't no- ticed. He set the place up—he *likes* it here. And there's a guy called Brink who you've not met yet. He's here because he found out a bit too much about a new weapons system the allies have developed."

"Christ. I didn't know we had gulags."

"Mustn't let the Russians get one over on us, must we? Anyway, I think he was quite glad to have the choice. He told me that several of his colleagues had topped themselves when they found out."

The water vole kept darting from his hole. I threw a stone at him, and missed. Two scientists' histories remained, and I could sense that it wasn't simple oversight on Whitehead's part that he hadn't ex- plained them. The question sat there, blocking all conversational exits, so I asked it.

"I was hoping you wouldn't," he said. "After all, you've got to work with them. It might make things a bit strained."

"They're strained already. Tell me the truth."

"All right. Sit down first."

I smiled at this bit of melodrama; Whitehead did not. So I sat down.

"What do you know about matter transference?" he asked.

"Nothing. Except 'Beam me up, Scotty.' "

"Good, then you know as much as anybody else. It's an impossibility, and always will be. But some scientists, the mad ones who read comics and play Dungeons and Dragons, believe they've cracked it. It's a bit of a twentieth-century philosophers' stone. Loewick and Evens thought they'd cracked it, too. And that's how they came to be here."

"And?"

"Oh, you don't want all the details do you? They're very tedious."

"There's no need to patronize me."

"I'm not patronizing you, I'm trying to spare you. Loewick and Evens won't do it again. You're quite safe with them."

"They won't do *what* again? Stop pissing me about."

"Are you sure you don't want some stuff? I do downers, you know."

I laughed at this, and the slight lightening of atmosphere seemed to give him his way into the tale. Still, he continued to affect the studied carelessness of someone about to tell an effective ghost story.

"Well, Loewick and Evens built some kind of machine. It was half successful, in that it did disassemble objects. If you think about it, that's not too hard—even a stick of dynamite does a good job *disassembling* things. However, those two imagined they were halfway to matter transference. Now, if you built a machine that only made things disappear, you wouldn't think you'd solved the problem, would you? And neither did Loewick and Evens. The trouble was that they *did* manage to make something reappear. Something, but not the same thing that had gone in. At that point they got very excited and waved bye-bye to their scientific principles, not to mention their sanity. They started putting live things through their machine. Dogs, mainly."

"And then they were arrested?" I said eagerly.

"Of course they weren't. Dogs are pretty expendable to scientists. And if you put a dog in one end of a machine and dog *meat* comes out the other, who knows what it was in the first place? No, dogs weren't their downfall. They put a kid through. And I don't mean a baby goat, I mean a baby person."

"Fucking hell. They just snatched some poor kid off the street and minced him? I don't believe this."

"They didn't snatch a kid off the street, they hadn't lost all touch with reality. They knew that would cause a fuss, a search. No, they used Loewick's daughter. And now you know."

Decently, Whitehead did not examine me for a reaction; he just stood up and began walking back through the wood. I suppose I should have thrown up, or screamed, or fainted. Instead I did the oddest thing: I ate a handful of grass. When I'd finished I took another, but found it wasn't needed. Whitehead was nearly out of sight, so I cast the grass on the breeze and hurried after him, still without my plan of the grounds.

· · · · ·

"That was a long walk, Whitehead," mumbled Loewick as we rejoined the picnickers. He had one end of a sausage hanging from his mouth and I was unable to prevent a Grand Guignol image from prancing across my mind. It looked like a child's limb.

"Well, you know what it is, Kevin. We were having such fun pulling the wings off butterflies that we just didn't notice the time."

Loewick, lolling on the grass, slightly drunk, with smeared lips and foody teeth, seemed the type of monster I had stopped believing in at age seven, along with Santa. Funny how angels and devils both disappear with the birth of morality. Suddenly I knew that Alison's prediction was right, that I would escape that afternoon.

Whitehead, for whom the horror had long dulled, set about eating some lunch. Considerately he prepared a plate for me, but it looked too vivid in the light of my carnal knowledge. Instead I smoked a cigarette and guzzled two bottles of hot beer. Everybody else lay on their backs beneath the buckling dome of the sky, except Ryemann who strode around like a father at the wrong wedding breakfast. I felt a

195

fleeting desire to take proper leave of all these people I'd hardly met; but already they seemed to be figures in a dream. Good-byes could draw me in for ever.

The professor's distressed meanderings led to a sudden outburst. "Ladies and gentlemen. The leather and the willow," he announced, as though about to sing a rustic ballad to lute accompaniment. There was a general complaint about this, except from Evens, who trolled off to fetch the cricket set. When he returned, Ryemann allocated positions in his orotund way, which seemed to take longer than some entire cricket matches. While he was doing so, William drew me aside.

"So, you're hopping it?" he asked, shadow bowling like all men of his type do the moment a cricket ball is in their hand.

"That's what Alison tells me, though God knows how."

"He might not, but we do. Ryemann's batting first. When he hits a six, which he usually does straight away—and he will today because I'll make it easy—you field it as normal. But, and this is the important bit, when you get to the ball, just keep on running. Savvy? We'll do the rest."

"What do you mean, keep on running? There are guards and probably an electrified fence."

"Oh yes, there are, both. You'll just have to trust us, and when you get to the gates, whatever you do, keep on running."

"I don't even know where the gates *are*. This is ridiculous."

"Don't be wet. Round the front of the house. Just follow the drive, it's not far—about two hundred yards."

Ryemann was calling us to the game. "Cheerio, Nick. All the very best of British," said William, sounding even more like Kenneth More than usual. He shambled away, polishing the ball on his trousers, and I felt the loss acutely. Then he turned and came hurrying back.

"Nick, I've got to say this. We're going to miss you. All of us, but me and old Joe especially. You don't know how grateful I am for what you did yesterday."

196 {

"That's all right. I didn't do very much."

"Well—thanks, that's all. You've really turned out a lot better than your father. Don't forget us, eh?"

It seemed a bit late in life for me to be having orphan fantasies, but as William ran to open the bowling I wished very much that he could have been my father instead of the dim, greedy snob I'd been given. For a moment I considered remaining at Rose Cottage, where human virtues seemed still to hold, but a sudden proud bellow of "Six!" from Professor Ryemann started the machinery of fate, and I was running.

Loewick, of course, was the first to understand my intention. No sooner had I run past the ball than he had broadcast my intentions to the guards. Crazy at the prospect of a lab animal escaping, he soon caught me and snapped shut his fingers on my rump. Though the flesh obliged with its stretching trick, allowing me to continue running, I was slowed enough for guards to take aim with their pretty rifles. I turned. Loewick was waterskiing across the lawn, holding reins made from my flesh. My energy was almost sapped with the effort of pulling him; then for no visible reason his legs were pulled out from below and he slurried to the ground, exactly as though he'd been rugby tackled.

"Well done, Joe!" I heard William shout as Joe became visible, his arms wrapped around Loewick's calves. The guards switched their attention from me to the wailing Loewick, and I used the diversion to dodge past them and around the front of the house.

The drive curved sharply to the left about a hundred yards ahead, obscuring whatever lay in wait. I picked up speed on changing from grass to shingle and soon rounded the bend, where I was met by enough firepower to stage a coup. Guards knelt, lay, crouched; tensed to discharge their years of training like athletes of death. I was surprised at my expendability, and as they took final aim decided to give myself up.

"Keep on running! Keep on running!" came the combined voices of Millie and Florrie in my head. It was probably their first successful performance, and it made me carry on, even as the fence loomed, impassably high, with no way through and the guards being ordered to fire, and the ground sloping away beneath me as I was flown over the fence and placed on the other side, running. It can only have been Melvin, doing somebody a good turn at last. Or perhaps he was having one more attempt on Alison's affection. Whatever, he had saved my life.

My troubles were hardly over, even if my body was. The guards soon grasped that I was on the other side of the fence and gave chase. They ran in step, ten or so of them, giving the impression of one huge pursuer. Fee, fi, fo, fum, I said to myself as the ground pulsed behind me, my sole consoling thought that at least they couldn't run and fire guns at the same time. But they were gaining—my own desperate energy was no match for their steak-fed motors. I'd had enough. It was a good try, plucky but foolish. Perhaps in a few years I'd get another chance. In the meantime there was at least physical comfort, and pleasant company. Or maybe I'd choose the operation and start a new life somewhere. God knew there wasn't much left for me in London. I slowed to a submissive trot, then an ataxic jog, then a halt. Then something happened.

First came the noise, from nowhere. The sound of a thousand broken trumpets, played as if by children—not for the music, but for the sound alone. The raucous power of it could have stopped any pursuers, but it was only a harbinger. A second later I watched the guards disappear amid a madding crowd of African elephants. The terrified animals' screams and brays were mixed with those of men. One fired his rifle, exciting the herd into a stamping frenzy, and I heard no more human noises. A thin red stream of Chateau GI trickled through the gravel, and I caught the gaze of a grizzled bull. He studied me dubiously: was I the cause of his family's misery, and if so, did I deserve to die? His single tusk showed he wasn't afraid of a fight. I was, though, and ran with all the sap left in me. I hoped that Loewick had his instruments ready, for Mavis had truly excelled herself.

At first it was just a small black beetle, crawling toward me across the perspectiveless fen. Drawing nearer, it more clearly became a London cab and I could hear its homely chug, then smell its rancid diesel on the prim rural air. I wondered why I'd bothered to hide in a ditch since escaping Rose Cottage, now that Benny Sweet was arriving in a vehicle less discreet than a camel in sunglasses and a fez.

In fact I'd seen nobody since escaping, so lying in the ditch had been my own bit of Len Deightonish skulduggery. When I'd made it away from the elephants and through the deceiving ring of poplar trees around Rose Cottage I'd been surprised to find myself in East Anglia. The flat land frightened me: it seemed like a game board, with myself as the only piece remaining to be taken. For a few minutes I had skaddled about in a panic, certain of being intercepted, hoping somehow to conceal myself with movement. By chance this technique had led me to a road and, like an apparition, a telephone box. I couldn't see why it was there, with no apparent community to serve (unless the field mice had relatives in America), but it was, and the grass outside it was trimmed, and inside there were blue carpet tiles.

Somebody drunk had answered Benny's telephone and refused to accept the charges. He'd found it extremely amusing, unlike the operator and myself, until he yelled with pain and Benny came on the line, full of apologies and Scotch. My begging speech went unsaid: he'd been awaiting my call and wanted only to know where I was—something easily provided by the IN CASE OF EMERGENCY notice in the plush box.

"Shall I bring Ashtray?" he'd asked.

"What? An *ashtray?* Why?"

"Never mind—just stay there, son. Benny's comin'!"

· · · · ·

And now he had. When the cab stopped nobody moved—Benny stayed in the back and the driver, who'd obviously had enough of this particular fare, rolled a lazy cigarette and sucked on it like the last man in an opium den. Just as his features relaxed and he began to resemble someone who might have a family and hobbies, Benny leaned forward.

" 'Ere, you! Knobhead! I ain't given you three ton to go rollin' fags— open my farkin' door!"

The cabbie visibly considered physical violence, but settled for a meaningful exhalation of smoke and did as he was told. Benny, after all, was old and eccentric: the cabbie could see that from his clothes. So could I: if his appearance at our first encounter had been offbeat, when he climbed from the taxi it was more off-*world*.

His hair was lashed with purple glitter gel, his eyelids with parrot-green shadow, and his beard obscured by Christmas "snow." But how drab they seemed, compared with his clothes. A quilted aluminum jacket with planelike shoulder pads hovered on his torso; plastic-mirror trousers wrapped his kinked old legs, making them look like vital plumbing from some gleaming machine; and on his feet were metalized platform boots set around with lights, like office blocks. I wasn't sure if he was taking off or coming in to land.

"What am I, then? Eh? What am I?" he asked, swaying on his illuminated foundations. "Go on. Guess."

I fumbled for a compliment. "Um . . ."

"Can't guess?" he said, hopefully.

"Not really," I admitted.

"Right. I'm a deus ex farkin' machina, ain't I?"

"Oh. Of course."

"Look, you knob end. I'm done up like a god, ain't I?"

"Are you? Which one?"

"Never mind *who*. I just *am*. And here," he said, indicating the taxi, "is my *machina*. Get it?"

The cabbie looked to me for confirmation that he wasn't going mad. I could offer nothing. Benny seemed pleased.

"Like me clobber, then?" he asked, smoothing down the lapels of his silver suit. "Got it at one of them charity auctions. Gary Glitter's his-self, it was, but I reckon it looks better on me. Don't you?"

I laughed. "Yes. I think it does."

"Yeah. Hang about, though. You ain't had the full effect yet," he said, tottering back inside the cab and re-emerging with a ghetto blaster the size of a small fridge. Touchingly, he couldn't find which button to push, and we got the shipping forecast from Radio Four before the music started. I'll admit to recognizing the song immediately: "Hallo! Hallo! I'm back again!" Despite my early attempts at cool, I sneakingly liked Gary Glitter in the early seventies. Now Benny, a man actually *in* his early seventies, mimed for our pleasure.

As he mouthed the words he wiggled his rickety bum at the cabby, then Betty Booped for unseen cameras. By the time he reached the second verse we were his. In reply to the song's question about us being good little girls I cried, "Yeah!" and so did the cabbie.

Benny pranced around, a Baco foil satyr, defying gravity to pull him from the Manhattanesque boots. He ripped open the jacket to tease with a chest wig like a barbershop floor, projected his groin for yards, and finished on one leg. Even then, when he fell over, he continued wiggling his electric boots at the sky. When I picked him up he seemed weightless. The cabbie had been applauding but Benny's fall brought him back to the world of roll-your-owns and mortgages.

" 'Ere you, my meter's still runnin'. You payin', are ya?"

"Piss off—you saw me money. I dunno, Nick, us artistes, eh? Don't nobody appreciate us no more?"

I carried the ghetto blaster to the cab. Benny went to follow, but not before doing a little encore, making constant reference to the time by holding out his wrist and waving his watch at the cabbie.

"See?" he said. "I'm pay-*in'*."

Before climbing into the taxi he blew a raspberry, then asked osten-tatiously, "Wanna go for a ride anywhere, Nick?" I knew he wanted me to help him tease the cabbie, and say "Timbuktu," but I was almost asleep.

"Home?" I offered. He looked disappointed.

"All right, then. 'Ome."

· · · · ·

"Faaarkin' Ada! I'll have that bastard Ashtray's guts for garters—'e's gone and drunk me dry, the guzzlin' gunt!" yelled Benny, slamming shut an arid drinks cupboard. He clattered off on his perpendicular boots, leaving me alone in the dusky room to contemplate the odd connectedness between us both. First there had been the business with the tramps at Marcus's warehouse party. Then when the taxi had arrived at Benny's house and he'd woken me up, I realized I'd seen it before.

Two years previously ZZD had won a big air-freshener account. I wasn't on the team but had gone with the creatives on their search for the right location. They were looking for somewhere blatantly smelly; somewhere—as the art director had put it—"with visual stench," the better to show the aerosol working its sweet miracle. Delhi was first choice, rejected for being tastelessly expensive, and nowhere closer offered the right qualities. The team reconciled themselves to shooting on set. But then someone discovered Spitalfields, a part of London barely touched by the nineteenth century, let alone the twentieth. They couldn't believe their luck: Georgian terraces, dying from within like beggars' mouths; real rot on the pavements—not just newspapers and chocolate wrappers, but vegetables, animals; and the whole area teeming with local color—thousands of Bengalis, layered in bursting sweatshops and swarming on the streets. It was a creative's gift. For less than a clapper loader's wages they got their location, the top floors of a "picturesquely subhuman" sweatshop; the workers grinned for the minimal baksheesh of immortality, and the aerosol is now brand leader.

Benny's house was next-but-one. I remembered how we'd squinted through the muddied windows, incredulous to find that it was someone's home and not another rickety machine for making money. What kind of lunatic chose to live in such a place, we'd wondered? And now I was sitting in the first floor of it, on a sofa upholstered in Turkey carpet, awaiting the return of the lunatic himself.

"Fooled the bastard!" he said, waving a full bottle of Scotch. "The one place 'e never looks is under the cover on me bath. You dirty Arab, Ashtray! Wanna snifter, Nick?"

"Please."

He tipped Scotch into serious tumblers and handed me one. "Still, we've all got a cross to bear, eh? Mine's Ashtray, the gunt."

"I forgot you had a friend called Ashtray. When you mentioned him on the phone I thought you meant a real ashtray."

" 'E is a real farkin' ashtray. You *wait.* Cheers!"

"Cheers. And thank you."

"No, don't go thankin' me. Not yet awhile, I ain't been paid yet."

"Oh. Um . . ." I patted the pockets of the dead farmer's trousers. "I don't actually have any money on me right now—but I could get hold of some. How much are we, er . . ."

He chuckled. "Not money, you knob. Somethin' else. You'll see, by the by. You'll see."

"Couldn't I see *now*?" I asked, wondering if Benny was leader of some press-gang for Help the Aged.

"Nope, you can't. So drink up." He poured himself more Scotch. My own swigging had hardly moved the contents of the crystal bucket.

"Like me gaff, then? Been here years, I 'ave. I used to call it squalor but now they tell me I'm a *New Georgian.* Two geezers come knockin' the other month, wanted to know if they could make a film. 'Oooh, Mr. Sweet,' one of 'em says, 'What lovely *dirt.* Do you apply it by brush?' 'Mmmm, yes,' says 'is pal, 'and how very *echt* to have your electricity supply removed.' *Echt?* What the bleeding 'ell's the meanin' of that? I told 'em to sling their 'ooks. Echt! Fark. 'Ere, give us an 'and with these boots."

He poked his tinned legs at me and I yanked at the oil platforms. The colored lights around the soles continued to flash.

"Pretty, ain't they?" he said. "I dunno how to turn 'em off."

"Shall I?"

"No, don't matter—leave 'em. Easier than lighting the candles. I'm not on the electric, see?"

"I can see it would spoil the atmosphere, rather."

"Atmosphere? *Bollocks.* It's the computers I don't care for. Don't like me name on 'em, do I? Reckon one day someone'll push the wrong button and we'll all disappear up some computer's arse'ole. More Scotch?"

I noticed that the bottle, which I assumed to be the only one remaining after Ashtray's binge, was two-thirds empty.

"No, I'm fine. Thanks."

"Go on, don't be polite. There's plenty more in me bath."

"Really, I've got lots left in this glass. But I'd like something to eat, if that's possible."

"Food? Never touch the stuff. Tell you what—I'll getcha a bit of fruit later, when we go round the market with the boys."

It was clear, from the way he concentrated on rubbing his feet and drinking his Scotch, that he was not going to reveal his plans for me. I knew that I was free to walk away if I chose: but what to? My own world had been changing, even as I left it, and was certain to have become more hostile since. For all I knew a media caravan remained encamped outside my flat, emissaries of Rose Cottage lurked in the lobby with silent weapons, Herman Coprolite had arranged a European tour, and Lucy was married to Marcus, expecting twins.

My stomach was complaining. I shut it up with a burning slug of whisky. For some reason I had nothing to say: the impetus was all with Benny, who continued rubbing at his girlish feet. Lit by the single spear of evening sun which pierced the plankton of dust in the ancient air, his preposterous getup gave him a mysterious dignity, like an alien sage. Or perhaps it was hunger, whisky, and my having seen *The Day the Earth Stood Still* once too often. Whatever, when he finished fiddling with his toes, leaned back, and looked at me, I was prepared for the solution to the enigma of life. At least.

204

"Farkin' athlete's foot. Drives me barmy. You ever 'ad it? Terrible."

"No, I haven't," I said frustratedly. I wanted an end to mysteries.

"Don't wannit, neither. Take my advice—always wear plimsolls to the swimming . . ."

"Benny."

"That's me."

"Yes. Who are you?"

He went to rub his foot again, but didn't. "Yeah, you're right. 'Bout time. Good question. I ain't sure meself, sometimes . . . I've done so much, been so many people . . . I mean, I am Benny Sweet, I ain't no con merchant—but it's funny how many lives you can fit in one stupid monicker. The full version is Benedict *Erasmus* Sweet, by the by. Anyway, I shuffled on me mortal coil in 1916, in 'Ong Kong, where me old man worked for Jardine's. They 'ad plenty of dough, so they did the sensible thing and packed me off to school the minute I could walk. Prep school first, then Eton."

Here he paused, waiting for the gasp of surprise that this part of his story had probably caused many times before. But I was prepared to believe anything about his origins; a stable in Bethlehem would not have been entirely out of the question. However, he wasn't going to continue without some reaction from me, so I raised my eyebrows.

"Knew that'd shock ya, didni? Eton. Not for long though, 'cos when I'm fourteen I get a telegram. 'Orrible things, telegrams. Never 'ad a good 'un in me life. I can still remember the exact words. FATHER LOST STOP RETURN POST HASTE STOP MAMA STOP, it said.

"Now when she said *lost* she don't mean they couldn't find him, she means lost to *opium.* Very common in them days—they did it for a bit of relaxation, on account of their jobs. Like them boys I see today, round the corner in the City. I can see it in 'em. Terrible things, drugs . . . ," he downed another quarter pint of Scotch, ". . . terrible. Things never got no better. Me old man was a vegetable—an 'appy one, mind you—we lost all our money and then me old woman cracked up under the strain and done 'erself in. And do you know how?"

I prompted again, with a wide-eyed shake of the head.

205

"I'll tell ya. By lickin' the numbers off playing cards, that's 'ow. Yep. Full of arsenic. Took her months. Funny, eh? And shall I tell you what was funnier? Her name was *Patience.*

"So there I was, in 'Cng Kong, with no mum and a mad dad. Then one day me uncle arrives from England to take the situation in 'and. What an 'orrible old bastard 'e was—I weren't goin' back with 'im, was I? So I took a job on a ship.

"Now, what was I saying about telegrams? The ship got one—or whatever it is ships get. Cables? It got a cable, sayin' that the company what owned it 'ad gone bust. So we put in at the nearest port, Port Elizabeth in South Africa. I tell ya—them coons reckon they got a bad deal now? You should've seen it then! I saw a geezer—one of them Dutch bastards, I'm glad to say—make a coon lay down on a patch of mud so's 'e could walk over 'im and not get 'is shoes dirty! That is gospel.

"So I got out, toot sweet. Came back to Blighty. I'd 'ad me education —not a lot, but more than most in them days, and I'd learned a bit about real life an' all—so I got a job in a bank. Did that for quite a bit, I did. It was me normal period. Even got engaged to a lady of the opposite sex. But it was no good—I mean, can you see me as a married bank manager?"

I tried to picture this man, dressed like a transvestite turkey, dandling grandchildren or withholding my overdraft.

"Not really."

"There you go. No, 'Go west young man,' I said to meself. So I did— *well* west. Texas. And *that* is 'ow I come by a bit of the foldin' stuff. I was what they called a wildcatter—I looked for oil. Most of 'em doin' it was just fools or nutters, but *I* weren't. I struck it lucky an' found some oil—farkin' *loads,* if you wanna know. It weren't all mine—I was in a syndicate—but enough was. An' I didn't piss it all up the wall, like some. No sir, I kept it. You thought I was talkin' bollocks when I said I was an oil millionaire, didn't ya? Well I *was*! I ain't no millionaire. But I ain't broke, neither. So drink up, I'm goin' for a piss an' another bottle."

206 { The original bottle wasn't quite empty, but Benny had obviously planned to leave me alone at this point. I needed an interval to take things in. When he returned he was wearing a sailor's cap which said HMS BLEAN.

"So guess what I did next. Go on, guess."

To please him I pretended I couldn't. He danced a hornpipe.

"Now d'ya know?"

"Um . . . you were in the war?"

"Correct! Splice the mainbrace!" he said, waving a bottle of navy rum.

"I won't mix them, if you don't mind."

"No, you're right—bad idea on an empty stomach. I found this, if you wannit," he said, producing from within his jacket a giant bacillus masquerading as an orange. "A bit moldy. But I thought . . ."

"Thank you, I can wait."

"Yeah, we're goin' out soon. Anyway, the war. I was in Texas when it broke out, an I s'pose I could've dodged it, but them Krauts—what a shower, eh? So I did me bit for king and country, till the second time we got torpedoed. I bust both me eardrums and got invalided out. What did you think of me singin', by the by? No—stow it, I know—an' ever since then, 1942, I've pleased meself. An' that, in my opinion, is all that's worth doin' in this life. Cheers!"

He drank dark rum from the bottle while I eyed the furry orange and wondered how long it would be before we went out.

"Oh yes, I've been in some scrapes," he continued, "and that brings us back to you, don't it?"

"Do it—I mean—does it?"

"Well, if you ain't in a scrape, I'm a monkey's uncle. Or don't this 'orrible illness what you've got bother you?"

"Oh, I'm getting used to it. Besides, how do you know?"

" 'Ow do I *know?* You're famous! You been in the paper every five minutes, an' whenever I seen a telly you ain't been off that. The coppers want you, on account of some damage you did . . ."

"Not that bloody hole in the road?"

"That was it. An' some geezer called Copper . . . Coper . . . ?"

"Coprolite."

"Yep. Says 'e's your manager. An' I don't mind bettin' them scientist blokes you were telling me about are after you an' all. So that's 'ow I know. *Now* d'ya fancy a drop o' Captain Morgan's?"

I loathe dark rum; I get a hangover *while* I'm drinking it. But I agreed.

"Have you seen my girlfriend in any of the papers? Lucy—she's quite small . . ."

"Nope, definitely not."

"Oh. Or any of my friends? Marcus Trilling, for instance—he's the presenter of *Simply Trilling*?"

"Now that *do* ring a bell. Short-arsed fatso?"

"That's him. He's a very good friend of mine, actually."

"Is he now? That is interestin'."

"Why?" I asked with an eager smile.

" 'Cos he says you ruined some big party, an' that you owe 'im money for somethin', an' that 'e always thought you was weird."

"I hardly . . . I really . . ." I sighed. Benny took off his sailor's cap, placed it on the floor, and shook the fake snow from his beard.

"Not very 'appy, are you, son?"

"No, Benny, I'm not."

"No. But don't worry. Come alonga me. Meet the boys."

ooooooooo E I G H T E E N ooooooooo

For my sake, not wishing to draw unnecessary attention, Benny had changed out of his silverwear and into a relatively discreet outfit of hobnail boots, Biggles helmet, and fluorescent orange flying suit. I was the one decked out as the more convincing tramp, in laceless plastic shoes, vomit-stiff Crimplene trousers, and a beer-soaked old roué of a jacket.

While Benny progressed with another of his odd dances, a sort of goose-stepping minuet, I had adopted (unconsciously) a hopeless shamble. Thus two tramps—one young, beaten, ruined, the other old, alive, orange—moved through the bright summer darkness of Spital-fields. I looked back up the street, now surprisingly quiet after the populous day, where the boot lights still flickered on the first floor of Benny's house.

"Jack the Ripper done 'is business round 'ere," he said, indicating a pub of the same name on the corner. I asked if that was where we were meeting his friends. "Fark, no. We're banned. We're meetin' the boys up the market. Come on, this way."

As if to taunt the ghost of the Ripper a preposterously obvious hooker stood outside the pub, wearing dominatrix stilettoes and a skirt as concealing as a perished elastic band.

"'Allo Benny," she called, "lovely night for it!"

"For what, Vera?" he chuckled.

209

"Yeah," she said, stamping her feet naughtily. *"Yeah!"*

"Fings don't change, eh?" he said when we had moved on. "Come up 'ere for the lorry drivers, they do. Poor cows. I used to give 'em money once, but it don't do no good. They ain't poor, see? They just can't 'andle money more than one day at a time."

This novel analysis of the vice problem kept me thinking for the next few yards, while we crossed the road amid maneuvering lorries arriving with their produce. Several drivers called out greetings to Benny, who replied to each by name. Once across he led me into the vaulting iron halls of the Edwardian fruit market, where his first act was to approach one of the traders and get me the promised fruit. He returned with an entire branch of bananas slung over his back, like a side of meat.

"Here y'are! Bit o' fruit."

Daintily I plucked one.

"Well, that's no farkin' good, is it? I'm only little—you take the bastards. I only got 'em for you!"

"Yes, of course," I said, lifting the plantation onto my back. In truth I was no longer hungry—the smell of rotting fruit in the covered market had smothered my appetite—but I undid and ate a banana, to keep Benny happy.

Suddenly he was off, dancing between the towers of crates, beckoning me and my load to follow as best we could. Then he disappeared behind a stand. When I got there he was nowhere to be seen. I called his name.

"Over 'ere, you knob!" he said, very close but still invisible. I peered around from beneath my fruity carapace. "Through 'ere! Where the walls join!"

There was a small gap, not much more than a foot wide, between the original wall of the market and some later addition. Its narrowness gave me the excuse to dump Little Jamaica before I could squeeze through, into the oddest gentleman's club since the Round Table.

By an architectural accident a sort of room had been created. Four corners formed a tall space, like the inside of a square chimney. Four maroon leather armchairs, a card table, and even a Christine Keeler cocktail bar had been placed there. And in the chairs, lit by an Argand lamp, sat "the boys."

As is the way with many clubs, nobody acknowledged the presence of a stranger, and Benny was content to stand aside, letting me take in the scene. There were three men. Two were holding a sort of conversation. It seemed very drunken, though I could see no alcohol. The first would say "Frazier, cunt, *Frazier*," while the other repeated "Ali, *bastard*, Ali." Both men were small, not much taller than Benny—though fatter—and tramping had somewhat blurred the physical distinctions between them. But one, the one favoring Ali, seemed familiar. My first thought was that he, like Benny, had been abused at Marcus's warehouse party, but then I felt sure he had not been there. It was something else—the feeling that I actually *knew* him.

Before I could get a fix on him, my attention was drawn by a series of bullfrog-shaming belches emanating from the last man, who sat away from the other two. I looked over in time to see three lighted cigarettes shoot from his mouth, through the air, into a distant bucket. Instantly he lit two more and blew some classy smoke rings before manipulating the cigarettes into his mouth using only tongue and lips. For a moment he calmed, lowering his eyelids like hydraulic doors, but a second later his eyes, mouth, nostrils snapped open terrifyingly and with another belch he projected the burning cigarettes into the bucket. This, I supposed, was Ashtray.

Benny stood laughing, as though this were the first time he'd seen the performance. Ashtray began laying Swan Vestas along his thigh, in preparation for some unspeakable encore.

"No, don't, not now," said Benny. "Meet me mate."

Ashtray put the matches back in their box, then stood up to shake my hand. He was the only man of full height and close up I could see the effects his hobby had wrought. His hands were hatched with new burns and old scars; his face, as befitted a human flue, was choked and sooty. For all that he looked as though he'd enjoyed doing this terrible damage to himself.

211

"Nick, this is Ashtray," said Benny.

"Thank God for that," I said to Ashtray. "For a minute I thought you might only have been the warm-up."

He grinned, exposing teeth like Turkish toilets. " 'E's all right!" he said to Benny.

The other two men were making slow progress with their discussion of boxing. They still shouted "Ali" or "Frazier," though more vehemently than before; and then it seemed they would settle the argument with a little boxing of their own. As they struggled from the chairs and took up stance, Benny waded in.

"All right, you two gunts! I don't want no fightin' tonight. It was *Frazier,* Nobby. All right?"

Nobby, the man I felt I recognized, froze midpunch.

"It were *Ali!* 'n your cunt an' all! You wanna fight? I'll avva fight!"

Although his remarks had been addressed to Benny he turned to me, dukes raised. He was that type who had been spoiling for fights all his life but never got one. Like the cowardly lion, he wasn't worth beating. I stared him down, as generously as possible, and he went over to the corner to take a pathetically flagrant piss. The other man had adopted a hand-wringingly ingratiating manner when he'd noticed Benny. Throughout our exchange with Nobby he'd sucked his teeth and clicked disapprovingly. Now he scraped like a probationary footman.

" 'Allo Ben, 'allo mate, sorry bout that, I tried to tell 'im, sorry 'bout that . . ."

"At ease, Spike," said Benny. "This is Nick."

Spike was cringing so deeply that I almost had to kneel to shake his hand. Once this formality was over he did straighten a little, though he kept his eyes focused above my head.

"Have you, er, been tramping long, sir?" he asked in a new voice, a sort of batman posh.

"Not long, no."

"I see, sir. And how is you finding the life?"

"S'all right, Spike," interrupted Benny, " 'e ain't Viscount Montgomery. Just come an' sit down."

· · · · ·

There was no spare armchair, and Benny's friends asserted their rights by sitting down before me. I stood to one side, quite content to be alone. When Benny noticed this he turned to Nobby.

"You're in disgrace, you. So get up and let Nick sit down. Go an' get us some bottles."

Nobby moved past me to the bar, flashing a look that might have been frightening, had I not been so fascinated by it. His face had a soft-focus malevolence I recognized perfectly, but from where, or whom, I simply could not tell. It was as though he were just too familiar to register, in the way one can fail to recognize one's father in the street, or oneself in a mirror.

Spike and Ashtray said nothing while Benny told them my story. They nodded gravely throughout, accepting matter-of-factly another biography from the Twilight Zone. Ashtray, after all, was the man who Benny once told me imagined triple-uddered radioactive cows, and the prime minister copulating alfresco in Whitehall.

When the tale was told, Benny hollered at Nobby for the belated booze. There was a long pause. Spike and Ashtray gave each other a nervous look.

"Ain't none," said Nobby.

"What! I gave you a ton yesterday to get some in! What 'ave you done with it?"

Nobby surled. "Spennit," he said, his stone cladding falling away to reveal the pitiable council-built personality beneath.

"Well?" demanded Benny. "What *on?*"

"Postal orders."

"Postal orders?"

Nobby's soft little lips vibrated with trapped tears. "Yeah! Fuckin' postal orders, you cunt!" he shouted, and ran off into the market. Benny removed his flying helmet and looked into it, as if for an explanation.

"Well," he said, "I've 'eard it all now. What's 'e want postal orders for?"

213

"If I could, Ben, like . . ." muttered Spike, ". . . they was for 'is boy. It was the kid's birthday, see . . ."

"The kid? The *kid*! From what I've 'eard, Nobby's boy is thirty years of age, an' fuckin' loaded! 'E ain't even *spoke* to Nobby for ten years! Fark, I dunno."

"Yeah, right, you're right, Ben, mate. But y'know, Nobby feels cut up about it, y'know, it's 'is boy . . . and well . . . no, you're right, mate, you're right . . ."

Benny sighed. "If I live to be twenty-one again I won't understand that bloke. Anyway, it's done now. Spike, you come with me up Liverpool Street. Nick, you stay 'ere with Ashtray. You'll 'ave to suck your tongues till we get back. Come on, Spike."

The two men went off, Benny trotting and Spike serfing along behind, virtually on all fours. Which left me alone with Ashtray.

· · · · ·

We sat, finger-drumming on the arms of our chairs. Unlike Spike and Nobby there were remnants of a social creature in Ashtray. Once, I felt sure, club-chair conversation had come easily to him, perhaps in an officers' mess somewhere. Now his only interface with the larger world was his talent with cigarettes; a talent that probably drew the attention of many passersby while producing few invitations to dinner. Beneath his tarred, scarred surface—more like a road than skin—there remained a handsome man of the sock-suspenders-and-Brylcreem sort chastely dreamed about by entire Women's Institutes. But the road surface took a lot of imagining away. His sticky dirt looked about as attractive as midsummer flypaper.

After a couple of minutes' searching for an opening gambit, all I could manage was, "Have you known Benny long?"

Before he answered, Ashtray went on a prolonged scratching expedition to the Valley of the Buttocks. Then he said, "Yeah. 'Bout three weeks."

"Three weeks?" I echoed, unable to conceal my surprise.

"Three weeks is a long time when you ain't got no 'ome."

"But if Benny's lived in that house all these years . . ."

"He ain't. Nobody lived in that house till three weeks ago. It was derelict."

Now it was my turn for a scratch. I settled for my head.

"Benny told me he'd lived there for years. He told me his whole story. Hong Kong . . . the war . . ."

"The war?" laughed Ashtray. "That's funny! Benny ain't never fought no war."

"But I . . . He told me he'd been in the navy. He showed me his cap."

"What, *HMS Blean?* That's mine."

"He might have been in the war, though," I said emphatically. Somehow I didn't want reality moving underfoot yet again.

"Listen," said Ashtray, leaning into my face and fixing me with his tarry breath. "I'm tellin' you, 'cos I know. Ain't nobody ever seen Benny Sweet round here till three weeks ago. I don't know who he is. Don't even know *what* he is. But he's always got plenty of booze and he don't mind spreadin' it about. Now, call me a liar."

I could see that Ashtray was desperate to believe in the miracle of Benny. He didn't want to start picking at the story, in case it should unravel and leave him naked. But I couldn't let it alone: Ashtray only stood to lose his supplier of free drink; I was trying to keep my whole life in one piece. So I carried on.

"But who do you think he is?"

"I don't. Fucking. Care."

"Aren't you even curious? This man comes out of nowhere—does all these things for you, but doesn't want anything back. Don't you want to know *why*? Aren't you even curious?"

"Curious?" laughed Ashtray sarcastically. "You know what curiosity is? A luxury, that's what. A luxury you can afford when you don't spend all your time workin' out how you can get to the next day. And even if I could afford it I wouldn't bother—'cos that's the other thing about curiosity. It killed the fuckin' cat. Right?"

His fear had begun to turn to anger. I could see I was risking one of those violent outbursts we always half-expect from street people; the outbursts that never seem to happen, except in our nightmares and the Sunday newspapers. Still I pressed on.

"But if he came from nowhere, Ashtray . . . he'll probably go away again . . ."

"I'll BELT you in a minute!" he shouted, trembling. "I KNOW he's goin' away, don't I? I'm a drunk, not a fuckin' idiot!"

"But if you know . . ."

"Oh, Christ! You're the reason why he's goin'! Ain't you worked that out yet? He said you'd 'ad a proper education! You're as thick as shit! You're the reason. All this is somethin' to do with you! So now you're 'ere he'll be goin' soon, won't he?"

I didn't carry on. Not because his potential violence really threatened me: in the end he was a wrecked old drunk and I was not; but because I saw the truth in his little speech about curiosity. It *was* a luxury, and I'd indulged it too far at his expense. He was wrong, though, about me being stupid. I was merely confused. Benny made as much sense to me as to him. Less. My mind could produce nothing but banal explanations of the man's identity. A long-lost relative? A curator of extraordinary human phenomena? A supersubtle version of Herman Coprolite? A mystery, that was all I knew.

An atmosphere of loss had come between us since Ashtray's outburst. I had made him look into the void and now he sat, staring wild-eyed and angry. I felt ashamed, but incapable of breaching the chasm.

Finally it was he who broke the atmosphere by producing his cigarettes. He held the pack in his left hand, flicked his fingers underneath, and launched two cigarettes to his mouth. Then he took a gas lighter and, cupping his hands tightly, filled the receptacle thus formed with butane. In a swift movement he drew his hands to his face and ignited their contents. A jet of flame burst from his fingers and the cigarettes were alight. I clapped. He shook his head to indicate there was more to come.

"Benny don't like me doin' this next bit, 'cos it goes wrong, sometimes. But I'm all right tonight. Watch."

He opened his mouth wide. The cigarettes hung from his lips like tusks. He breathed out all his air, sucked it back, and the cigarettes were gone. I looked around for them, but Ashtray pointed to his throat. Smoke drifted from its carbonized depths and there, glowing like the eyes of some infernal dog, were the tips of the cigarettes. I applauded again. Ashtray bowed; smiled; bowed again; and began to choke.

I thought at first that it was a hoax, that he would writhe around for a while before producing the cigarettes from his ears, or another unexpected orifice. When he had writhed for a minute, and longer, I saw that he was in real trouble. By then it was too late: he went into spasm, vomiting a rill of bloody tar. A second later he stopped breathing.

I had always imagined that when I met my moment for performing the kiss of life the urgency of the situation would blind me. After all, kissing a corpse is no fun, no matter how attractive it looked when walking. When I'd had that conversation ("But what if it was your mother? Yurk! Or your grandmother? Yeech! Or your grand*father*? Yeeargh!") I'd always insisted that it wouldn't matter. One simply wouldn't notice at the time. Ashtray, however, was living—*dying*—proof of the uselessness of theories. There he lay, a lavatory with lung cancer. I wouldn't have touched him with a bargepole. I wouldn't have touched somebody *else* touching him with a bargepole. And somehow, if I were to prevent his death, I had not merely to touch him, but to put my mouth over his: an orifice less alluring than an arsehole in a land without paper.

I knelt over him. No, I'll admit it—I ran around yelling my head off for a while, and *then* I knelt over him. First I had to clear his mouth of gory sludge, a substance that looked like the result of a collision between an oil tanker and a butcher's van. There was nothing to clear it with, so I had to use my fingers. How do people store such stuff within them and *live*? I wondered as I scooped out the stinking bitumen. When that was done I had a proper view of Ashtray's mouth. Lucky me. There was no trick I could use, no technique to displace reality. My senses were about to take an assault course in a sewer.

Tearfully I took a deep breath and clamped my mouth over his. When I removed it I realized that I hadn't actually had the courage to breathe *out* again, so I repeated the process. Ashtray remained ungratefully lifeless. I did it again, and this time something positive happened. I threw up. My half-empty stomach made it a dainty puke. Compared with Ashtray's industrial effluent, my own tablespoon of mashed banana looked like Fortnum's baby food.

I set to my grim task again. After several minutes of virtual coprophagia I sat back to look at my reward for effort. It was, undoubtedly, the corpse of Ashtray. Filthy, sick, exhausted, raw, and weeping, I beat the bastard on his chest; not in a last effort at resuscitation, but to punish him for not having had the decency to wake up and say thanks. My frustrated wailing masked the return of Benny and Spike.

Far from seeming shocked at the sight of his dead friend, Benny came steaming over in a rage.

" 'As that farkin' stupid bastard been doin 'is suck-'em-down-the-throat trick again?"

"Yes. He was only trying to entertain me—I didn't know it would . . . he's dead . . ."

"Dead! Gunt! Sit 'im up. Sit 'im up!"

I propped Ashtray's torso, which rose in an eerie, cantilevered way. Benny kicked him square between the shoulder blades, and he came alive. Without so much as a cough he stood up and wiped the remaining gurk from his mouth.

"Sorry, Ben," he said. "I know I shouldn't do it, but I thought, what with Nick bein' new . . ."

" 'Ow many times 'av I gotta say it? You're too farkin' old for that. Your lungs ain't what they was. Right?"

"All right, Ben, I won't do it again."

"Nah," said Benny, "not till the next time, eh?"

· · · · ·

When Benny asked what I had done while Ashtray appeared to be dying, and I told him, he refused to believe me.

"What, you put your gob over . . . nah! That's 'orrible! We better get you down the 'ospital for a tetanus injection. Did you 'ear that, Ashtray? Nick gave you the old kiss of life."

Ashtray showed off his mouth, by way of a smile. I couldn't believe what I'd done either, but it was wrong to suggest I might need a tetanus injection. Chemotherapy was nearer the mark.

"Ta, Nick," said Ashtray. "That was decent. I'm chuffed. Anytime I can do the same for you, just give us a shout."

"I can't see 'im wanting *that* in an 'urry," said Benny, "but 'e do need a bit of 'elp, as it 'appens. Don't ya, Nick?"

"Well, I suppose . . ."

"Suppose? Farkin' Ada! You got no mates, no bird, no job, and worst of all you're a farkin' human cartoon. Now, do you need 'elp or what?"

"All right. Of course I need help. But what can you do?"

"Ah, see, I got it all figured out, 'aven't I?"

"Have you?"

"Yurp. Me 'n' the boys is gonna give you a party!"

"A party? How the hell will that help? I told you what happened at the last one."

"But this 'un'll be different. F'ra start it'll be at my gaff, and when it's all done I guarantee you'll be all right. I guarantee!"

"Can I serve the booze, Ben? Can I do that?" asked Spike.

" 'Course ya can. An' Ashtray can swallow as many farkin' fags as 'e likes, an' Nobby is gonna be a very special guest, if we ever find the silly tosser. In the meantime, Spike, fetch some more of that booze we just bought. I ain't even a quarter cut yet, never mind 'arf."

Spike scraped off to fetch drink, and I attempted to press Benny further on the subject of the party. But he was at his most annoyingly coy. All my questions were met with winks, sly taps of the nose, strokes of the beard, and, mostly, unrefusable demands to knock back more alcohol. Within ten minutes I was too drunk to be inquisitive about anything except the location of my mouth.

· · · · ·

I awoke, what felt like ten years later, with an intensive-care hangover. Daylight played on my eyelids, delicately as a chainsaw, and when I managed to unglue my mouth to yawn a gust of cryptic air farted forth. Actually opening my eyes was too painful to contemplate, but I braved a glance through gummed lashes and saw that a man in a chalkstripe suit was standing at the foot of the bed. For a moment I thought that some fresh misfortune had befallen me, that I'd been kidnapped by a City consortium, perhaps to be floated on the stock market by lunchtime. Then he spoke.

"Good morning. I represent the unfortunate Mr. Taig's solicitors," he yarred.

"What? I am the unfortunate Mr. Taig," I said, sitting up, screaming with headache, and lying down again.

The man laughed. It didn't match his suit.

"'Ad ya fooled there, didn't I?" said Benny.

To confirm the truth I cranked open one arthritic eyelid. It was Benny. Just. The suit was shock enough, but he had gone the whole way. His hair was neat on his head and missing entirely from his chin. I gasped gangrenously.

"Good, eh? Look, I even got a buttonhole," he said, poking the rose in his lapel at me. "'Av a smell, go on."

"I've already got a smell, thank you."

"Yeah, you 'av a bit. Bit like stale booze an' a bit like Ashtray."

Sour stomach contents clawed up my esophagus at this reminder of what I'd previously managed to forget.

"What you need," said Benny with a pointed sniff at his rose, "is an 'air of the dog."

"What?" I moaned. There were at least five dogs inside me already. Dead ones. "I need morphine."

"Course ya don't. Sit up. You'll be right as rain in a minute."

"I can't sit up. Fetch me a priest."

"Dear oh dear. It's only an 'angover, you ain't dead."

"No, it's worse. I think I'm undead."

"Look, just drink this an' I promise you'll feel better," he said. "It's a glass of Benny Sweet's special formula pick-you-up."

I could not bring myself to look at his remedy, but God, thoughtfully, had heightened my sense of smell.

"It stinks," I said.

"No worse than you do. Just drink it. There's nothin' terrible, just tomato juice, egg . . ."

"All right, all right! If you promise not to say what's in it, I'll drink it."

"Good boy. Open your gob, then, an' I'll give ya the glass."

I did as I was told. The drink certainly did pick me up. By the hair. Then it plucked out my guts and blowtorched them, before removing my brain, passing it through a blender, and reinserting it via my nostrils. My tongue rattled in my head like a clapper. Gases from the dawn of time parped frankly from all exits, roaring and fizzing from fissures I didn't know existed. I felt like something about to be launched. I was dying. I was dead . . . and it was over.

"There you go," said Benny. "Never fails."

"Except when the patient dies, perhaps?" I asked, patting at my body to ensure it was still there.

"Nah, nobody's ever died. Anyway, you can 'av a look at me disguise now you're better. Good, eh?"

It was. Perfect, in fact: the trousers were just beginning to shine at the seat. Benny could have walked into any London solicitors' office, sat down to work, gone for a business lunch with his colleagues, and never have been noticed at all. The question was why he'd adopted the look at all.

"Obvious, innit? If I'm givin' you a party I'll 'ave to 'ave your address book. An' that is in your flat. I can't go there in me usual gear, can I?"

"You weren't serious about this party? What the hell will it achieve?"

"You want all this aggro to finish, don't you?"

"Of course. It's just I don't see how a party will help anything."

"Nope. And you won't, neither. Not right till the moment."

"What moment?"

"The moment when you get better."

"Benny, I don't mean to sound ungrateful, but could you stop being so fucking mysterious?"

He rolled his eyes, mysteriously, and pressed his fingers to his lips. I'd had enough. "You silly old goat!" I yelled. "I don't know who you are, or what your plans are, or why we met, but I do know one thing: you are not a doctor! And I've got a physical *illness* that's turned me into Mickey fucking Mouse and you're proposing to give me a fucking *party*? I DON'T WANT A PARTY! Do you hear? I don't want one!"

He took it with smiles. "You're the worst so far, you know," he said in a voice halfway between his own and the suit's. "The most awkward."

"The worst *what* so far?" I sulked, a little guilty now that my anger was vented.

"The worst toon-o, of course. You're not the first, you know. Just the worst case."

"You expect me to believe that? People turn into cartoons every day of the week, I suppose?"

"Nah, more like once a year. In a place like London, anyway. New York's worse, I 'ear—though it ain't my patch as such. An' Los Angeles is the world center for it. You're a very bad case, though. Like I said."

I snorted. "And who are you? The ghost of Walt Disney?"

He ignored me. "As a rule, when I 'ear about one, I find 'im—or 'er, though it's more often a bloke—and I 'ave a chat with 'em. Then they get better."

"I see. You have a chat, then they get better. How cozy. Why don't you prove it and have one of your nice little chats with me? You're raving mad."

"Well, I were goin' to. But I soon saw it wouldn't 'elp. I can't just tell ya, can I? You gotta find out for yourself."

"Christ almighty! Why don't you just sing 'The Impossible Dream' and have done with it?" I yelled. "Find out for yourself, follow your quest—what utter crap! I've lived next door to a dead hippy for three years, Benny, and if he's an example of 'finding yourself' I'd rather stay lost."

"Anyway," he went on, unperturbed, "that's why I'm throwin' the party. Now could you tell me 'ow I can get into your flat?"

His eyes looked cleaner than ever that morning, and when I looked into them there was neither approval nor disapproval. Only honesty. I mumbled instructions for finding my hidden doorkeys at Brecon Mansions.

He thanked me, then straightened his tie to leave. As he opened the door I called him back.

"Can't it wait?" he asked.

"I don't think it can, no."

"But I know what you're gonna ask, and I ain't got time."

"What am I going to ask?"

"Oh, you're gonna say you're sorry for shoutin' at me . . . then you're gonna say: Who are you? Where did you come from?"

"Benny, I'm sorry for shouting at you. Who are you? Where did you come from?"

He sighed. Shrugged. Sat down on the bed.

"You'll only shout at me again."

"I won't. I promise. I just want to know."

"Well, let me see . . . what d'ya fancy? Shall I say I'm an angel? 'Ow about a wizard? I already *told* you what I am."

"When?"

"Yesterday, if you think about it. When I got out of the cab."

"I can't remember. What did you tell me?"

"It'll come back to you . . . but anyway, it don't matter. See, there's nothing to tell, in the end. I am what I *am* . . ."

"Oh, Jesus. You're Gloria Gaynor."

He laughed at that, but came no closer to an explanation. After perhaps a full minute he spoke.

"Trouble is, see, I've only ever told you the truth. But you don't wanna know. What can I do?"

I remembered a moment, weeks earlier, when Lucy had challenged me similarly. "Prove it," she'd said. And I hadn't been able to. When I'd tried I was believed even less, though I'd never been more honest in my life. Remembering all that, I propped myself up in bed and said to Benny, "Prove it."

He smiled. "Made your 'angover go away, didn't I? 'Ow much proof d'ya want? And anyway, what is it you want me to prove?"

"That you're not just a mad old tramp who happens to have a lot of money and spare time. That you really can help me."

"Well, like I said—you're the only one who can do anything about that."

"All right—forget that. Prove the first part. Show me you're not just a rich wino."

"All right," he said, simply, folding his hands in his lap.

"Well?" I demanded.

"There," he replied.

"Whe—"

223

In the corner of the room stood a pillar of light, around six feet high.

It had a quality quite unlike any light I'd ever seen. One moment it radiated with a brilliance that made the very walls disappear, illuminating the houses across the street; the next it became a sort of anti-light, draining every photon from the room. This second, dark phase filled me with the most primitive fear, the sort I'd never felt, even as a child. I couldn't understand why, until I realized that it was removing not only the light from the room, but even the *idea* of it. Light no longer existed when the pillar turned its black face toward me. It was the darkness of death itself. And as it turned, light-dark, light-dark, life-death, I found myself more and more afraid of the nothingness—so afraid that I offered up my soul to any being who could let me remain in light.

Benny unfolded his hands. The pillar went away. I couldn't speak.

"Get back in bed, you silly gunt," he said.

Without realizing it I had stood up and pinned myself at the head of the bed, arms and legs flattened against the wall like a bearskin. I was also in tears. Slowly I inched down the wall, into bed, then pulled the sheets up around my nose. Without thinking I blew my nose on them.

"Charmin'," said Benny. I blew again. " 'Ow was that?" he asked, as though he'd just performed a little card trick. "Want me to do a bit more?"

I shook my head, or perhaps my head shook me. I was shivering too much to tell.

"What was *that*?" I managed to ask. Benny smiled.

"I reckon you know the answer, eh?"

"But I don't!" I cried, squashing my face into the pillows childishly, but without shame. "You keep saying I know all the answers. But I don't!"

"Yeah, you do," he said. "But I don't mind if you don't wanna admit it. Ain't many who can. And like I keep sayin'—you're the worst yet."

He stood up and brushed at the lapels of the immaculate suit, then turned and left the room without a glance. Two seconds later he returned.

"Sorry to do this to you, Nick, but it's for your own good. I'll be lockin' you in for a few days. Just till the party, like. I'll see you get your grub. There's some pens and paper over there on that dressin' table. Per'aps you oughta write it all down. Give you somethin' to do. You never know, it might do the trick, an' you won't need a party at all. Tata!"

He left and locked the door quickly. But he needn't have bothered. All I did, from then until nightfall, was lie on the bed, stare at the corner, and fear the return of the pillar of darkness and light.

When Benny had locked me in I'd thought he was joking. He wasn't. For three days I didn't wash; I hardly slept and I ate nothing that couldn't be pushed under the door. Admittedly it was an old house, and the door frames had moved over the centuries; but we're still talking omelettes. There aren't many people who've eaten an omelette after it's been pushed under a door. It's especially entertaining if the floor hasn't been washed for a hundred years or so.

At least he'd left me the pens and paper, which I'd put to good use. Well, not *good* use—but after three feverish days with nothing else to occupy me I'd managed to write a lot of things out of my system. It was rambling, meditative rubbish about the meaning of my life, and re-reading it was a nightmare in purple: somewhere below the artistic achievement of a lovesick teenage chimpanzee. All the same it had made me feel a lot better; and the illness had left me alone the whole time. I even caught myself thinking that perhaps Benny had been right: I wouldn't need a party at all.

Such delusions were short-lived. On the third evening it happened. Around eight o'clock I began to hear the upholstered sound of expensive car doors closing. The particular hum of privileged voices grew in the rooms below. Around nine, live music was added to the mix, and something told me I was getting a party.

In a dreamy way I wondered if there was anywhere in the room to hide from the inevitable, but there was not. Even the Invisible Man would have become so quickly covered in ancient dust that a myopic bat could have discovered him in seconds. Then suddenly nothing mattered anymore. Not my illness, or everything that had happened, or what the future held. All that *mattered* was that Benny was outside the door of my garret, rattling his keys ostentatiously, while all the people who were ever significant to the decade waited downstairs. For *me*. And I was about to greet them unwashed, stinking, and so poorly dressed that nudity would have been far preferable. Perhaps I could die, I thought. Could I just die—please? Or at least have a *shower?*

He came into the room, still without his beard, in white tie and tails so dazzlingly clean that God could have worn them to a bar mitzvah. He was slightly drunk, in his particular controlled way, smiling at me like a deb's father. If he says I look beautiful, I thought, I shall strangle him.

"Faaaark!" is what he said. "You look like dysentery in an overcoat!"

"What did you expect?" I hissed. "Beau Brummel's nattier brother?"

"Dunno. Not this bad, though. You could've combed your barnet."

"No, Benny, I couldn't. There isn't a comb in here."

"There is, too. On the dressin' table."

"Oh, *that* comb. It hasn't got any *teeth.*"

"Yeah it 'as. I can see 'em from 'ere."

"Oh, I'm sorry. So it has. Two."

"There you go. So why didn't you comb your barnet?"

I looked at him lolling impishly against the doorframe, and decided not to play the game.

"Stop fucking me around, will you? You want me to look as terrible as possible—isn't that the idea? I didn't want to disappoint. Should I piss down the front of my trousers? Would that make it even better?"

He stroked on his now-phantom beard, pretending to take my suggestion seriously.

"Nah. There's so much crap down the front of them strides you couldn't see a bit of piss. Now, per'aps if you threw up on 'em . . ."

I made a sudden move toward him, fists clenched, but he side-

227

stepped, giggling. For some reason I was suddenly breathless, and had to rest on my hams, like a runner. He closed the door and crossed to the dressing table.

"So you did write it all down, then?" he asked, flipping through the pages I'd written. He picked one up and began to read.

"No!" I shouted, snatching it from him.

"All right," he said, "don't get all shirty again."

"It's very private—that's all. I didn't write it for other people."

"That's no good. You was s'posed to write it for other people, not *you*. I knew it wouldn't 'elp, leaving you them pens and paper."

"What are you talking about now?"

"I was 'oping you'd write down the truth, see?" He shook his head. "Yep, I was definitely right about you. The worst I've ever come across. Never mind, soon be over."

"You know, I really can't believe you're keeping this up," I said.

"Keeping what up?"

"Your fucking Archangel Gabriel fantasy, you loopy old bastard."

"Did I say I was the Archangel Gabriel? Dear me. I'd get my wrists slapped for that."

"You see? You're doing it again. Get your wrists slapped by whom? God? Merlin the magician? Who?"

"Don't start all that again," he said.

"No, come on—let's start. I'm not in any hurry to go to this so-called party, even if you are. I've had a lot of time to think about you these past three days—especially that little trick you pulled with the light. And do you want to know the cruel professional truth, Benny?"

"Tell me," he yawned.

"You're no better a magician than Uri Geller. Only he isn't mad, he hasn't got a drink problem, and he doesn't insult our intelligence to the point where he pretends to be a fucking *elf*!"

"Hang on, I thought I was the Archangel Gabriel?"

"You're a cunt, that's what!"

"Dear, dear. Language. You must've been keepin' bad company."

"No, bad company's been keeping *me*. Against my will, I might add."

"Never mind. Fancy comin' to a party? You're dressed just right."

I didn't. I never did. But I followed him all the same. There was nobody else to follow.

Fortunately, the twist in the staircase let me see the party before it saw me. For once, Benny wasn't playing games: all the guests were indeed dressed as vagrants, though none looked quite so convincing as I did. All the same, I had to admit the joke was rather neat: it was an exact reversal of Marcus's infamous "Laugh on the Dole" party. Where Marcus had employed a disused warehouse, Benny's house, which virtually *was* a disused warehouse when I'd last been outside my garret, had been transformed into a passable imitation of Versailles. Where Marcus's guests had dressed in their finest, tonight they were dressed in their worst. No, not *their* worst: the worst of people they usually stepped over in the street. And where Marcus's servants had been real winos, employed for the price of a bottle of Thunderbird and humiliated for our amusement, Benny's servants were the same winos, dressed in the sort of clothes they had probably never even touched, let alone worn. Benny, Spike, and Ashtray each wore identically glowing white tie and tails. The only other person similarly dressed was Victor Silvester Junior, the bandleader, whose little orchestra perched precariously on the stairs, playing old hits.

"See?" said Benny, "Told you you was dressed just right, didn't I?"

"How did you get them all to come?" I marveled.

"Easy," he replied "told 'em who the guest of honor was."

"Is Lucy here?"

"Err . . . dunno."

Desperately I scanned the throng for Lucy's face. It was hard to spot people quickly, beneath the rotten clothes and the Burlington Bertie makeup, but I already knew she wouldn't be there.

"Sorry, Nick," said Benny. "I did ask her."

"No, no. Don't worry. Maybe I'll see her when . . ."

"When you're better?"

"Yes. When I'm better."

Benny led me a little farther down the stairs. I was surprised nobody looked up. All the expected faces were there: Marcus, managing to look campy in castoffs, had brought his camera crew from *Simply Trilling.* I

229

noticed the crew were not in fancy dress, but it hardly showed—like most film and TV support staff they seemed to take a delight in looking as filthy as possible. Eddie Geary, my newscaster acquaintance who always gets his Giorgio Armani for nothing, now wore a denatured parka. I imagined him going into some charity clothes store and doing his usual speech. "Hello, I'm Eddie Geary. I read the *News at Eight.* What? Oh, you know me . . . anyway, I'd like to wear some of your delightful secondhand clothing on the show . . ." I bet he had, too. Herman Coprolite had come with Allegra Assai. She, unable to resist the opportunity for exposing her breasts, wore—or almost wore—what looked like a consumptive's handkerchief. He, drawing somewhat tastelessly on his childhood experience of the ghetto, was clothed in reprints of Polish newspapers from the late 1930s. Rory McKaine was lolling against the banister, showing a woman his muscles. In his sackcloth posing pouch and his suntan he looked less like a tramp and more like Arnold Schwarzenegger in a remake of *Robinson Crusoe.* And no Christian. Where was Christian? Why were the only two people I wanted to see not there?

Looking across the room was like surveying my own personal solar system. A little farther away stood the minor planets: James Custer; then Dickon, Kerry, Piers; then people from work, even Akron Darkly himself, and the terrible Anthony Android; then, even farther out, at the far reaches of my personal space, stood people I hardly knew, except in the sense that I ought to have—anybody, everybody, who built the eighties out of themselves. Stylists; Celebrities; Producers and Bimbos . . . Copywriters; Art Directors; Photographers; Designers . . . Graphic Artists; Typographers; Liggers and Deejays . . . Commentators; Pundits; Journos and Byliners . . . New Right; New Money; New Women; New Men; New Romantics . . . Foodies, Yuppies, Preppies, Guppies, Twinkies, Dinkies, and Buppies . . . Docklanders, Topsiders, Insiders . . . Management Consultants, Image Consultants, Color Consultants; Moneymen . . . Coke Dealers, Futures Dealers, Insider Dealers, Property Dealers, *Life* Dealers. . . . I swooned against the banisters, faint with meaningful categories. Benny supported my elbow.

"See?" he said. "You don't look so terrible after all, eh?"

"Please, Benny. It isn't too late. Let me go."

Oh, but he was wise that night—the pure smile playing in his eyes—and I wasn't to be excused my destiny.

"Bit late, ain't it?" he said.

"But I've got nothing to get me through. Not even *clean hair,* for Christ's sake!"

"Yeah, you have," he said, "this." From his trouser pocket he took a matt black box, about the size of a cigarette lighter. It was rather intriguing, the kind of thing that might once have attracted my attention across some chilly Soho restaurant.

"Take this. From me."

"What is it?"

"It's something to say good-bye with."

"Good-bye? To you?"

"Nah. To All That, as they say."

"But what is it?"

"Nothin' much. A box o' tricks. It solves all your problems. Or it will, when you press that little button on the top."

Of course I pressed the button immediately. Nothing happened. Benny chuckled.

"But not just yet awhile."

"*NIIIICHOLAAAAAS!!*" screamed a familiar, thin, indulged voice. Trust Marcus to see me first. Victor Silvester Junior silenced his band, and the guests fell silent too, incapable of chattering without an aural backdrop. The television crew craned their mike booms and sun guns at me. There was nowhere to go but down.

As I began my descent, manic xylophone music accompanied me. It was a touch of sarcasm I could have done without, but when I looked angrily at Mr. Silvester he only shrugged his shoulders. Then I realized that the sound came not from the band, but from *myself.* It was cartoon music. Some of the guests applauded my talent.

231

"Come on, Nicholas. Don't keep us waiting," said Marcus, advancing with his crew. I was suddenly frightened by these people, as though they might want to take pieces home. My teeth were chattering. I knew they were, because they leaped from my mouth and chattered right down the stairs. I ran after them, but they were already on their way back. They shot into my mouth with such force that the back of my head expanded, to the ironic sound of a cartoon trombone.

"Did you get that?" yelped Marcus at his cameraman.

"Too quick, sorry," said the cameraman without a trace of apology.

"My God, can't you even do your job for a grand a week, you half-breed?" said Marcus, and turned to me without waiting for the pre-scribed two-fingered answer. "Nick Taig. This is the first time you've aired your much-talked-about act in public. And thanks for giving *Simply Trilling* your first interview . . ."

"Sorry, Marcus, what? What's going on?" I said, clamping my hand to my mouth to keep my traveling teeth in place.

"Hold it, hold it!" he said to his crew. Then to me, but loud enough for everyone, "Remember, Nicholas? You owe me an interview. You owe me lots of things. Like a new fucking coke spoon, and the antique Bavarian quilt you pissed on. All right? So let's play ball, shall we?"

I didn't want to do as he asked, but Marcus knew that, so I nodded dumbly. The technicians readied themselves once more; Marcus pulled his man-of-the-people smile; turned to camera . . . and a hairy hand dragged me off into the crowd. It belonged to Herman Coprolite.

"Kid!" he grinned. "Meet Allegra."

Allegra smiled. I'd never seen her do anything else. It's probably an implant, like her famed tabloid tits, which point skyward, no matter what position her body is in.

"Looks great, don't she?" asked Herman. "What a tramp!"

Allegra smiled again, adding a giggling sound.

"Thanks for rescuing me from Marcus," I said.

"My pleasure. That little peckerhead. We ain't talking these days."

I looked over my shoulder. Marcus seethed in a corner, but didn't approach. I wondered why Herman and he weren't friends any longer.

"Anyway, kid. Great to see you. What a great idea this party was! You really went all the way with that costume. What *is* that smell?"

"It's me, Herman. Naked me."

232

Allegra tittered disbelief, but Herman thought he had my measure, and laughed.

"Glad to see you ain't lost your sense of humor these last coupla weeks, kid. And your act! You really did some fine tuning there."

"How many more times? It isn't an act, it's an *illness.*"

"Yeahyeah. Act, illness—whatever. It's great TV! You know what I'm gonna say next, don't you?"

"You're going to say that you just happen to have a contract about your person, and if I could only manage to put my signature at the bottom . . ."

"That's right! How 'bout it?"

He pulled the contract like a gunslinger, along with a diamond-studded fountain pen. I was really too tired to protest. Why didn't I get it over with? The diamonds winked money at me: a little consolation in my new life. I reached for the pen.

"Champagne, gentleman?" said Ashtray, appearing behind Herman with a silver salver.

"What could be better?" said Herman. "We're celebrating."

While Herman was taking champagne I folded the contract in four and put it back in his pocket unsigned. A way of avoiding the deal had just occurred to me.

"There you are, Herman," I said, patting his pocket. "To us."

"To us!" he said. Chink chink. Allegra, I noticed, had disappeared for Herman. He gazed into my eyes as though I were his long-lost wallet.

"Herman," I said. "How would you like to sign *two* new talents tonight?"

"Two? There's two of you?"

"No, no. Not quite—but there is someone else with a most unusual talent. A real crowd-puller, I'd say."

"There is? Who? Where? Waiter, give me more champagne."

I waited until Ashtray had started to pour, then said, "This is the man himself. Ashtray, meet Herman Coprolite."

Ashtray fumbled with his tray, attempting to shake hands. I took it from him, then Herman asked what his talent was.

"I do funny things with fags," replied Ashtray.

Herman looked disappointed. "So what else is new? Half the guys in this room do that."

"No, Herman," I intervened. "Cigarettes. Show him, Ashtray."

Ashtray took out his packet and began inserting a row of cigarettes between his lips. He was a real showman, a natural. Herman was fascinated already, and even Allegra had a dimly puzzled knot in her brow. While Ashtray began filling his cupped hands with butane I took my chance to slip away.

It got no better. There was nobody who wanted to see *me:* it was just my fame they'd come to greet. And worse, they all wanted to know what it might do for *them.* Akron Darkly, for instance, actually put his arm around my shoulder. I thought he might ask when I was coming back to work—but no, he wanted to know if I'd promote a range of children's toys. I staggered away, into a phalanx of hairdressers begging exclusive rights to my mane. I spotted three reassuring faces— friends from school, now stolid City types—but when I got to them they only wanted to invest my unearned fortune. A record producer actually performed, unaccompanied, the Hi-NRG song that would take me to the top of the Hot One Hundred. A property developer told me of his prime apartment complex, built especially with the privacy of the famous in mind. Three publishers bid for my autobiography, and twice that number of writers offered to ghost it. On and on I stumbled, through a nightmare of celebrity. "Nick, over here!" "Nick, if I could just . . ." "Nick, when will you . . ." "Nick, I'd like you to meet . . ." "Nick, have you thought about . . ." Nick, Nick, Nick, Nick, Nick, like they'd known me for years. And of course, they had—at least, they'd known the thing I represented. I felt like a golden pinball, kept in play on the flippers of others' ambition. And throughout this breathtaking trip on the switchback of avarice Marcus shadowed me with his crew, waiting for the moment when I was too tired to repel his intrusion.

I felt in my pocket for the black box, but when I pressed the button again nothing happened. I suspected that nothing ever would: the box was just another of Benny's answerless clues. I propped myself against the little stage where Victor Silvester's orchestra played music so inappropriate for the spirit of this age, and wished I'd never been born. Marcus, I saw, was about to exact his dues. He advanced across the room, and there was nowhere for me to hide. I looked at him in a way I never had before: pleading, as vulnerable as an opened oyster. But he is a Tartar of television, his microphone his pitiless sword, and he pointed it at me without compassion. Then a voice came over the loudspeakers, and everything changed.

"My son! My boy!" it said. I'd heard it before. So, evidently, had Marcus. He dropped his microphone and his pretensions. They hit the floor together. His cherub face, always held just this side of evil, seemed to collapse on itself; I could see only the spiteful, gorging maggot within. And then I realized why it was that Nobby seemed so familiar.

When I turned to look at the stage I saw that Nobby was wearing his everyday clothes, not white tie like the other tramps. But there was no mistaking the difference between a real down-and-out and the costumed crowd. He couldn't conceal the failure at his very center; and failure, in that company supremely, was a spiritual leper bell.

Nobby clung to the mike stand and stretched out his hand to Marcus. To his child.

"Duane . . . Duane . . . !"

Some people, the ones who always did want the dirt on Marcus, quickly grasped what was happening. "Duane??" I heard someone snigger. It was enough.

"Duane . . . you've come for me!" said Nobby. His face was flushed with love, and his tears caught the light from the sun guns.

Marcus walked forward. He seemed more in control. Nobby half-fell from the stage, into the arms of his son. Marcus pressed his mouth to his father's ear. To the guests it looked like a kiss, but I was standing very near.

"When this is over," I heard him say in a voice like a viper's, "I'm going to have you murdered. While I *watch.*"

Ironic applause started up at this touching reunion, which Marcus pretended to take graciously. As he led his sobbing father from the room, Victor's band played "Congratulations."

I saw that attention wasn't focused on me right then, and thought it

235

might be my moment to escape. I edged toward the door, but the music stopped again. I heard Benny tapping at the microphone.

"Sorry to stop the fun and games," he said, "but I've got a special announcement to make."

I knew who his special announcement would concern, and his wink to me confirmed it.

"Now, you all know why you're 'ere," he went on. "To welcome back a friend." He paused, but there was no response. "And I know that you what don't know him, soon will. Now, before I get him up 'ere, I thought I'd better say a few words. . . . I first came across this freak of nature in a pub near Victoria Station. He tried to pretend 'e wasn't 'imself, but me old peepers ain't that weak yet! I knew who 'e was, an' I saw right away that 'ere was a golden opportunity for makin' money."

I was so shocked by this betrayal that I hardly heard the noises of agreement from the crowd. I couldn't believe what Benny had just said.

"Now the trouble was, 'e 'ad this daft idea about runnin' away. I could see there'd be no stoppin' 'im, so I took precautions. I knew 'e'd get in a fix sooner or later, so I give 'im me business card."

There were yelps of approval at this financial acuity, but they seemed to come from another place. How could Benny do this? How could he be this? All his trickery, all his charm, all his *love*: it had all been employed to this end. Was there not one person left on earth I could trust?

"And sure enough," he went on, "it worked. So it was *me* what rescued 'im, *me* what give 'im shelter, and *me* what got this." He held up my handwritten pages. No, this was impossible. He must have snuck back to my garret to get them.

"Yep," he went on, like a man selling snake oil to snakes, "this is the official truth, written with 'is own fair 'ands. An' *I'm* the lucky geezer takin' bids! Now the rest of you can take what you can get. Nick, come up 'ere, son! Say a few words."

236

I had no will anymore; no power to shape my own life. It was all in the hands of these people. Why resist? I stepped up on the little stage. Benny grinned at me, that innocence still in his eyes, despite the truth about him. I took the mike, but there was nothing to say. My mouth dropped open and my tongue flopped down two feet, then tied itself in a knot.

"Ooop!" said Benny, taking the mike. "I think 'e's a bit tongue-tied! Go on, Nick. Give 'em a show! Don't disappoint the punters."

And what a demanding audience they were. I wanted to give them my usual speech about this illness not being under my control—but that would have been like the diva appearing on stage to explain her acute laryngitis. They expected entertainment, and they weren't used to waiting for it—or for anything. From sex, drugs, and food, down to taxis, tickets, and haircuts—these people could never wait. And I couldn't perform.

Their expectant smiles began to droop. They were never real smiles anyway—just the muscle reflexes of the massively bored. Was I about to fill that emptiness for a minute? That's what they wondered, and their mouths stretched up in hope. But now I was disappointing them, like everything always has, like everything always must. How else would they drive themselves forward, if not to search for pleasure?

Nobody made a sound, but the weight of their disappointment advanced on me visibly. If they could have turned their thumbs down with effect, they would have. Somebody started a slow handclap, which was oddly relieving. Others soon joined. Some started to stamp. The vibrations pulsed through my body so strongly that the molecules themselves seemed to change. I saw the room and its occupants in a series of freeze frames. *Stamp:* the walls hung with blue and pink silk. *Stamp:* the balloon-filled netting strung beneath the ceiling. *Stamp:* Marcus, now returned, his mouth tensed to jeer.

"Freak!" someone called. Oh, they liked that. "Freak! Freak!" Look how clever we are: stamping, clapping, and shouting, all at once. *"Freak! Freak! Freak! Freak! FREAK! FREAK! FREAK!"*

And as I looked at them, it was not me, but they who seemed to be cartoons; with their heads thrown back in impossible attitudes of disgust, and their thighs pumping disapproval like engines. I clung to the mike stand, not knowing what would happen next, as those emperors

237

and empresses of Ego stomped their anger to the floor. *"FREAK! FREAK! FREAK! FREAK! FREAK! FREAK!"*

Benny, my old friend, my new enemy, remained onstage. He looked worried, and kept gesticulating at me. I ignored him: he should have calculated for my nonperformance. If it was going to result in our mutual demise then so be it. I'd take him with me. *"FREAK! FREAK! FREAK!"*

Then he was next to me. "What do you want, you evil old shit?" I shouted above the noise.

"The box, you silly gunt!" he yelled. "The box! Before it's too farkin' late!"

"What, this?" I asked, producing the mysterious box. "It doesn't do anything, does it? It's just another trick!"

I threw it into the melee. It was caught by Rory McKaine.

"You quiverin' twat!" gasped Benny. "You was s'posed to push the button. Now we're done for! Don't you understand *nothin'*? It weren't s'posed to work till the right minute, and that is right bloody *now!*"

He had me by the collar, and only then did I see his plan. I started to laugh.

"No good laughin'," he shouted. "This lot are out for blood!"

Rory had the black box in his simple palm. Already he was using it to social advantage, lighting a pretty boy's cigarette. He stretched out his thick arm. His thumb was on the button. Benny gripped my shoulder, but I knew he needn't worry. McKaine was too stupid to imagine any other purpose for the box: he would do as predicted.

He did, but even Alison from Rose Cottage could not have foreseen what happened next. It started with the net under the ceiling falling away, and the balloons drifting down. Even though they'd seen it a hundred times before, most people in the room turned their faces to the ceiling. That was unfortunate, for the balloons were only a cover. Something else lay above.

A man screamed first. For an instant he drew attention, before they were all shouting, swearing, coughing, retching, and otherwise articulating revulsion. Not at me; I was forgotten for the moment—but at the truckload of horse manure that was once on the ceiling and then was not.

Benny, the architect of the mayhem, looked amazed.

"Fark," he said. "You don't arf get a lot of shit for two 'undred quid, don't you?"

I don't think I've ever seen a man look more pleased with himself than Benny did at that moment. The guests, on the other hand, didn't seem to have such a developed sense of value. They might well have spent many giggling hours gearing themselves up like down and outs, but rotting shit was that bit *too* down and out to be funny. Even real tramps don't tend to see it as day wear. The commonest reaction, especially from women, was a sort of breathless denial. They threw their arms above their heads, shut their eyes, and panted, "Oh God! Oh God! Oh God!," as though The Man Himself might suddenly appear with a J-cloth. Quite a few of the men, including Rory McKaine, immediately tore off all their clothes. Allegra Assai seemed to have taken a particularly unfair load. She fainted outright, probably beneath the sheer weight. Herman, with surprising gallantry, knelt down in the mire and wiped at her turd-encrusted breasts with his Polish newspapers.

Dangerous as I knew it was to linger, I could not stop watching the Augean scene. Benny, too, looked like the sorcerer's apprentice: pleased with his own power but unsure of its results. For as yet the crowd were too busy with their immediate problem to be angry—but one or two were tending that way. Benny took the microphone again. I wondered what smoothing words he could possibly say.

"I'm sorry about that, ladies and gents," he said. "But I s'pose you're all used to bein' *full* of shit, and now you're *covered* in it. What's the difference, eh?"

"Oh, thanks very much, Henry Kissinger," I said. "Give me that bloody microphone!"

239

Benny handed it to me. Miraculously, the entire room fell silent, but it was only the silence of a gathering storm. Each body quivered with the violence of humiliation; each eye started vengefully from its dungy orbit; each caked lip curled back to show the sharp and hungry dentistry behind. I knew I was about to be eaten alive; yet still I spoke.

"Erm . . . would anybody like . . . would anybody like . . . a taxi?"

"You *cunting* bastard, Taig! I'll kill you!" guttersniped Marcus. It needed only one person to stir the group instinct, and as he lunged for me a kind of charge formed at his rear. I wanted to wait and pulp his face, but I was pulled backward from the stage by Benny and Ashtray. With the maddened pack baying at our heels we clattered through the house: Benny in front, me in the middle, and Ashtray behind. As we reached the front door I managed to fall over. Marcus literally screamed with the thought of tearing me to shreds and I thought the game was up until Ashtray turned around and barked a gust of flame in his face, like a combination Saint George and dragon. Marcus, to his infernal credit, hardly flinched in the chase, but the moment's grace was all we needed: Benny shoved me through the door onto the street.

We'd had no time to close the door behind us, so the mob was only a moment in coming. I was free of the house, but with no idea what to do except run; and when I turned to ask Benny's help he was gone. Then I heard it: the unmistakable toot of the stupid horn on my stupid car. It was parked not fifty yards away, engine running. But fifty yards was still too far: though most of my pursuers could not match my speed, fueled as it was by mortal fear, one did: Marcus. He advanced on me with a power greater, perhaps, than fear; the power of a man with nothing to lose. His unfit little lungs squealed like dying animals at the inhuman demands being made of them, and as he drew close I felt his hot, dry breath on my neck, like the blast of a crematory oven. Don't worry, I thought, as his vicious claws sank into my shoulder, you'll stretch. I did not. Marcus brought me to a halt then spun me around like a doll. His face, black with exertion and caked with beasts' feces, was terrible enough to kill me on its own—but that wasn't his idea at all. From his coat—and even in that desperate, crazy moment I was amazed—he pulled a knife. Not a kitchen knife, or a mean little switchblade: a maniac's knife, a knife made all of hatred and perversion; an

240

under-the-counter knife—secret, sexual, and pitiless. As he lifted the
blade above his head I watched with a kind of innocent intrigue. He no
longer held me, yet I did not move—did not even want to move. Perhaps this was always how it would end. Then a hand, a big hand on a
big person, closed around Marcus's deadly wrist.

"Marcus Trilling?" said a voice so perfectly Essex it could only belong to a policeman. "I'm arresting you on suspicion of trading in ille-
gal drugs."

Marcus spat straight in the policeman's eye. Probably a bad move,
because twenty other policemen were standing right next to him.
Three of them picked up his fat sac of a body and threw it in the back
of their van, where yet more officers waited. I had a feeling they
wouldn't be asking Marcus whether they could get his clothes dry-
cleaned for him.

Only Benny could have tipped the police off—though how he knew
about Marcus's drug-dealing was as much a mystery to me as everything else about him. And of course, there he was, leaning in the
shadow of the church at the end of Fournier Street, tapping the side of
his nose.

"Better get goin', son!" he shouted, pointing at the crowd. Marcus's
arrest had stopped them only for a moment. It was still me they
wanted.

"But who *are* you?" I pleaded to Benny. He reached into his pocket
and threw a scrap of silver through the air. Defying the breeze it came
right to me.

"I'll leave you me card," he called, as it dropped into my open palm.
"Now *faaark* off!!"

I smiled. Looked up. He was gone.

Then the animals really were upon me, and I saw I must move
straight away, or not at all. My car was just ten yards distant. And who
else *could* it have been at the wheel but Christian?

"Come on, Nicky!" he called, revving the engine. "This is all too ma-
cho for me!"

241

I had no time to open the door: hands were upon me. As Christian
pulled away I managed to throw my torso through the open back win-

dow, and that is how we escaped: Christian swerving wildly down Commercial Street while I struggled to keep more of myself in the car than out.

"Good party?" he asked, when I had managed to drag myself through the window.

"Shitty," I said, leaning into the front to get a better look at my friend. I don't think I'd ever loved someone so much.

"Rory there?"

"Yes. With a woman, I'm afraid."

"Was he? Couldn't care less, I've chucked him for good."

"Three cheers! This is a day for happy endings. Or it would be."

"Why, what's wrong now?"

"I don't suppose Lucy's said anything about me?"

"Nah. Sorry, Nicky—I reckon she'd had a bellyful. I think she found a new boyfriend."

"Oh," I said. It seemed so ungrateful to be wanting more than I had right then, but I wanted Lucy.

"I know you haven't seen Christian for a while, but I thought I might get a kiss."

And there she was, there she was! Curled up small in the shadow of the back seat, dressed in that same cream crepe de chine she wore on the night she first put a name to my illness. I wanted to take her in my arms, but it seemed like a dream.

"Are you real?" I asked.

"Of course I'm real, dopey. Come and find out."

"I can't," I said. "I'm scared you won't be there."

"Oh, please, give it a *rest*," said Christian. "There's no room for two dopey queens in one car. Give her a fucking kiss."

That broke the spell. We kissed. When we were done, about two hours later, I pressed my face to her breast, just breathing her in.

242 }

"I love you," I said, hoping she knew how much more it meant than ever before.

"I know. I love you, too."

A familiar pain stabbed inside my ear. No more, I thought. Please, no more. This is over, don't let it start again. Lucy pulled the wet balloon from the side of my head, laughed, and threw it from the window.

"Wow," said Christian, "some condom."

"I wanted to read that," I said to Lucy.

"It was terribly corny," she said. "Just give me another kiss."

"Hang on," I said. "There is something I really *have* to read."

From my stinking jacket pocket I retrieved the silver card Benny had thrown my way in the street. The message was hard to make out, like writing on a steamy mirror. Then a streetlamp caught it just so, and the words lit up with the same light that had pinned me to the wall, three days earlier.

BENNY SWEET, it read. DEUS EX *FUCKING* MACHINA.

But this time there was no address.

ABOUT THE
AUTHOR

Greg Snow was born in 1959, in Bermondsey,
London. He was educated at Brampton County
primary school and Corpus Christi College, Cambridge.
He has written extensively for radio and television.
That's All, Folks! is his first novel. At present he is
working on *The Red Nylon Heart,* a theater play, and a
new novel.